A LIFE BETRAYED

Sydney Rutherford

Published by Black Hat Publications

ISBN: 978-1-0670159-2-3

This one's for you, Dad.
Miss you always.

Author's Note

This story contains scenes of violence and references to drug use, death, and suicide. If needed, a content guide for this book is available at sydneyrutherford.com/contentguide

Midway upon the journey of our life
I found myself within a forest dark
For the straightforward pathway had been lost.

— DANTE ALIGHIERI, *The Divine Comedy*

1

Frances Allen flicked through the photos, the glossy paper stock sliding between her fingers. Before her sat a stack of files she'd spent the last month poring over. The folders were stuffed so full they threatened to spill their contents across the conference room table at the RCMP's Quebec divisional headquarters in Montreal.

As an inspector for the federal police in Ottawa, she'd been working a migrant-trafficking case linked to a Mississauga-based recruitment company when the deputy commissioner had tapped her to replace the head of a beleaguered investigation across the border in Quebec. The investigation had been running for almost a year, and the divisional office had little to show for their efforts. With funding dwindling and government attention beginning to stray, they'd brought her in from the Organized Crime Branch as a last-ditch attempt to help things shape up. Because if there was one thing Frances was known for, it was getting shit done.

"No one in the city will say anything. The municipal police won't touch him with a ten-foot pole," Sergeant Alexandre Gagnon said, sitting across from her at the table and fiddling with the adjustable armrest on his chair. "Montreal is insular. Everyone knows who runs the show. We can't get decent informants because they fear the repercussions. I don't think you understand the name the man has made for himself, Inspector."

Frances stopped at the photo on the bottom of the pile. It was a close-up shot taken two and a half years earlier outside the church at Giorgio Russo's funeral, the subject looking directly at the camera as if issuing a challenge. She tossed the rest of the photos on top to obscure the man's piercing gray stare. She wouldn't admit to it, but something about that stare made the hair on the back of her neck stand on end.

Frances was well acquainted with the Montreal mob—or the family, as they were more commonly known. Their dealings were the subject of lore at the OCB. Decades of exclusionary politics meant the RCMP—the country's national police service—had been largely shut out of Quebec, allowing Giorgio Russo's criminal organization to reign unchecked. But all that was changing. The recent election of hardline Anthony

Piper as prime minister had put crime back at the top of the national agenda and given the federal police the backing they needed to start taking names.

"Then we need to look farther afield, find someone from outside the city," she said. She reached for her cup of cold break-room coffee and took a reluctant sip. The provincial branch was located in a plain concrete building in the city's Westmount suburb. Funded by taxpayer money, it was as stripped-down as the offices at the RCMP's Ottawa headquarters and had few office perks—including decent coffee. "We know he's got ties to the cross-provincial drug trade—we've intercepted shipments from the Hamilton docks, headed for the ports of Montreal. Surely, someone has a beef to pick with him."

"Not one they're willing to die for," Gagnon said smugly, folding his arms. It was no secret that he resented her stepping on his turf.

The sergeant had been a long-standing fixture at the Quebec office and had followed the mob's dealings in Montreal for years. Frances also had a hunch he'd been gunning to fill Inspector Lapierre's shoes before she so unceremoniously replaced him. He'd been thwarted by a big shot from the capital—and a woman, no less.

"Find someone," she said, shutting down the conversation and swiping the photos back into one of the overstuffed folders. She ignored the sour look Gagnon gave her and tucked the stack of files under her arm before leaving the conference room.

A tip-off had launched the investigation, and despite her extensive research after taking on the case, Frances hadn't been able to determine the source. That meant it had come from up high—the top brass obscuring any information that might lead to the exposure of their most valuable informants. The tip-off had provided details implicating several Montreal mob figures in a series of short narcotics sea shipments and the laundering of funds derived from the enterprise. But to date, the RCMP had succeeded only in apprehending a handful of smaller players: runners and dockworkers who were far removed from those calling the shots. What they sorely needed was to land a big fish. And Frances had one in her sights.

As she wound her way through the maze of cubicles housing the divisional office staff, her polite smiles went unreturned. She'd grown accustomed to their frosty reception. Her French was excellent. She had studied the language at university level and spoke it often in her dealings in bilingual Ottawa. But she was an Anglo and one of the suits in the capital who thought they had jurisdiction over the entire country. It didn't help that she'd supplanted an existing manager who'd been well-liked by the tight-knit, fiercely Quebecois staff. Still, she couldn't let office politics distract her from the chance to take down one of the most notorious criminal figures in the country.

Frances stepped into her small windowless office and dropped the stack of files onto her desk. She sat down and turned to the wall behind her, where she'd pinned a map of the province heavily marked up with intersecting red lines. Beside the map was a hierarchy she'd constructed—headshots of key players, accomplices, and allies arranged according to their purported clout. Giovanni Bianchi, the reigning boss, sat at the very top, and directly below him were the members of his advisory group—the Four Horsemen of the Apocalypse.

She narrowed her eyes at the newest addition to the mob boss's council as he looked back at her from the photo. Intimidation, extortion, racketeering—Mathias Beauvais had spent the better part of a decade writing his own rules into law. But Frances was here to accept his challenge. When she was done with this investigation, the infamous mafia captain would be off the streets and behind bars, where he belonged.

2

It wasn't unusual for Rayan to discover Mathias was in town by waking in the middle of the night to find him in his bed. Sometimes he'd feel the weight of the man above him, hands already rousing him as he emerged from sleep.

That night, Rayan could smell the alcohol on Mathias's breath—it clung to him like cologne—and see the dullness in eyes that were usually so sharp. This version of Mathias was different from the one who occupied their daytime reality. The nocturnal Mathias moved slowly and deliberately and spoke of things never mentioned in the light of day, his voice a low murmur close enough to Rayan's ear to make his skin shiver.

Rayan stared at Mathias lying beside him, still in his shirt and slacks, hair splayed across the pillow, and studied his face in the dimness. He liked him here in his bed when the world was still, before the crank turned and lurched the day into motion like clockwork.

"How long can you stay?" Rayan asked.

"Only for today. I'm leaving tomorrow."

"It is tomorrow."

Mathias closed his eyes and exhaled loudly. "I swear, that ape will grind me down before the end."

Despite his rise to the Quintino, Mathias still held himself responsible for maintaining the alliance between the family and the Hamilton-based Reapers. His semiregular meetings with William Truman also served as an excuse for him to make the hour-long drive across the lake to see Rayan. And to Rayan's immense pleasure, Mathias didn't seem particularly keen on giving that up.

"The gift that keeps on giving," Rayan teased and moved his hand to Mathias's chest, slipping a thumb between the buttons of his shirt to graze his skin.

"You're still too far away," Mathias muttered, a shadow crossing his face.

"I'm right here," Rayan said softly and leaned in to kiss him.

The snow started early in the morning and grew heavier as the day wore on. By the time they emerged from bed around lunchtime, it had blanketed everything outside in a thick layer of white. As Mathias readied himself to leave and make the drive back to Montreal, Rayan turned on the television in the living room to check the forecast.

"With the blizzard touching down earlier than expected, we've received reports of up to twenty-three centimeters of snow in parts of the Greater Toronto Area. The Don Valley Parkway and sections of the 401 have been closed, and motorists are asked to seek shelter where they can."

Images of the storm battering the province flickered across the screen. "The roads are closed," Rayan said, turning to Mathias, who was pulling on his coat by the door. "You won't make it anywhere tonight."

Scowling at the presenter on the screen, Mathias grudgingly slipped off his coat and hung it back up on the hook. He took out his phone and slid a thumb across the screen as he stepped into the bedroom. "You'd better have enough booze," he called over his shoulder.

Rayan lifted the remote to mute the TV and listened for Mathias's voice through the wall. If it was English, it would be Giovanni on the other end—the boss himself, on speed dial—with Mathias devising carefully worded excuses for his absence. If it was French, he would be speaking to Jacques, imparting a brisk set of instructions, no questions asked.

Rayan knew better than to eavesdrop, but he couldn't help himself. He was still desperate for any part of Mathias's world, even that which he'd left behind. He heard a snatch of clipped French in a tone he remembered well and smirked. Jacques had his sympathy.

Turning his attention back to the television, Rayan stared at the buried cars— the people whose lives had ground to a halt—and tried to stem his growing sense of elation. As selfish as it was, he could think only of the fact that he had Mathias to himself.

"There's only one thing to remember about cooking pasta." Mathias, shirtless, stood before a steaming pan of boiling water, a wooden spoon in one hand and a cigarette in the other. "You'll be forgiven for not knowing, *estraneo*."

Rayan snorted, loose with pleasure, Mathias having moments ago fucked every coherent thought from his brain. "Go on," he goaded.

It was past midnight the following day, and they hadn't yet eaten dinner. Time seemed to have lost its temporality while, outside, the snow refused to let up. It heaped along the windowsills and piled up on the balcony. Mathias had taken it upon himself to give Rayan a condensed lesson in Italian cooking. Despite having drunk his weight in scotch, the man had a steady hand and moved about the kitchen like a pro.

"Always take it out just before you think it's done. That's when it's done."

Mathias took the pan off the stove and tipped it into a colander in the sink. Then he fished out a piece of penne with a fork, stepped over to where Rayan was seated at the counter, and pushed the pasta into his mouth. Rayan ate it dutifully.

"If it's mushy, you fucked up," Mathias said.

Rayan nodded, not overwhelmed. He'd always preferred rice to pasta, and he much preferred Mathias's lips to food—lips that now pressed against his. Rayan reached instinctively for Mathias's neck, and he felt himself once again begin to stir.

It was ridiculous, the sex they were having, as though they had nothing else to do while snowed in. He had a hunch Mathias was using it as a distraction from his gradual nicotine withdrawal. He'd been forced to ration his remaining cigarettes as long as snow barred the building's entrance and the street, making a run for supplies impossible. Even if they could leave, nothing was open. The official word was that the plows were prioritizing important routes, but the storm was delaying clearing efforts. "Stay inside and hold tight" was the general message.

Mathias refused to watch television and had instead raided Rayan's bookshelves, leaving a trail of books strewn about the apartment, each abandoned after barely a chapter. Rayan had made several attempts to get started on the readings for his classes but got only a few pages in before Mathias, restless and irritated, would appear and jump him. Not that he wasn't a willing participant. They'd exhausted their usual repertoire—the hurried release that typically characterized their coupling during Mathias's too-short visits to the city—and moved to a whole new playing field. Without Rayan realizing it, Mathias had begun to manipulate him like a finely tuned instrument, knowing exactly what got him off and how to hold him at bay, edging him so that when he finally came, he was so far gone he couldn't speak.

Earlier that afternoon, when Mathias had him bent over the bed, coring him slowly, he'd pressed his mouth to Rayan's shoulder and spoken in a tight voice. "What do you think about when I'm not here?"

Mathias was deep, pushed hard up against him, and Rayan could only groan as the pressure built, threatening to spill over. Mathias, whether he was there or not, was all Rayan thought about. Lying with him afterward, Rayan realized he couldn't remember what day it was. He brushed his fingers against the layer of stubble on Mathias's cheek, taking pleasure in his private dishevelment.

"You'd think they'd know how winter works by now," Mathias scoffed and raised his arms above his head in a lazy stretch. "What a fucking joke."

When this is over, don't bother driving back, Rayan thought. *Just stay here.*

"What are you plotting?" Mathias asked, giving him a curious look.

"Nothing," Rayan mumbled.

They'd spent two years like this, capturing days and weekends between the long stretches of time they were apart. If it took a snowstorm to ground Mathias for a couple of days, Rayan would take it. He'd known what it was to lose Mathias completely and was forever grateful to have him at all. But it didn't stop him from harboring covert imaginings of a life in which each day began and ended with the man's face, as it was now, turned toward him.

At the front of a gaudily decorated hotel ballroom, the wedding party was seated along a large table draped with white lace. In the center of the table, Enzo Carbone's youngest daughter and her new husband—neither of whose names Mathias knew or cared to remember—crossed arms to tilt flutes of champagne into each other's mouths. Enzo sat beside his daughter, grinning broadly, his face flushed from the free-flowing booze and the heat of more than two hundred guests packed into the airless room.

Weddings, funerals, christenings—an endless rotation of mindless engagements. Here he was, finally accepted into the family's inner circle, and Mathias felt more out of place than he had as a grunt. He'd left Toronto as soon as the roads had cleared but now wished the snow had lingered another day, if only so he could avoid this teeth-pulling spectacle.

Mathias scanned the sea of attendees, his mind elsewhere. He was growing concerned that the time spent with Rayan, fractured as it was and never long enough, was beginning to eclipse the rest of his life—threatening to render it meaningless. Because to be with Rayan was like a long breath out. In every other aspect of his life, Mathias rotated the pieces of himself out of view so that the full picture remained obscured. But Rayan knew it all: his work, his past, who he liked to fuck. He hadn't realized how heavy the armor had been until he'd taken it off, and it was becoming harder to walk through the world as he once had.

In the end, Mathias had only himself to blame. Up until recently, he'd managed to navigate life by avoiding this. He'd thought the risk of getting close to someone lay in its ability to compromise him. Now he knew the real danger was how good it felt—waking to Rayan's mouth, feeling the brush of his slick body against him in the shower, watching him appear uncannily with the exact thing Mathias needed a second before he needed it, whether it was food, coffee, or a hand around his cock. Something this good made everything else pale in comparison.

Still, Rayan remained a puzzle to him. There were long silences when he disappeared into himself, and Mathias could only guess at what he was thinking. In bed, the man was mercurial. He liked to be dominated but was equally roused when he was the one in control. His impatience meant he often wanted things fast and rough—yet he would sometimes melt into Mathias, pressing against him as though they shared the same skin. Then it had to be slow and all-consuming. Mathias didn't possess the same ability to intuit what Rayan needed, unaccustomed to giving people what they wanted without expecting something in return.

"When are we going to see you up there?" Gabriele Giordano asked from across the table. He gave Mathias a tipsy grin and leaned forward in his chair as a waitress appeared beside him to refill his glass.

Mathias was seated with the remaining members of the Quintino and a handful of older family stalwarts. The boss had chosen not to attend. Giovanni retained the ability to opt out of various functions as he pleased, whereas Mathias was bound to them.

"I've negotiated enough deals to know a bad one when I see it," Mathias replied coolly.

The men around the table chuckled. "Perhaps you could convince a nice Italian girl to take your name," Armando Bernardi offered, gesturing at the room dotted with an array of young female guests.

Mathias was not oblivious to the attempts. Eligible girls from good families were sent to sidle by his table at events like these—all with the same empty faces and cloying laughs. Their fathers assumed his proximity to Giovanni Bianchi would boost their clout. Mathias had to be careful not to think too hard about the life these old men envisioned for him.

"Or you could take hers," Gabriele quipped.

The mood at the table chilled, and Mathias turned to look at Gabriele. The remark wasn't lost on him. Mathias's tainted lineage was not exactly a mark in his favor on the marriage market.

Gabriele cleared his throat and reached clumsily for his glass. "A joke. Come on, Beauvais. It's a fucking wedding."

Conversation turned to the track numbers, and Mathias caught Enzo beckoning him from across the room. He stood and navigated his way through the maze of tables toward him. As he walked, a woman in a purple gown appeared at his elbow. He recognized her from the bridal party, a sister or friend, rabid with wedding attention.

"I'm not sure if you remember me—it's Bianca," she said with a bright smile. "We met at Carlo and Stella's—"

He crossed in front of her without a word and rounded the head table to where Enzo was seated. The woman had enough sense not to follow.

"Congratulations," Mathias said when he reached the beaming father of the bride. He pulled an envelope of cash from inside his jacket and handed it to the man.

Enzo took the gift and stood to shake his hand. He gestured for Mathias to sit in the empty chair beside him. "Might as well keep it for myself, what with everything I've spent on this fucking thing. Lace from France." He gave a snort. "And you think we run a racket."

"Anything for the happy couple," Mathias said wryly, taking a seat.

"Ain't that the truth. But it's a relief, I tell you. Took the girl forever. We were afraid we'd be stuck with her."

Mathias glanced over at the horse-faced woman clutching the arm of the exceedingly sweaty man sitting beside her at the table.

"Heard you just got back. What did Truman have to say about the latest seizure?" Enzo asked.

That had been the reason for Mathias's trip to Hamilton. They'd had two shipments seized in the past six months, and he was growing tired of Truman's indifference toward the increased scrutiny. Mathias had a feeling their shared success had gone to Truman's head, and he was seriously considering pulling the plug on the whole operation. Over the past year, the volume of the Reapers' shipments had noticeably dropped, and it was becoming apparent that the additional risk they were shouldering was not worth the decline in profit. It wouldn't go down well with Truman, but with all the unwanted attention, Mathias couldn't afford to have him distracted at the wheel.

"We're going to have to do something on our end," Mathias said. "I'll speak with De Luca."

Enzo clapped him on the shoulder. "Good man. Did you get stuck in that mess over the weekend? No worse place to be snowed in than Hamilton."

Mathias shrugged. "A chance to catch up on my sleep."

Enzo chuckled and raised his wineglass to his lips. Mathias cast his eyes around the room, thinking of the other things he'd caught up on.

The councilman took a long swig and set the glass down. Then he leaned in, his voice lowered. "I've got some news about the investigation. Lapierre is out. It appears they've brought someone in from the capital."

Mathias frowned. They'd been aware of an ongoing federal investigation for some time, the divisional office making a show of sticking their noses into the family's activities with renewed vigor, but so far, nothing had come of it. It wasn't the first time either. The RCMP went through cycles like this, drawn into the group's dealings in Montreal only to pull back when their leads eventually petered out. It helped that the family maintained several friendly connections at federal level—Inspector Philippe Lapierre among them.

"With our old friend given the boot, there goes our sway. I've looked into his replacement and put something together." Enzo retrieved a folded sheet of paper from his jacket and slipped it to Mathias. "Figured you could use the info."

"Who is he?" Mathias asked, pocketing it.

"He?" Enzo sneered. "They've sent a broad. Brownie points for this government—they think some tart in tights is going to topple us."

Must be more to it than that. They wouldn't take Lapierre—who'd been a well-regarded figure at the Quebec divisional office for the past twenty years—out of commission for some Girl Scout who looked good on paper.

"There's something else," Enzo continued, glancing around quickly. "Turns out the whole thing came about from a tip-off, not just bad timing as we'd suspected. No clue as to who or where it came from, but it looks like we have a leak."

Mathias set his jaw grimly. "And the nature of the tip-off...?"

"No info there either."

"I'll look into it."

Enzo's face darkened. "Last thing we need's some bitch from Ottawa poking around when we've got a squealer on our hands."

Mathias looked out at the crowd of guests growing more inebriated by the minute. It could be anyone—in or out of this room. One thing was clear: they couldn't afford to give the Feds any more ammunition. He needed to figure out where the leak was coming from and plug it.

3

Rayan had just stepped out of the lecture hall after his morning class when he heard his name being called. Glancing over his shoulder, he saw Professor Hofstein threading his way through the mass of departing students.

"Glad I caught you. Can we speak a moment in my office?"

Rayan hesitated, pondering his escape. He could make an excuse and say he didn't have time. Something about the philosophy department's wood-paneled corridors and plush faculty offices made him feel uneasy, like he was out of his depth. But he didn't have anywhere else to be, and whatever this was would be better dealt with now than later.

Rayan nodded.

The professor smiled. "Great, I'm down this way." He fell into step beside Rayan, and they headed along the hallway to his office.

Once inside, Professor Hofstein gestured toward the armchair across from his desk and closed the door behind him. "You always seem in a hurry to leave," he teased. "Got much else on?"

Rayan's eyes flitted about the room, taking in the shelves of books and the framed certificates on the wall behind the professor's head. His mind filed away the details, the way it had for very different reasons in his former life.

"Not really." Rayan didn't see the point of lingering in the department building with the other students who stood around, making small talk about grades and upcoming assignments.

"Looks like you're on the accelerated stream. So you've only got your thesis left before graduation," Hofstein said, taking a seat behind the desk and pulling out a folder from one of the drawers. "Quite impressive. Not many students complete their bachelors' in five semesters."

Studying had proven an efficient activity to absorb the time, and with the money Mathias had left him, Rayan didn't need to hold down a job. He'd spent the summers taking courses instead.

"You wanted to see me?" he asked, evading the professor's praise.

Hofstein chuckled. "A man of few words, it seems. I got an email from the faculty admin informing me that you'd requested I act as your supervisor. To be honest, I was a bit surprised. I hadn't noticed you much in tutorials. But then I went and read this."

He opened the folder and took out Rayan's thesis proposal. Rayan had been instructed to attach it to the supervisor request so they could determine whether he was a good fit. He'd only selected Hofstein because he was taking his class on virtue ethics and admired his thoughtful observations. Otherwise, he didn't really have a preference.

"Circumstantial morality." The professor shook his head with a grin. "It reads at a PhD level."

Rayan shifted uncomfortably in his chair. He hadn't meant for the proposal to be so long, but he'd found himself caught up in the subject, entangled in a compelling web of reason.

"What are you, mid-twenties?"

Rayan nodded. He would be twenty-six in two months. The number seemed ancient. There had been a time when he'd thought he would never make it this far.

"Older than most of the undergraduates in the program," Hofstein continued. "Bit more life experience, I'd imagine. What were you doing before this?"

Rayan stiffened. "Nothing, really. Odd jobs."

The professor nodded. "And what brought you to philosophy?"

Rayan had struggled with that question. He remembered staring at the list of degrees and feeling nothing. He'd considered something practical, but he had done enough with his hands. He figured it was time to do something with his mind.

"A good argument can explain any number of sins," he said finally.

Hofstein laughed. "That it can, but what it can't do is change how we feel about them. That's the whole dilemma, isn't it? We can use the logic of philosophy as an explanation, but do we really believe it..." He lightly tapped his fist against his chest. "In here?"

Rayan crossed his arms, suddenly defensive. "You don't agree with the thesis?"

"No, that's not it. I didn't mean to get off track." He laughed again and absently thumbed through the pages of the proposal. "Nagel certainly does, as did Williams. The idea that morality comes down to an element of luck can be appealing to certain people."

Like me?

"You've made some good points about the fallacies of the argument, as well as subsequent theories that it's spurred. I'd like to see you bring in more practical examples, maybe touch on a few modern musings of redemption to add color to the concept."

"Redemption," Rayan echoed. "What do the scholars have to say about that?"

Professor Hofstein was silent for a moment, observing him with a kind smile. "Well, Mainländer argued it could only be achieved through death or complete annihilation, which I think is a tad heavy-handed. Nietzsche's idea of redemption takes the form of an altered understanding of past events. Personally, I'm rather fond of the Hebrew model, where redemption is pursued through mitzvahs—good deeds. Whether they cancel out prior misconduct, that's another argument."

"*Sadaqah*," Rayan said quietly, the word materializing on his tongue.

"That's right, the equivalent in Islam. Religions tend to position themselves more leniently on the subject than philosophers." Hofstein sat back and pressed his thumbs together reflectively. "What are your plans after graduation? Where are you headed?"

The question set off a flicker of panic. He had no idea where he would go or what he would do after this. Rayan still felt like he was in limbo, as though he was waiting for something—perhaps for his life to truly begin. He shrugged.

"Because you might have a pretty decent shot at academia if that's something you want," Hofstein said.

Rayan didn't know if it was.

"This is compelling stuff, Mr. Ayari. I think you've got a few ideas here. I'd be more than happy to supervise if you'll have me."

"Thank you," Rayan said, relieved that the professor hadn't pulled the thing apart. It felt personal somehow, a piece of himself woven in amongst the dry scholarly language.

"Wonderful. I'll go ahead and put my name down, get that signed off." Professor Hofstein picked up the proposal and handed it to him across the desk. Then he clicked his fingers. "Utilitarianism," he announced triumphantly and caught Rayan with his high-beam smile. "Bentham's theory on utility. Look that up."

Tony and Mathias's father were buried in the same cemetery, not by some strange coincidence but because the Italians of Montreal had long considered Cimetière Notre-Dame-des-Neiges to be their preferred final resting place. While Mathias had never bothered to seek out his father's grave, he'd come by Tony's a few times to pay his respects.

He made his way through the wrought iron gate and walked slowly down the rows of tombstones. Not one for maudlin gestures, Mathias had found his sense of obligation to do right by the former Collections boss unsettling, yet more than two years after the man's sudden departure, it lingered.

The office remained a virtual shrine to all things Tony. Mathias was still finding notes in his illegible scrawl, crammed at the backs of drawers and under piles of paperwork that had taken him months to organize. Tony had employed his own system, which, while lacking in order, had apparently made perfect sense to him. Mathias had done what he could to decipher it, but anything he couldn't figure out, he'd gotten rid of.

While technically responsible for the division, Mathias was not so precious—as Tony had been—as to refuse outside help. The thought of spending his days poring over the minutiae of each contract and chasing up incremental amounts of money was nauseating to Mathias. Once he'd gotten his head around the basics, he'd brought in Lucio Gammin—one of the Betting division's talented bookkeepers— to run the administrative side of things. He still spent more time than he cared to at the Collections office but only as a nominal head. He wanted baseline numbers, intel on difficult clients, and oversight on a few high-profile contracts. The rest he left to Lucio, who then delegated the work to Franco, Sonny, and the remaining team. Despite the time that had passed, it felt unnatural to occupy the role Tony Giraldi had guarded like a mutt with a bone, so Mathias came here occasionally as a nod to Tony and the space he'd left behind.

The grave was well tended. The headstone was clear of weeds, and a small glass vase with flowers had been placed on top. Mathias stood before it and reached into his jacket for his cigarettes. He waited for the tobacco to light before drawing a pull of smoke into his lungs.

Arrogant little bastard. Those had been Tony's words when Mathias had first shown up at the Collections office all those years ago.

The words hadn't been far off the mark. Mathias had been turned away from every other division and hadn't realized getting a job in Giorgio Russo's army would prove so difficult. He'd assumed they would want all the muscle they could get. But it was his first introduction to the layers of tradition that existed beneath the face of the criminal organization.

He'd been adamantly against using his old man's connections—however tenuous—and wanted to get the job on his own merits. Mathias had found out very quickly that, in the scornful eyes of the family elite, he had none. By the time he made it to Tony's office, he knew there was nowhere else to go, so he refused to take no for an answer. If Tony was stubborn, Mathias was even more so. And he was smart—he knew what he was getting into and had no qualms about what was required of him. This had been Mathias's opportunity to finally prove himself, and he would not let some graying old goat deny him that.

Of course, now he knew what a gamble Tony had made on his behalf. Mathias's background was a magnet for all the wrong kinds of attention. That was where Tony had differed from the rest of them—he hadn't given a shit what people thought. Not that the old man didn't put him through the wringer. Mathias's initiation of Rayan was nothing compared to what Tony had made him do. Baptism by fire. But Mathias had been ready for it. Hungry, even. Back then, he'd felt like an agent of chaos, as though the accident of his birth had somehow granted him immunity. It was by a fluke he had this life in the first place, so what did it matter what he did with it?

Mathias took another drag on his cigarette and peered at the inscription on Tony's headstone: *Beloved by all who knew him.*

He smirked. *Graveside humor.* There must have been a book of epitaphs, vague and sentimental, a catalogue of niceties to choose from. Beloved was one thing Tony most certainly wasn't. He remembered a time, shortly after Tony had officially brought him on, when Mathias was still some grunt the Collections boss would have liked to be rid of. Mathias had been called into Tony's office, and the man had slapped a piece of paper down on the desk between them. He began berating Mathias for changing the terms of a client's contract without his permission. The thing read like it had been written by a monkey and then passed from hand to hand without ever being corrected.

"It's trash," Mathias said in his defense. "I'm not peddling shit someone's been too lazy to fix."

"That someone is me, smart-ass," Tony growled, his face turning redder by the second. "You think you're clever, don't you, college boy? It's not the contract—it's you who's the worthless piece of shit. Don't forget you're only holding onto this job through my good graces—"

Mathias slammed a hand down on the desk, and Tony's eyes bugged with fury. "Now I'm going to talk, and you listen," Mathias said quietly. "You haven't accounted for statutory interest. It should be cumulative based on time in arrears. My version brought in six percent more than the outstanding amount. That's five grand, on a throwaway client. Think about what that looks like for our regulars."

Tony stared at him, no doubt with a torrid of insults brewing behind his closed lips, but Mathias could practically see the gears whirring in his head. It wasn't an overly complicated accounting concept but something that had occurred to Mathias when he'd attempted to decipher the gibberish that had been handed to him.

"If you want a shot at snaring the heavy hitters, at least make it look professional," he continued.

When his boss finally spoke, it was clipped and matter-of-fact. "Professional, huh? Go on, then. Let's hear it."

That was the moment Mathias went from being a troublesome lackey to an asset, someone worth listening to. He'd proven his value not with how eager he'd been to get his hands dirty or because he'd shown up each day despite the stream of crappy jobs but because instinctively, he knew how to make things better and if he had something to say, he wasn't afraid to say it.

Mathias tapped the ash from his cigarette, and it sprinkled across the pavers at his feet. Tony had taught him to trust that instinct and to use it for his and the family's benefit. The man might not have been beloved, but he'd had a lot to do with Mathias's success—far more than Mathias had given him credit for.

His eyes moved from the epitaph to the dates engraved below, that fateful day carved forever in stone. Sometimes, when his fingers brushed the dimpled scar on Rayan's chest, Mathias thought about what he might have done differently. He wondered if there was some decision he could have made that would have changed the course of that night.

Mathias brought the smoke back to his lips. The answer still eluded him.

4

Frances watched the girl reach beneath her fake fur coat to adjust the strap of her corset, her impressive décolletage straining against the gauzy fabric. She'd just come off a shift and looked out of place in her vinyl skirt and too-high stilettos as they stood by the entrance to the late-night diner Frances had suggested.

"Sure you don't want to go inside?" she offered.

The girl shook her head, clutching an overstuffed purse to her side. "I'm good here."

Frances had gone through the list of potential informants Sergeant Gagnon had compiled and was surprised to find that none of them were connected to the array of adult clubs the family operated across the city. One establishment in particular, Le Rouge, was known by local authorities to be a hotbed of mob activity. Yet from what she'd gathered, the divisional office had never tried to infiltrate the place from within.

There weren't many women in Frances's position at the RCMP. There were plenty at the agency—receptionists, administrators, researchers, and assistants—but few who'd climbed the ranks like she had. There were barriers, of course—men who'd held roles longer than she'd been alive and would give them up only if they were forced into retirement or keeled over entirely. But the federal police were beginning to see the value of a quick-witted female officer in the field. Early on in her career, she'd discovered that women had far more ways than men to slip into the criminal underworld unnoticed.

Frances had cast her net wide and asked the research team to put together a record of girls who worked at Le Rouge. Then she'd cross-referenced the names against the schedule of cases awaiting trial at the local courts, hoping to find an opportunity to exploit. She'd found one in Lauralie Duquette, a doe-eyed eighteen-year-old who'd submitted a character reference for her boyfriend, who was facing criminal charges for a string of home invasions. Frances had reached out and arranged a meeting, one Lauralie had cautiously agreed to, on the premise that Frances might help make her boyfriend's unfortunate situation disappear.

While the tip-off had implicated several mob figures, Mathias was by far the most high-profile among them, and that was where Frances had decided to concentrate her efforts. With what she'd learned about him, his involvement in the cross-provincial narcotics shipments was likely just the tip of the iceberg.

She'd been trying to put together an idea of Mathias's movements in the city, but so far, he'd proven elusive. If Frances had someone on the inside, she'd be able to get a better read on the man and his weak points. And if he was anything like the other crime bosses she'd put away, those points involved women—the younger, the better.

"George's court date is coming up soon, isn't it?"

Lauralie nodded, rummaging in her purse for a silver container of breath mints. She knocked several into her palm. "Next month. The eighteenth."

"It must be so hard on you both," Frances said, infusing her tone with just the right amount of sympathy. The boyfriend—George Lanore—had been behind a series of violent burglaries targeting houses in the city's wealthy Outremont suburb. George had finally been arrested when an unsuspecting homeowner had caught him red-handed in his kitchen and taken to him with his kid's baseball bat.

"He's a good guy, honestly," Lauralie seethed and popped a handful of mints into her mouth. She crunched them between her teeth. "He's just really impressionable, you know? One of his friends roped him into it."

Frances suppressed a scornful snort. She'd seen George's rap sheet. This wasn't his first brush with the law. Lauralie's conviction that he was innocent was likely a product of her own imagination.

"That's the thing, though," Frances said. "He's the only one placed at the scene, so it'll be hard to argue that he was coerced."

Lauralie looked at her from under her thick black lashes. "So what are we supposed to do? I don't want him to go to jail."

"Well," Frances began judiciously, "there are ways I might be able to assist in obtaining a more lenient sentence."

"You're saying you can get him off?" she asked brightly, brushing back a strand of golden hair.

"I'm saying when it comes to informants assisting with a federal investigation, there are some liberties we can take."

"What federal investigation?" Lauralie asked, scrunching up her nose.

"How much do you know about your employer?"

The girl's mouth quivered before she quickly masked her discomfort with an easy smile. "I'm not sure I understand."

"The mob," Frances said curtly, abandoning the sympathetic pretense. "The mafia runs Le Rouge, your place of employment. I have a hard time believing you had no idea."

"We're not supposed to talk about that," Lauralie said, glancing around the parking lot. "Especially not to someone like you."

"Quid pro quo," Frances said with a shrug. "You help me, and in exchange, I help George with his current situation."

Lauralie clasped the handle of her purse with a white-knuckled fist. "What do you need?"

"I need you to get close to Mathias Beauvais."

The girl's eyes widened, and she shook her head. "I can't—not him."

"How many years did George's lawyer say he was looking at?"

Lauralie stared at Frances, looking torn. "Seven to nine," she whispered.

"That's a long time, isn't it, Lauralie?"

"He's a good person!" she cried, her cheeks flushing.

Frances kept her face neutral. She knew better than to contradict the girl. "I'm sure he is. And you're in a position to help him. Think how grateful he'll be."

Lauralie's eyes darted nervously to a group of men loudly exiting the diner. "I'll see what I can do."

Frances hid a smile. If Lauralie succeeded in gaining Mathias's confidence, she would finally have an in. And why wouldn't she? The girl was pretty and eager. If Frances had learned one thing during her time on the job, it was that men like Mathias—men who sought status and power and believed themselves above the law—were easily ensnared by a young woman's wiles.

Mathias was steps away from the Collections office door and mere moments from freedom when his phone rang. It was Giovanni's minder, Henri Rossi.

"Boss wants to see you."

"At the house?" Mathias asked, his eyes narrowing as he saw Sonny making his way across the office toward him.

"No, somewhere different," Henri said cryptically. "I'll send through the details."

Mathias hung up, and Sonny sidled up beside him. "Boss, I'm having problems with the Carlisle contract."

Knowing Sonny, they weren't problems, just symptoms of his staggering ineptitude. "And...?"

"His partner croaked, and he's selling the business. Doesn't think the money's going to cover what's owed."

"All I'm hearing is that he's got issues. What's that got to do with us?"

"I don't think I can get the money."

Mathias stared at the man in silence, watching him fidget with discomfort. "The less you think, Sonny, the better," he said finally. "There are as many ways as there are bones in his body. Pick one."

"But, boss—"

"Don't come to me, expecting I'll do your work for you," Mathias cut in, fighting a growing irritation. "Carlisle is a cheat. His family has the money. You just need to go out and find it."

He pulled open the door, strode out onto the landing, and headed for the stairwell. If Sonny had half a brain, he would know that Carlisle's son was on the city council. That was where Mathias would start—he'd see how quickly the story changed when the councilor's life got a bit more interesting. But that wasn't Mathias's job anymore, and Sonny had been doing this a long time. He could figure it out for his fucking self.

In the parking lot outside the building, Mathias made his way over to the Bentley and got in behind the wheel. He'd sent Jacques out on his own to correct a few problematic contracts. These days, his second doubled as an unofficial captain for the division. Jacques was more useful when he was getting work done rather than trailing Mathias from one tedious family commitment to another.

A second had once been a necessity—an extra set of eyes and a partner in intimidation. Mathias had little use for that now and preferred, instead, to move about on his own. It was less stifling that way and allowed him the freedom to go where he wanted. But having a second had never felt tiresome with Rayan. The man had been quiet, sure, but he'd had a knack for keeping pace with the procession of Mathias's thoughts, occasionally adding his own eagle-eyed observations to the mix.

As he drove, Mathias mulled over the information Enzo had given him about Lapierre's replacement. The sheet of paper had included a thumbnail photo of the woman in uniform—stern-faced, her auburn hair pulled back tightly behind her head. Inspector Frances Allen. The single-page bio listed her credentials, her personal background, and the high-profile cases she'd worked on. She'd been transferred from the Organized Crime branch at the RCMP's Ottawa headquarters and assigned specifically to head the divisional office's investigation.

Since the election of the current prime minister three years ago, there'd been a noticeable shift in attitude toward the family's various activities. Anthony Piper had campaigned on a platform of getting tough on crime, and since taking office, he'd pushed to expand the powers of the RCMP and implement harsher sentencing. There'd been talk that, with a government more inclined to crackdowns, Quebec— a province long ignored—would be subject to increased federal scrutiny. That was why they'd brought someone in from the capital—the divisional office in Montreal had become too accustomed to collusion and partial to generous bribes, which was what had kept the family—and Mathias—safe for so long.

After receiving the news from Enzo, Mathias had reached out to his contact at the Quebec office, who'd hinted that Inspector Allen wasn't well-liked by the local team. That could work in his favor. He'd been unable to gain any insight into the source of the tip-off. His informant had revealed that all identifying details had been scrubbed from the record, which meant someone at the RCMP was keeping that information close to their chest.

More concerning was the fact that the tip-off included details of the short sea shipments he'd been running with Truman. While they didn't yet have anything solid to tie Mathias to the arrangement, this explained the recent string of seizures. Mathias already had a list in his head of those who were involved in the operation— peripherally or otherwise. He would have to be proactive at stamping out any potential source who might be funneling information to the inspector.

The address Henri had sent him was located in a new building at the center of downtown. Mathias parked the car outside and walked into the swanky office tower, which boasted a roster of high-profile clients on the mezzanine directory. Mathias rode the elevator to the thirty-first floor and stepped out onto a walkway lined with windows. It smelled of fresh paint, and the carpet beneath his feet was pristine.

The walkway split off into two corridors. Mathias turned left and walked to the glass doors of an office suite with a numbered placard affixed to the wall. He pulled open the doors and stepped inside. He spotted Henri first then the boss, who was standing in the corner of the unfurnished office, staring down at the street below.

Mathias moved to the window and saw how high up they were. The cars below looked like toys on a child's play mat. "Considering a new career?"

Giovanni turned to him with a slow smile. "Take a good look, Beauvais, at the future of Collections."

Mathias cast his eyes about the empty office. "What am I missing?"

"While I appreciate the hard work, I think we both know you heading the division was temporary. Christ, you've complained about it enough. In truth,

Collections has been in transition ever since Tony left us, and I think now's the time to remedy that."

Mathias couldn't deny that the division had been a thorn in his side since he'd grudgingly agreed to take the helm, but what exactly had brought this on?

"Russo, God rest him, built this organization up from a gaggle of street criminals. We've moved beyond that, and it's time we looked the part," Giovanni said, peeling away from the window and stepping past him into the center of the room. "You know as well as I do, the country's changing. It's getting harder to keep the law from interfering in our various... endeavors."

Mathias understood then where the boss was heading. "You want to move things aboveboard."

Giovanni's eyes crinkled in amusement. "Always so quick, Mathias. You never fail to impress."

"There's a lot about this business that doesn't exactly fit onto a spreadsheet," Mathias scoffed.

"Of course, but there's a hell of a lot that will."

Mathias kept the skepticism from showing on his face.

"I've been in discussions with BCF Holdings, the company who owns this building, about a generous lease agreement," Giovanni said. "In the words of our dear departed friend, money talks. And there are some very large organizations looking for a confidential cash injection. Why waste our time hassling mechanics for small change when we could be lending millions to the big players and making a killing?"

It was ambitious and not entirely out of the scope of reality. Mathias himself had considered the possibility of legitimizing certain family business ventures. "You've looked into the legal implications?"

Giovanni shrugged. "There are firms out there whose business it is to make dirty look clean. The current government isn't going anywhere, and soon Quebec will be expected to fall back in line. We've grown beyond a small annoyance. We need to remain one step ahead and pivot before they try to shut us down."

Mathias slipped his hands into the pockets of his slacks. The afternoon sun streamed through the window, projecting his shadow onto the blank wall beside him.

"Think of it as an upgrade, a step into the future. We'd create a shell corporation with a shadow director and a respectable board lineup, use consultants to muddy the trail," Giovanni continued. "Tony was one of the old guard. He stuck to what he knew. We're taking Collections in a new direction."

Mathias had found an old ledger at the bottom of one of Tony's desk drawers. It dated back to the early eighties and was filled with a meticulous record of the division's profits for that year. Tony had just been starting out and was tasked with molding a fledgling branch into a well-oiled machine, a task he'd made it his life's mission to accomplish. He would have hated the idea of selling out to some faceless schmuck in finance.

"Don't tell me you're old-school as well," Giovanni goaded him, misinterpreting his silence. "You would know well enough, Mathias, this is the way forward."

"I don't doubt it," Mathias said. "But the trouble with working with a bunch of slippery suits in the Caymans is that it's hard to find a neck to squeeze when things go wrong."

Giovanni chuckled. "Trust you to get right to the point. And you're not wrong—it does leave the issue of compliance. But there are paper-based ways to extract the desired response."

Mathias had been doing this long enough to know that a piece of paper wasn't nearly as effective as a clenched fist.

"The real money is to be made where the fat cats sit, and we've accumulated a sizable investment portfolio to run with the big boys," Giovanni continued. "More profit for less risk, and we keep our noses clean in the process."

If the boss wanted Collections to run like a high-end investment firm, it would mean dismantling the street teams and placing control into the soft hands of consultants who didn't know a thing about the realities of their business.

Giovanni waved his hand as if swatting an errant fly. "I'm talking long-term here—future planning. There's a lot to be worked out before then. But I figured..." He gestured around the pristine office. "Why not get started now?"

Mathias nodded noncommittally. A thought niggled in the back of his mind, remaining unasked: *where does that leave me?* But there would be time for questions. He'd learned, in his role as the boss's counsel, that it was best not to contradict the man when he got an idea into his head. It was far easier to let the dust settle and then present a compelling counterproposal.

5

Rayan remembered the flour on his mother's hands as she kneaded dough on the kitchen counter. He could hear the chatter of the TV from the living room, where his brother was stretched out on the floor in front of the screen. Even cartoons couldn't lure Rayan from the joy of standing on a chair by her side and watching as she dipped her slender fingers into the flour jar. She would sprinkle a delicate layer of white across the lump of unshaped dough and work it in with the heel of her hand. Sometimes she broke off a piece and gave it to him to roll into little balls, which he would lay on the tray alongside the perfect circles of flatbread. While the bread baked, she mixed oregano, cumin, and sumac to make za'atar, which she would spread across the top and douse with olive oil.

On Saturday mornings, she ruled the house. Their father wouldn't be up until noon, sleeping off a hard night at the local tavern after his pay packet came in on Friday afternoon. They listened to Najwa Karam, and his mother spoke to them in her native tongue, her voice sounding different from how it did in French—more melodious, as if this was the real her and the other woman simply a character she played.

He wondered how much of his mother's life had been spent playing a character—the dutiful wife, the assimilated immigrant, the happy mother. Perhaps it was a trick he'd learned from her. But hiding had only left him starving with need.

In darker moments, Rayan feared she'd believed she was doing them a favor, relinquishing him and his brother to the system. After leaving his father, she had struggled to find work and keep their small family afloat but was unequipped to navigate the expectations placed on her by an unfamiliar society. If there were services, she didn't know about them, and if there was help, she didn't ask for it. The thought that his mother had decided he and Tahir were better off without her was too painful to imagine.

In the kitchen of his apartment, Rayan pushed his knuckles into a ball of dough on the counter. He kept his movements slow and even, in no hurry to get the dough onto the tray and into the oven. It wasn't Saturday but Sunday, and he'd woken with an overwhelming urge to make his mother's flatbread. Recreating the dishes from his childhood had become a strange sort of medicine.

Recently, he'd found himself able to remember things again, the memories floating into being as though released from the murky confines of his mind. He wondered if it was because, in the last few years, the tenor of his life had so drastically changed. When he'd first come to Toronto, Rayan had felt like he was still in hiding. He'd barely left the apartment except to go to classes and had kept to the same nearby stores. Then, as time went on and nothing happened, Rayan began to shake free of his self-imposed exile. Still most comfortable on foot, he started to explore the city, walking from one neighborhood to the next, taking it all in.

He'd never felt such freedom before. Even when he and his brother had been loose on the streets of Montreal, with no responsibility to anyone or anything, it hadn't been true freedom. Details about what they'd eat and where they'd sleep had been contingent on the events of the day—he'd planed down his ability to imagine the future and see past the task of keeping one foot in front of the other.

Rayan realized now how ruinous such uncertainty had been. With each new neighborhood he discovered, each course he completed, each purchase he made for the apartment, he fought to counter the voice of warning in his mind. It told him not to be foolish, for everything could once again be taken away.

After setting the dough aside to rise, he opened the pantry to discover he was out of oregano. Rayan grabbed his keys and walked to the door to pull on his coat. He left, locking the apartment behind him. During the week, the streets around his building bustled with commuters and school children, but on weekend mornings, they were virtually empty. Rayan preferred it like this. In crowds, he tended to let his paranoia get the better of him.

A store run by an Iranian couple, several blocks from his apartment, sold a selection of specialty foods—spices, grape leaves, and ajwa dates, along with cans and jars that he recognized but didn't know the names of. The couple were friendly and spoke often of their family back home, cousins and nieces and uncles who were always promising to come visit. Sometimes they put things aside for Rayan that they thought he might like.

That morning, someone had set up a small table covered with stacks of glossy pamphlets outside the store. It was manned by a young boy wearing a yellow hat and gloves, perched on a metal foldout chair.

"Sir, did you know...?" the boy called out.

Rayan stopped and looked at the kid, whose plump cheeks were ruddy from the cold.

"On any given night in Canada, 3,491 women and 2,724 children sleep in shelters because it isn't safe at home." The boy spoke in a practiced voice as though he'd carefully memorized each statistic. He picked up a pamphlet in his gloved hand and held it out to Rayan.

Rayan stepped over and took it, glancing down. On the cover was a picture of a woman holding a little girl close to her chest. Beneath the image was the name of an emergency shelter.

"How old are you?" Rayan asked.

"Six and a half," the boy said, grinning proudly. "My mom works there."

A woman with two bottles of water emerged from the store and sidled up beside the kid. "We're actually just around the corner," she said, gesturing toward the end of the street. "This time of year always seems to bring an extra demand for our placement services."

Rayan took out his wallet and removed a clump of bills from the fold. He pushed them into the slot at the top of the collection box on the table.

"Thank you so much," she said with a smile. "Your donation will go toward food and clothing to help families get back on their feet."

Rayan nodded and continued into the store, the pamphlet still in his hand. After his meeting with Professor Hofstein, he'd looked up utilitarianism—an ethical theory promoting actions that ensured the greatest good for the greatest number of people. Rayan had never really adhered to a life philosophy. He'd always found living hard enough without the luxury of determining how he went about doing it. But living hadn't been hard lately, and in the absence of struggle, he'd felt a growing need to make sense of where he stood.

Hofstein's mention of redemption had caught on something, tugging like a hook. Maybe it was childish fantasy to think a future of good deeds could cancel out those of the past. *How much good would it take to cancel out mine?*

Mathias sat in one of the VIP rooms at the back of Le Rouge, tapping out a cigarette from the pack in his hand and placing it between his lips. Across the table, Narcotics head Filippo De Luca leaned forward to light it for him. It was unusual for Mathias to find himself at the club on a Monday evening. Or any evening, for that matter.

If there was one positive thing about being on the council, it was that Mathias had to frequent Le Rouge far less often than he used to. Lucio stood in for him as the Collections rep at division head meetings, and Mathias didn't make an appearance unless a particular item of business called for it. As for the Quintino, they preferred their meetings to be held during daylight hours, opting for places that served better food and less pussy.

"Two shipments in six months?" De Luca shook his head, bringing the flame to his own smoke and taking a pull. "No longer looks like a coincidence."

"The man's blasé about it, too—doesn't seem to think it's a concern," Mathias said. "Give me the numbers. What are we looking at?"

"They're down. Have been for months now. What with the seizures and the flood of product making its way up from Colombia—at two-thirds of the cost, mind you—the arrangement's no longer proving as lucrative as it was when we began."

"So you'd recommend pulling the plug?" Mathias asked, exhaling a stream of smoke.

De Luca splayed his hands. "I mean, we could sit on it, see if things pick up. But if they stay the same, we're better cutting our losses."

Mathias tapped the end of his cigarette against the ashtray in the center of the table.

"Obviously, in this situation, there are wider implications with that course of action," De Luca added carefully.

"Truman."

"Exactly."

"If he's underperforming, not keeping his eye on the ball, we're well within our rights to terminate the agreement. There might be hurt feelings, but this isn't fucking summer camp," Mathias said. "I'll discuss it with the boss. I wanted to get your take first."

De Luca nodded and moved to top up their glasses.

"While I'm here," Mathias began, "do you know of anyone involved who's caused issues, kicked up some attention?"

De Luca cocked his head. "Not that I'm aware of. What's this about?"

"Turns out the Feds received a tip-off about our little operation."

"You're serious?" De Luca's eyes widened. "You don't think it could be...?"

Mathias paused, his drink raised halfway to his lips, the possibility only now occurring to him. "No," he said, dismissing the idea. "He's stupid but not that stupid."

Yet the thought lingered. After he'd finished up with De Luca, Mathias walked out to where Jacques was waiting in the hallway, and together, they made their way toward the entrance of the club. One of the hostesses stopped him when they reached the door.

"Mr. Beauvais," she said, throwing a glance over her shoulder. "One of the girls wants to see you."

"I'm not interested," Mathias said brusquely and stepped past her.

"She said it was important," the woman said, lowering her voice.

Mathias stopped, immediately suspicious. He gave her a short nod and turned to his second. "We're done here."

As Jacques peeled off, Mathias followed the hostess to one of the private enclaves around the back of the main stage. She shut the curtain behind him and disappeared without another word. He stood in the middle of the cramped room, unwilling to sit, let alone touch anything. It had been years since he'd last been back here, and he was in the enviable position of no longer having to prove himself. His status afforded him the ability to wield *no* as a power play, and he was free to act as though he was above the club's inferior offerings. Still, the room conjured a familiar unease in his stomach.

The curtain parted, and a slight girl with wavy blond hair slipped into the room. She wore a sheer robe over top of her skimpy outfit and clutched it to her chest as though shielding herself. "Sorry to bother you," she mumbled nervously. There was a rough edge to her Quebecois, revealing a small-town pedigree. "I-I just thought you should know."

"About...?" he asked curtly.

She shrank and refused to meet his eye. "She was the one who contacted me. My boyfriend's court date is coming up, and she said she could get him off—"

Mathias knew where this was headed. "In exchange for what?"

The girl's eyes, wide with panic, flew to his face. "I didn't agree to anything. I didn't tell her anything!"

Mathias tempered his agitation. He had little patience for hysterical women. "What's your name?" he asked evenly, changing tack, which appeared to calm her somewhat.

"Lauralie."

"Now, Lauralie, what did this woman want you to do?"

The girl ran her tongue across her lips. "Get close to you. Give her information."

Mathias almost laughed. To think he would confess his sins to a piece of ass. "Did she say who she was with?"

Lauralie shook her head. "No, but she was definitely a cop—Anglo. Her French was prissy. And she mentioned something about a federal case."

"She gave me her number so I could get in touch," the girl added. "Said her name was Allen something."

Frances Allen. So his suspicions had been correct. The inspector wasn't a chump, like Lapierre, and she wasn't here to play games. "Well, we wouldn't want to disappoint," he announced.

Lauralie balked. "What?"

"Call her," Mathias instructed. "Tell her you have some information and you'll meet her at the dep across the street." He pulled a roll of bills from his pocket and held out a handful to the girl.

She took them gingerly. "Now? What if she can't—"

"She'll be there."

Lauralie grimaced. "You're not going to do anything?"

"That depends on what you've told her."

"Nothing," she whispered, shaking her head vigorously. "Honest to God."

"Then I'm not going to do anything." Mathias watched as she slipped her hand into the robe to pull out her phone. *Not yet.*

Frances peered at the gloomy contents of her fridge and weighed up her options. She'd meant to pick up groceries on her way home but seemed to be leaving the office later and later each day, only to bring work back with her anyway. The kitchen table was currently piled with filing boxes of records that she'd spent the last few nights trawling through. She was looking for someone close enough to Mathias to have the inside scoop but motivated enough to risk turning on him to cut a deal. She was beginning to understand why the investigation had gotten nowhere—an informant like that might as well be a fucking unicorn.

She closed the fridge and scanned the empty kitchen as though a warm meal might magic itself into existence. The rest of the apartment was equally sparse. Work was paying for it while she was stationed in Montreal. The place was nothing special—a simple studio that came with a bed and basic furnishings. Frances was still living out of the duffel bag she'd brought with her when she'd left Ottawa. If there was anything she happened to need—clothes, cutlery, a decent frying pan— she went out and bought it.

She gave a defeated sigh and reached for her keys. It would have to be takeout again. That was one thing she did like about Montreal—there was always something open, and it was almost always good. Even in the depths of winter, the city managed to maintain an air of vibrancy, its residents conditioned to simply carry on as usual despite the relentless pummeling of snow.

Frances was pulling on her boots by the door when her phone rang. She saw who it was and fumbled to pick it up.

Lauralie spoke quietly, her voice almost a whisper. "Can we meet? I have something to tell you."

Frances glanced at the clock on the wall. It was late. She must have just come off a shift. "Of course."

"Do you know the Beau-Soir across the street from the club?"

"I'm on my way." Frances hung up and felt a jolt of excitement in her stomach. This was what she loved about the job, the slow-motion pursuit—each move bringing her one step closer to an endgame. Maybe she'd found her unicorn.

Frances pulled her car into a space at the far end of the convenience store parking lot. She got out and waited beside the driver's door, stuffing her hands into the pockets of her winter coat. The place was relatively quiet for this time of night. There were two cars parked by the building and one idling off to the side. She checked her phone for missed messages, and when she looked up, she saw Lauralie approaching on foot across the parking lot toward her. The girl stopped when she reached Frances and glanced around distractedly, hugging her calf-length coat against her tiny frame.

"Cold night."

Lauralie just nodded, chewing on her scarlet-painted bottom lip.

Frances was vaguely aware of a car door slamming and the thud of purposeful footsteps. Lauralie's mouth gave a panicked lurch. Frances looked past her shoulder, and there he was, only meters away, heading straight for them. If she'd found his photo intimidating, she was even less prepared for how formidable Mathias Beauvais appeared in person. He was tall, well-built, wearing an expensive-looking suit beneath a full-length black overcoat. His face was handsome—unnervingly so—but it was the way his eyes fixed on her, cold and hard, that made Frances draw back.

Lauralie turned as he came to a stop beside her. "That's her," she said, a quiver in her voice.

"You did well." Mathias gave a slight tilt of his chin. "Go on." Despite hitting all the local notes, his French was more polished than the average Montrealer's,

betraying his maternal origins and—from what she'd discovered in her research—
an expensive education.

Lauralie threw her a quick look before scurrying back across the parking lot, her
heels clicking on the pavement. Frances hid her frustration. She'd hoped the girl
would be her ticket into Le Rouge, but instead, Lauralie had gone straight to
Mathias and turned her in. She recalled Gagnon's warning: "I don't think you
understand the name the man has made for himself."

"Didn't pick the Feds for a bunch of pimps," Mathias said, his breath coming
out white. "She sucks me off for information, and you throw out her boyfriend's
conviction?"

"That's—"

"A misjudgment on your part. Unfortunately for you, Inspector Allen, my cock
doesn't do the thinking for me."

She froze. He knew who she was. Frances was suddenly aware of the delicate
position she'd put herself in. Not expecting company, she had left her weapon at
the apartment and hadn't informed anyone at the office of her plans.

"I hope you compensated the girl for her time. How does the RCMP expense
strippers' tips?" He clicked his tongue disapprovingly. "A questionable use of
taxpayer money."

"Assuming you've ever paid any," she shot back, some of her courage returning.
"It's nice to finally meet you, Mathias Beauvais. I've certainly heard enough about
you. Sounds like you've heard about me too. At least now, when I bring you down,
we won't be strangers."

Mathias raised an eyebrow. "Awfully confident, aren't you?"

Frances shrugged. "Why wouldn't I be? It looks like your luck has run out. We've
caught onto your little cross-provincial enterprise." She was bluffing—they were
still struggling to gather anything substantial in the case against him, but she
wanted to put a dent in that impenetrable exterior of his.

Mathias smirked. "You're not going to find what you're looking for, Inspector.
If I were you, I'd tread carefully."

"Is that a threat?"

"Why would I have reason to threaten you?"

"I know exactly who you are."

His gray eyes narrowed. "Then you would know to mind your step," he said, his
voice dangerously quiet.

Frances watched as Mathias walked back to his car, her hands clenched tightly
inside her coat pockets.

6

Mathias sat across the table from his mother in the kitchen of her apartment, tuning out the witless drone of her voice as his mind returned to the events of the previous evening. Frances Allen had been plain, barefaced, and not the slightest bit threatening. As soon as he'd laid eyes on her across the parking lot, it had occurred to him how entirely unremarkable she appeared. But she had a quick mouth, and during their conversation, he'd seen a steely glint in her eyes, giving Mathias the impression that she was a bulldog—once she got hold of something, she didn't like to let go. Clearly, he was what she'd gotten hold of, and he needed to figure out what she knew so he could remain one step ahead.

In his efforts to source the leak, Mathias had reached out to his contacts in the city and the wider province for information. Still, he'd been unable to brush aside De Luca's conclusion. Could Truman really have rolled over? It didn't make any sense—the shipments implicated both of them.

"Whatever happened to that lovely young man?"

Had his mother paused her prattling to actually ask him a question?

She looked at him expectantly, turning the handle of her coffee cup. "You used to send him around every month while you were out of town. It made such a difference with the little things."

Mathias frowned. "What are you talking about?"

"He'd shovel the walk, clear the snow from the stairs. He even unjammed the stuck window in the study. You know the one—polite, doesn't talk much."

That's for fucking sure. This is the first I've heard of it. "He came by every month?"

She nodded. "For the life of me, I still can't figure out where he's from."

Mathias fought the urge to roll his eyes. *An hour north of here.*

"Isn't his French marvelous? So integrated! You know these immigrants—they can be so stubborn, refusing to adapt, chattering on in their language as if it's our job to understand."

How quickly his mother had forgotten that she was an immigrant herself.

"I hope you paid him well for his trouble. He never took the money I left him."

Mathias hid a wry smile. *Of course he didn't.*

"Those are nice." She reached out to brush his right cuff link with her fingers. "Are they new?"

Mathias withdrew his hand and raised the cup of coffee to his lips. The cuff links had arrived at his apartment in an unmarked box in early November. Silver, a small opal set into each face—they were expensive and inarguably his style. Mathias had been surprised by the man's taste. The only clue was the note inside the box: *bonne fête.*

The gift had come about following a conversation he'd had with Rayan while in Toronto about a year before. Rayan often did this when Mathias was still wrapped in their warmth, his mind addled with pleasure—he ambushed him with questions.

"When did you know?"

"Know what?" Mathias asked.

Rayan, pressed naked against him on the sofa, raised his head to look at him. He often struggled to follow the current of Rayan's mind, the way it shifted, dipping below the surface into swirling depths.

"That what you liked was different."

Mathias preferred not to dwell on the subject. It brought up other, darker feelings that seemed to have died with his father but sometimes resurfaced in quieter moments, catching him off guard. "Who knows? Things went from either-or to equally appealing. Until recently—" Mathias stopped, shocked at his own carelessness.

"Recently?" Rayan echoed.

I seem to want only you.

"Christ, always with the questions," Mathias muttered, extracting himself and reaching down to the floor for his pants. "What's next, my first memory? My favorite color?"

"How about your birthday?" Rayan asked, sitting up. "You know mine."

He did—the first of March, a date his brain had oddly retained after seeing it on Rayan's police file. "What makes you think that?" he scoffed.

"My pay was always more that week."

Mathias set his jaw. "Misplaced optimism. Thought you'd actually spend some of it, I don't know, on bottle service and a lap dance."

Rayan let out a snicker.

"What did you do with all your earnings?" Mathias stood and refastened his pants. "You lived like a monk."

"I hid the cash under the floorboards."

Mathias blinked, incredulous. He picked up his shirt and pulled an arm through the sleeve. "And when you left Montreal? Stuffed down your shirt?"

"I gave it away."

Mathias stilled as he registered what Rayan was saying. The man had sold his soul to work for the family, only to walk away from all that he'd gained by the sacrifice.

"The money wasn't important." Rayan's face furrowed, and his eyes darted down with—was it remorse? "It's not that I... I'm not ungrateful."

"It was yours," Mathias said, beginning on the buttons of his shirt. "You could have set it on fire for all I care. What about the money I left you? I suppose that's funding some Cypriot war charity."

"No," Rayan said with a rueful shake of his head. "But it's more than I'll need in this lifetime."

Mathias picked up his lighter and cigarettes from the coffee table. "Then I suggest you start getting creative." He stepped across the living room and paused at the door to the balcony. He could see the outline of the man reflected in the glass— his tousled black hair, the slope of his bare shoulders. "And you?" Mathias asked stiffly.

Rayan was silent for a moment. "Since I was a kid. I don't remember knowing exactly, more knowing I had something to hide." He gave a soft laugh. "As if I didn't have enough to hide from my old man."

Mathias looked back to see Rayan staring off into the distance, lost in thought. He felt an unfamiliar pang. "November twelfth." Mathias pulled open the balcony door, the crisp outside air brushing against his cheeks. He caught the flicker of a smile on Rayan's face as he closed the door behind him.

When Mathias had been old enough to grasp the concept of birthdays, he'd come to the realization that he'd never had one. Initially, he'd thought, like most things, his mother had simply forgotten. But as the years wore on and the day came and went without note, he began to suspect she was actively avoiding it. So, as a point of pride, he did too.

They had enough money, but it was a while before Mathias fully understood where it came from. Part of his parents' strange arrangement included his schooling—perhaps his mother's only contribution when it came to raising him. She'd negotiated with his father to send him to a French private school. She would have preferred boarding school, but his father's generosity must have stretched only so far. By the time his old man cut her off for good, Mathias was making his own money. He'd been tempted to walk away and watch the woman who'd made him fall into the depths of her own unmaking. He didn't owe her anything, he'd spent most of his life reviling her, yet that was one final abandonment he was unable to subject her to—as much as he thought she deserved it.

His mother liked to appear regal, but she was plebeian at best. She'd been a headstrong girl who had left school at sixteen and absconded to Canada to shed the shackles of her parents' influence. From there, her life had followed the trajectory of many young women who found themselves alone in an unforgiving city. She'd always bemoaned the loss of her education, which Mathias found laughable, as if that was the reason she'd ended up where she was. He'd gone to university to show her how easily he could throw it away. Mathias knew she was secretly disappointed in his decision to join the family. He imagined she, like his father, had envisioned a different life for him.

He looked at his mother across the table. Marguerite had already launched into another topic, Mathias and the cuff links forgotten. She appeared to him like a crudely drawn sketch, a hollow pretense for a person. As a child, subjected to her coldness and her volatility, he'd been frightened by that emptiness. Now he no longer cared. He'd given up trying to understand his mother a long time ago.

"Jesus, can you keep this stuff away from the kids?" Diana slapped a pile of papers down on the kitchen table, where Frances was sitting, watching her niece, Brie, shape a heart out of purple Play-Doh.

"Where did you get this?" Frances cried as she realized it was the contents of a confidential file from her backpack.

"Timmy was pulling it to pieces in the hallway," her sister sniffed. "Must have found it in your bag."

Frances stood and attempted to shuffle the mess into an orderly stack, searching for the missing folder. Brie leaned over to look, and Frances placed a hand on top to shield her view.

She was back in Ottawa for a few days, putting the screws to her old contact Dave Villanova, who supposedly had an in with the Red Reapers and was attempting to get a message to the group's head, William Truman. The Quebec office had looked into who was facilitating the Ontario end of the mob's shipments and had narrowed it down to the Hamilton-based Reapers. While it was unusual for the family to be associated with the outlaw motorcycle clubs that dominated the Canadian criminal landscape, there had been rumors of an alliance with the Reapers following Giorgio Russo's death. She knew pulling off a meeting with Truman was a long shot, but she had a nice bit of leverage, and if anyone had dirt on Mathias they might be persuaded to divulge, it would be the head of the notorious Ontario biker gang.

"Oh my God, who is that?" her sister murmured, glancing over Frances's shoulder.

"No one." Frances briskly shoved the photo and the rest of the papers into the folder she'd found at the bottom of the pile. Timmy chose that moment to toddle up to the table with her car keys in his mouth. "There's my crime-solving nephew," she cooed, gently tugging the keys from his reluctant jaws. "Want to be like Aunty Frances one day?"

"Is he one of the guys you're after in Montreal?"

"Diana," she said pointedly, noticing Brie observing their interaction with wide-eyed curiosity. "You know I can't talk about it."

Her sister shrugged, a suggestive smile on her lips. "I wouldn't mind getting him alone in an interrogation room."

Frances recalled the quiet warning in Mathias's words. He'd looked at her with a kind of amused contempt, like she was out of her depth—a child playing dress-up. She scowled, and Diana raised her eyebrows in mock surprise.

"Why, Mommy?" Brie piped up as her sister breezed into the kitchen to finish chopping the salad for dinner. "He must be a bad guy if Aunty Frances is chasing him."

"You're right," Diana said. "If Aunty Frances is after him, then he must be bad."

Frances pocketed her keys and stepped into the hall to pick up her manhandled bag. She slipped the folder back inside and hung it on one of the coat hooks by the door, out of reach from prying fingers. She wondered how much Brie knew about what she did for a living. As her niece got older, Frances found herself entertaining thoughts of taking her into headquarters and showing her around. Maybe she'd even get some of the grunts to dress up in uniform. But aside from the odd question, Brie had never really shown an interest. She was like her mother in that way—she would much rather go shopping than tour the inside of a federal police station.

Frances returned to the kitchen as Diana pulled a casserole from the oven and placed it down on the island. She gave a disappointed frown. "It doesn't look anything like the recipe," Diana said, poking at the crusted cheese with a fork.

"It looks fine." Frances reached behind her sister for plates. In fact, it looked better than anything she'd eaten in the past week. She hadn't realized how much she'd been relying on packets of vending-machine chips for her weekday meals.

After dinner, having wrangled the kids into their pajamas and to bed, she and Diana sat in the lingering chaos of the kitchen. Pans and dirty plates were scattered across the counter. Diana poured them each a glass of wine then slid back in her chair with a sigh.

"Let Jeff clean it up when he gets home. I'm done." She took a gulp and set her glass down on the table. "So, you up for this one day? Or have I scared you off?"

Frances laughed. "What, kids?"

Diana nodded. "I mean, is it part of the plan, or do you see yourself doing this for the rest of your life?"

This? She could count on one hand the number of women under forty who were heading an entire federal investigation. "What do you mean?"

"I don't know, Frances. Work can't be everything, right?" Diana asked, raising her hand in exasperation. "I thought you had something there with Ethan. Are you meeting people? Going on dates?"

Frances bristled at her sister's appraisal of her personal life. *Does she think I'm lonely and pining, sitting around waiting for a man?* When she wanted one, she sure as hell didn't have to wait. That was the beauty of living in an era when men seemed to prefer the least amount of commitment.

"You don't need to go on dates to get laid."

"Please, you're thirty-eight," Diana said dismissively. "At a certain point, casual sex starts to look sad."

Sad, is it? Her sister's opinion of her prom dress had followed a similar vein. As had her opinion of Frances's first boyfriend and most of them since—Ethan being the notable exception.

"Honestly, I don't care what it looks like," Frances said, raising her glass and taking a pointed sip.

That was her sister's MO—husband, house, kids. Diana liked to make sure everything she did fit into a tidy little checkbox.

"Okay. Well, hear me out," her sister said, placing her hands flat on the table like she was about to launch into a sermon. "I have a friend of a friend, recently single."

Frances gave a snort. *It's not a sermon—it's a fucking pitch.*

"He's looking to meet someone, and we all offered to see who we could set him up with. I think you'd like him."

"Really?" she said mockingly. "And why's that?"

"He's got a great job, super-stable, and is into cycling, travel. Plus, he's easy on the eyes."

Frances wasn't sure what among those stellar qualities was supposed to appeal to her—and this from her own flesh and blood. She hadn't ridden a bike since she ripped her chin open falling off the Schwinn she'd gotten for her twelfth birthday. She still had the scar.

"It would just be casual—you know, coffee or a drink somewhere. You're in town for the next week, right? Can't hurt."

Frances gripped the stem of her wineglass. She'd always resented her sister's meddling. It made her feel like she needed to be fixed.

"I read this thing online about how, as we get older, our circle of acquaintances shrinks." Diana was incapable of taking a hint. "So I figured, why not share some of mine?" She talked about it like they were sharing appetizers off a menu. "Please, just do it for me," she whined. "I worry about you. This is what big sisters do."

Frances let out a defeated groan and did what little sisters did—she agreed.

After leaving Diana's, she drove through the darkened streets to her house across town. Even though she'd bought it a few months before meeting Ethan, he'd moved in shortly after they started dating, so it still felt like *theirs*. As she pulled her car into the garage, she couldn't shake the feeling that the place was eerie without his stuff. Ethan had constructed an elaborate hanging display for his landscaping equipment across one of the garage walls. He was the type to wake early on a Sunday morning to mow the lawn, which had both amused and annoyed her. Now the wall was empty, a white expanse in the dim light, punctuated by ominous metal hooks.

She got out of the car and headed inside. It wasn't just the garage that had been stripped after Ethan left. He'd owned most of the furniture in the house, and she hadn't got around to replacing it, mostly because it was too much of a hassle to pick something out and haul it home. It didn't help that she was barely home to begin with.

Frances dropped her keys on the counter and surveyed the state of the place. It was strange to be back among her things and stranger still to realize that she didn't miss any of them. She opened the fridge for a beer and popped off the lid. Taking a long pull from the bottle, she felt a buzz in her pocket as her phone began to ring. It was Dave.

"Please tell me you have good news," she said. She was desperate for some. Her usual tactics were proving laughably ineffective.

"It's good. I've got you a meeting."

"No shit!"

"You'll have to go alone, though. He only agreed to see you. And he insisted on picking the place. He'll get word to my man, and I'll get word to you."

"Awful lot of conditions," Frances grumbled, resting her elbow against the kitchen counter.

"It's William Truman, Frances," Dave said with a snort. "If he's seen meeting with you, the hit to his reputation will be the least of his worries."

"And I'm supposed to just go along with his demands? I'm the one with the dirt here. With what Border Services has on him, he should be bending over backward for a chance to meet with me."

"Truman has managed to avoid the cops for years. He's not afraid of you."

Frances smirked and took another swig of beer. "He will be."

"We'll see about that," Dave cautioned her.

"All right—thanks for coordinating. Keep me posted about the particulars." Frances hung up and gave a short laugh when she realized that, in the space of one evening, she'd managed to be set up twice.

7

Belkov had cleared out Château Suzdal for the evening, and he and Mathias sat together at a table in the corner of the empty restaurant. Periodically, a woman in a white uniform would come out of the kitchen, ferrying various dishes to their table. Mathias didn't often meet the Bratva boss out front. They typically conducted their business in the office behind the restaurant. But when Mathias called to set up the meeting, Belkov insisted he join him for a meal.

After the Russians had assisted in ousting Piero Russo and solidifying Giovanni's bid for succession, Mathias had found himself on better terms with Viktor Belkov. In the subsequent years, the two of them established somewhat of a working friendship, which consisted mainly of mutual back-scratching and the odd late-night bender. Mathias would not quickly forget that the Russian had come to his aid when he was adrift and desperate, following his transfer to Hamilton. At the time, he'd felt almost abandoned by the family and had leaned heavily on his alliance with the Bratva.

Mathias poked at a piece of questionable-looking meat on his plate and wondered how much he'd be expected to eat without offending the man. Belkov had heaped his plate full, pushing meat and boiled vegetables into piles on his fork.

"There's plenty here," the Russian remarked. "Why not bring him in?"

They both turned to the window overlooking the parking lot, which was empty except for Mathias's Bentley, where Jacques waited behind the wheel. Mathias had brought his second to drive him home in the rare event that he found himself incapacitated. With Belkov, that was difficult to predict. Mathias refused to let the man one-up him when it came to holding his liquor, and Belkov seemed to appreciate that he was up for the challenge.

"He's fine where he is."

Belkov gave him a knowing look. "You don't trust him."

"I'd be an idiot not to trust my own second," Mathias retorted.

"Then why does he always wait outside?"

Mathias didn't reply. He brought a forkful of potatoes to his mouth and chewed the claggy mess quickly in an effort not to gag.

"I liked the other one better," Belkov said.

So did I.

"You never said what happened to him," the Russian complained. "All of a sudden—" He splayed the fingers of his left hand. "Poof! He's gone."

"He stopped being useful," Mathias replied shortly. Abandoning the pretense of eating, he placed his fork down and picked up his glass.

"How cold-blooded." Belkov tutted. "To get rid of such a loyal dog."

"I don't run a fucking charity."

Belkov nodded. "I understand, though. Once you've been shot, you're never the same." He raised the bottom of his shirt to reveal three circular scars below his ribs.

"Now it makes sense why you're such a crazy bastard." Mathias downed his vodka.

Belkov grinned and poured them each an ample refill. "I suppose you came by so we could regale each other with tales of success."

"There's something you can assist me with," Mathias said, pushing away his plate and getting to the matter at hand.

The Bratva boss chuckled. "Why is it I only see you when you're in trouble?"

"I seem to remember receiving a rather panicked call from you last month, after the FBI detained four of your men across the border," Mathias said. After the call, Mathias had reached out to one of his contacts stateside to facilitate an amicable resolution.

"And your assistance was appreciated," Belkov said, raising his glass in salute.

"Time to return the favor."

"Does this have anything to do with the reshuffle at the Quebec divisional office?" Belkov asked coyly.

Mathias narrowed his eyes. "What do you know about that?"

Belkov shrugged. "Only that they've sent someone new from HQ. And that they're very interested in certain members of the family. Might one of those be you?"

"I need intel on Inspector Frances Allen. She's the one they've pulled in from the capital. She's taken over the investigation from Lapierre. I've got feelers out among my people here, but Gurin's better connected in Ontario. I want to know who she's talking to and where she's going."

The Russian took a swig of his drink. "That can be arranged. You're welcome to our eyes and ears. I'll let Gurin know."

"There's something else," Mathias began cautiously. "I've got a leak. Wondered if I might find it out there."

Belkov raised his eyebrows and turned the glass in his hand. "Are you saying…?"

"The man's got a big mouth."

Belkov laughed. "No doubt, but surely he's got more sense than that."

"Does he?" Mathias countered. "The more clout he gets, the bigger his head becomes. He's cocky, thinks the rules don't apply."

"Truman's been burned by the family before. He knows what that tastes like."

"Gets harder to recall the longer it's been."

Belkov gave him an amused smile and threw back the remainder of his drink. "You want to see if you can catch him with his fat fingers in the cookie jar."

"It wouldn't hurt to find out what he's been up to."

"Consider it done."

Mathias raised his drink in acknowledgment and knocked it back.

"After all," the Bratva boss said cannily, "where would we be if we didn't look out for each other?"

It took Rayan leaving the family for him to truly understand how different his life had been. He shared none of the hallmarks of adolescence that had shaped the cohort of fellow students bustling around campus. No school dances or sports games or keg parties. No parents who gifted cars for birthdays and helped with college applications and attended graduation ceremonies. While he didn't pine for these experiences, he felt the way that their absence had shaped him. Then there were the things he had done, which forced Rayan from the other students' naive little world altogether. He might as well have come from outer space for how little he shared with the kids sitting next to him in class.

Rayan was packing up after his last tutorial on a Thursday afternoon when the tutorial leader, a master's student named Lily, announced that the group was heading out for drinks.

"That means you, too, Ayari," she said, stopping by where Rayan stood, pulling the strap of his bag over his shoulder. "You've been suspiciously absent from our Thursday-night socials. Come chat with the group about something other than philosophy." She cocked her head, waiting expectantly, and Rayan felt he had no choice but to nod.

It wasn't that he didn't enjoy their company. For the most part, everyone in the group seemed able to form coherent, sometimes even compelling arguments. But he still wrestled with the need to remain invisible. The more involved he got, the more likely he was to be seen.

He was also impossibly lonely. He ached for Mathias in a way that seemed shamefully juvenile, and he thought constantly of what the man was doing and where he might be. Though small, his apartment seemed cavernous when Mathias wasn't there—which was still the majority of the time. Throwing himself into his studies helped some, but more often than he cared to admit, Rayan found himself unable to concentrate and itching for Mathias's touch.

When they'd worked together, he'd spent most of his days with Mathias and had been privy to his sparing yet withering observations on how the world operated. Now, surrounded by idealists, Rayan missed his pragmatism—the way he distilled even the most daunting situation into practical, manageable action. Mathias had taught him to work hard, keep his head down, and trust his instincts—tactics that had saved him from being swallowed by the circumstances of his past.

Rayan followed the rest of the tutorial group to a popular dive bar a block away from the university. On the walls hung signed photos of mildly famous Canadian celebrities and banners for local sports teams. They found a booth, sat down, and passed around a stack of beer-stained menus. While they were waiting for their drinks to arrive, a young man dressed in a burgundy smoking jacket approached the table, and Lily leapt from her seat to kiss him on the mouth. He was short, with close-cropped blond hair, and his blue eyes were rimmed with black eyeliner.

"This is Noah, everyone," she announced, and they all shuffled over to make room.

Noah raised a hand in greeting and slid into the booth across from Rayan.

As promised, philosophy was off the table. Instead, the group jostled from one topic to the next—college parties, faculty gossip, music concerts. Rayan sat nursing a soda he didn't want, while in front of him, Noah was knocking back beers like they were water. He kept looking at Rayan like he was sizing him up, and it was starting to get annoying.

"Rayan," Lily called from down the table. "Give us a reality check here. We could use a non-Anglo take on this."

Rayan shrugged. He hadn't been following the conversation. "I don't really have an opinion."

"I didn't pick you for a Quebecer," Noah said with a coy smile. "That is, until you opened your mouth. Love the accent."

Funny how it was the same assumption no matter where Rayan went, only presenting in different ways. In the family, the prejudice had been overt. There was a name for his otherness—*estraneo*. Here, they all thought it—they were just better at hiding it.

The conversation bounced past them, and Rayan met Noah's probing stare. "Why's that?"

Noah gestured at Rayan's face. "Just expected something else, I guess. Not that it's a bad thing or anything. I mean, you're stunning." He gave Rayan a rakish grin that didn't seem out of place among this group of mouth-kissing, bohemian-looking kids.

Rayan didn't reply and instead turned his head to listen to the increasingly tedious prattle at the other end of the table. Discussion had turned to politics, and Lily was spearheading a spirited takedown of the new government. He knew the right-leaning party in power had been making things difficult for the country's criminal groups, even in Quebec—a province that typically avoided the full scope of federal attention.

"It's cyclical," Lily was saying, punctuating the air with her hand. "They crack down on crime through a series of dubious measures until the next government gets voted in and repeals everything, and then we're right back where we started. You need to get to the root of why people offend."

"Why do people offend?" Rayan asked, unable to remain silent. Her confidence had rankled him.

The table turned its attention to him, and Lily grinned. "I promised no philosophy."

"It's not philosophy."

"Sure it is. Look at Nietzsche's view—that criminals are the result of society's suppression of man's animalistic drives. Society domesticates man, inflicting itself upon him, and the criminal is simply 'the strong man made sick.'"

"Or he's just hungry or poor," Rayan countered. "Less a philosophical tug-of-war and more basic economics." After he spoke, he realized how hard his voice sounded.

Lily gave him a curious look. "You seem pretty passionate about the subject."

"Excuse me," he muttered, getting to his feet. "I need to find the washroom."

In the men's room, Rayan stood in front of the sink and stared at his reflection in the mirror. When he and his brother had conned kids at the group homes out of their money, or when they'd started stealing cars, or when Tahir began using, people like Lily had sat around theorizing about why they did it, turning to Nietzsche to justify their moral failings. But then, he'd told Professor Hofstein that a good argument could explain any number of sins.

The door opened, and Noah slunk in, giving Rayan a slow smile. "I figured it was code." Eyes glazed, he stepped over with a drunken wobble and placed a hand on Rayan's chest. "I can't keep my fucking eyes off you."

Then Noah was kissing him, and it was as though Rayan was observing himself from across the room. The movement was oddly mechanical, flesh against flesh. He'd never really thought about how strange the act was when utterly devoid of feeling. With Mathias, it always felt like he was being swallowed whole, stripped to nothing but sensation.

Rayan jerked his head back. "What the fuck are you doing?"

Noah laughed softly and jutted out his chin. "I have a pretty good read on these things."

Rayan shoved him backward. He had to focus carefully to rein in the instinctual clench of his fist, ready to make impact. They still caught him off guard, these ingrained reactions wired to another reality. When someone cut in front of him in line or bumped into him as they passed, he flared with the need to correct the slight and ensure that he wasn't seen as weak. But this world was different. In this world, confrontation was to be avoided at all costs.

"You don't," he growled and moved to the door.

Rayan strode out of the bar. As he stalked down the street, he scoured the last hour for clues that he might have given the man, ways in which he'd inadvertently outed himself. Maybe Noah, drunk and arrogant, had simply projected whatever he wanted onto Rayan. A familiar fear gripped him. After a life spent being so careful, when had it started to show on his face?

8

The only place Truman would agree to meet her was at Copps Coliseum in Hamilton on the night of a home game. Frances hadn't picked him for a Bulldogs fan—let alone a hockey man—but he hadn't exactly proven easy to pin down. The stadium was packed. Rowdy fans in blue-and-white jerseys, with giant cups of beer in their hands, jostled past her as she followed the signs to the second floor Club Level.

Frances had little in the way of a traditional hockey education, and everything she'd learned about the game came from her male colleagues. Her father had been more interested in Hitler's tactical advances than the NHL. While she could talk her way through a conversation about stats and scoring with passable accuracy, she wasn't planning on wasting any of her precious time with the Reapers' head discussing sports.

By the time she reached the marked VIP area, the throngs of people had largely thinned out. She stepped through a set of heavy doors and found herself in an elevated section overlooking the rink. Lights flashed overhead, and the boom of an announcer's voice was intersected by pumping music and spontaneous cheers from the crowd. The seats in the VIP area were more spaced out than the rest of the stadium, and spectators dotted the rows in twos and threes.

In the far back row, sitting alone, she spotted a large man swigging from a plastic cup of beer. Frances approached him carefully, not sure he'd seen her. She didn't know why, but she'd expected him to be wearing his cut—the black leather vest with a distinctive scythe motif that she'd seen detailed in police documentation. Instead, the man before her was dressed in faded jeans and a forest green sports jacket.

Truman looked over when she was several steps away, his eyes crawling along her body before they reached her face. Frances felt her skin prickle. There was

46

something possessive about his stare, as though she was there for his viewing pleasure.

She recalled the heft of William Truman's file, which included a substantial section on the trafficking and prostitution activities linked to the Ontario Reapers chapter. Her attempt to penetrate Mathias's defenses by way of a honey trap had clearly been off the mark—she still smarted at the condescending way he'd spelled that out to her. But Frances got the sense, from the way Truman's gaze lingered on her chest, that he'd be more susceptible to such a ploy.

When he was done examining her, Truman gestured to the seat beside him, where he'd placed a cup carrier crammed with three more beers. "I would offer you a drink, but it'd be wasted on the likes of you."

"Pity," she said, cresting the final step and sitting down two seats over, the beers between them. "I am on the clock, after all."

"They let broads do more than pick up phones now? Guess a decent pair of tits can get you all sorts of places." His thin lips curled on his fleshy face.

"Oh, you have no idea," Frances shot back. She'd heard it all before. Something about a woman with a badge had the effect of rustling a man's feathers. "But enough about me," she continued, tiring of the predictable banter. "Border Services was kind enough to refer us a case they've been working on—a string of gunrunning activities over the past year that they believe are connected. Over twenty thousand illegal weapons smuggled into Ontario from across the southern border. While CBSA was able to confiscate a portion of that number, the rest is largely unspoken for."

Truman took a swig of beer, apparently unaffected.

"What they have been able to do, however, is trace it back to you," she said, trying to keep the smugness from her voice.

Apparently, the Reapers' affiliation with the Montreal mafia had resulted in a bad case of overconfidence. The Canada Border Services Agency had initiated a series of surveilled stakeouts and come away with video evidence of weapons being delivered to various Reaper-owned establishments across Ontario. In one video, Truman himself could be seen inspecting the contents of a crate as a delivery was unloaded into the storeroom at the back of the Iguana, his infamous Hamilton brothel.

"I assume you're aware of the situation, or you wouldn't have met with me today," Frances said. "A conviction of this nature carries a sentence of eleven to fourteen years. I can imagine the prospect of jail time might be somewhat unsettling."

"Can you?" Truman sneered. He brought the cup of beer to his mouth and chugged it back. "So, what—I hand over a couple of the boys, point you in the direction of the guns, and you get your little hoorah? What's the going rate—three to one? I got a few guys who could use a stint in the cooler."

"No," Frances said with a shake of her head. Below, in the rink, there was a flurry of movement as the Bulldogs burst out onto the ice, and a roar went up from the stands. She turned to fix Truman with a hard stare. "I want something on Mathias Beauvais."

Truman visibly stiffened. Then he began to chuckle, covering his misstep. "What the fuck are you talking about?"

"Come on, Truman. We've known about your little family-facilitated narcotics shipments for a while now. We know the two of you are working together. What we don't have is any evidence linking him to the operation. We'd like you to help us with that."

Truman tossed his now-empty cup to the floor by his feet. "Fuck off," he growled. "There ain't no way I'm helping you. Do you know the man? Fourteen years in the hole is nothing compared to what he'll do if someone rolls over on him."

"Don't worry about Mathias," Frances said, feigning confidence. "When we're done, he'll be put away for a long time."

Truman shifted so he was facing her, his bulky frame spilling over the edge of the seat. She hadn't realized quite how hefty he was until she'd sat down, and even with the surrounding crowd, she felt the menace of his physicality.

"Should've known some lady cop would be thick as a brick. You think prison will stop Beauvais? Do you know how many people he has in his pocket? He'd be running the joint before you know it—turn it into his own little fiefdom." Truman raised his arm and pointed a thick sausage finger in her face. "I ain't giving you that, sweetheart. Ask for something else, or we're done here."

Frances shrugged and got to her feet. "Then we're done. If it's not Mathias, you've got nothing I want." She moved to the stairs and stopped to address Truman over her shoulder. "I look forward to the trial. I hope you've got a good lawyer."

Armando Bernardi owned Le Châtaignier, an exclusive French restaurant in the cobblestoned Vieux-Montréal neighborhood that was open to the public only three nights a week. It catered handpicked events for the family's elite and hosted the occasional private function upon request. Apparently, even the boss was an admirer. He and his wife ate there every other Saturday.

It was also where the Quintino liked to hold their meetings. The aging councilmen were most comfortable when plied with a steady stream of rich food and expensive alcohol. They'd paid their dues and were no longer interested in margins and maximizing efficiency, only with how to maintain their station and ensure that the boss kept the ship afloat. It had proven a drastic change of pace for Mathias, who was wired to hunt out problems and aggressively resolve them.

They were seated in the private dining room toward the back of the restaurant and had just finished the fourth course of a seemingly endless lunch. Enzo interrupted a discussion on the increased customs presence at the Chartierville border crossing and turned to Mathias. "Did you look into that new inspector?"

"I did." Mathias placed his knife and fork across his half-eaten plate of seared duck. "I also had the pleasure of meeting her. I would be careful who you speak to at Le Rouge going forward." There was a low murmur of disquiet from the three men at the table.

"This the broad with the RCMP? I thought she was supposed to be some brainless paper shuffler," Gabriele grumbled.

"I wouldn't underestimate her," Mathias cautioned. "When was the last time the Feds tried to infiltrate one of our establishments?"

"The Quebec office would never be so brazen," Armando said with a snort.

"That's why she's here. She's got no qualms trying things the local office wouldn't dare," Mathias said.

"I don't like it," Enzo said, tapping his knuckles against the starched white tablecloth. "Do what you need to stay ahead of this."

The waitstaff came through from the kitchen and began clearing their plates. Mathias waited until they'd left before continuing. "What I can't figure out is who's behind the original tip-off."

"Who wouldn't benefit from us going through the wringer? I can't think of a single group that won't stand to gain," Armando said.

"Might not be a group behind it," Gabriele posited. "Could be a personal grievance, a targeted attack."

"Regardless, the Feds can't afford to keep this dragging on." Enzo raised his glass of wine to drain it. "My guess is they'll want something to show for their time, and we're an easy target."

Mathias didn't give voice to his suspicions about Truman, since they were still just that: suspicions. There was no need to get the council up in arms until he heard back from Gurin.

The servers chose that moment to return with ramekins of crème brûlée and cups of black coffee. The conversation at the table shifted as the men busied themselves with the final course. "So, Beauvais," Armando said, giving him a sly smile. "Has the boss shown you the office?"

Mathias pushed his dessert aside and considered the question carefully. "He has. It's ambitious."

"It's crazy, is what it is," Enzo retorted. "I was hoping you'd convince him of that."

"I can't say I'm entirely on board," Mathias said judiciously. "He seems dead set on corporatizing Collections."

"Thought you'd be happy to be rid of the division. It's no secret you can't stand it," Gabriele said, cracking the layer of caramelized sugar in his bowl with the side of his spoon.

"Giovanni has always had grand plans. Some of them are worth indulging—others not so much," Armando said with a snicker.

"And this one...?" Mathias asked, raising his cup of coffee to his lips.

"I say let him go down this fanciful path for now. He'll figure out soon enough that you can't run a successful division without boots on the ground," Enzo said.

Mathias took a sip of coffee. He hadn't had the impression that Giovanni was chasing a dream—it had sounded like he'd already thought all of this through. "There'll be pushback," he conceded. "Not everyone in the division's going to blend seamlessly into a swanky office."

"That's for fucking sure," Armando crowed, and the men around the table chuckled.

Mathias swallowed another mouthful of coffee and thought of the boss's warning—*soon Quebec will be expected to fall back in line.*

In the face of the unfolding situation with the Feds, he was beginning to think Giovanni's prudence might be justified.

Frances couldn't stop looking at the infinity tattoo on the underside of the man's left wrist. She'd first noticed it when he'd raised his hand in greeting after arriving at the restaurant for their ill-fated date. It was garish, like Chinese characters on someone's lower back, and laughably small, as though he'd wanted to be edgy but unobtrusive.

If you're going to get a tattoo, commit, God dammit.

"They offer these excursions in Bali where you can swim with dolphins," Louis was saying, and his green eyes lit up as though he was reliving the experience right there in the vegan tapas place he'd suggested over the phone. "It's incredible. You've got to try it."

She nodded and took another sip of her beer. They sat at a small table by the window, and she found her gaze wandering to the far more interesting people strolling by outside.

"Have you traveled much, Frances?"

"No," she said truthfully.

After graduating from university, she'd spent a month in Europe before starting cadet training at the RCMP academy. It had been an attempt to reclaim some of the fun she'd missed as a straitlaced student fixated on a future in law enforcement. But instead of partying and sleeping with foreign boys, she'd felt homesick and spent her time eating supermarket pastries in cheap hostels. This was the part where she was supposed to say that she would like to travel and planned to one day backpack through Asia or go bungee jumping in New Zealand.

"I feel like I haven't even done Canada justice yet."

"Tell me about it. Skylar and I—" Louis flushed and looked embarrassed to have mentioned his ex again. He'd done it twice already, and their food hadn't even arrived.

Frances pretended not to notice. She mentally cursed Diana and her own inability to say no. It wasn't that she didn't like the idea of having someone to share her life with, but she hated the process of getting there—marketing herself, the endless disappointing dates, all her own insecurities mirrored back at her. Because if she was honest, Louis was a perfectly nice person. He was friendly and enthusiastic and had worked in asset management at a well-known national bank for the good part of a decade. She was the one with the problem.

She imagined what Louis would say if she told him she'd once exposed a group of insurance brokers who ran an underground torture club. Or that last year she'd busted an international drug ring that spanned four countries and had led to the seizure of over eight hundred kilos of meth destined for the street. Frances lived in a world that most people would find abhorrent, filled with questionable characters and even more questionable motives. And she liked it—more than she liked the idea of swimming with dolphins. That probably made her what Ethan had so affectionately called her—a freak.

"So, you live in Montreal?"

"Temporarily," she said. "Just while I'm working this investigation. I'm originally from here. I plan on moving back to Ottawa once everything's wrapped up."

"How long does that usually take?"

How long is a piece of string? "Depends. Some investigations are more cut-and-dried than others."

"And this one?"

She thought of the hostile welcome she'd received at the Quebec office and the glint of intimidation in Mathias's eyes. "Not so cut-and-dried," she admitted.

"I've never met anyone who worked for the RCMP," Louis said with a grin. "Bet it's mostly guys, huh?"

Frances shrugged. He was right. She'd always used it to her advantage, though, as a way to stand out and push herself harder. "Mostly, but it's changing."

Fortunately, a young woman in a black apron appeared beside Louis and began setting out a series of small dishes on the table between them. Frances wasn't confident she could determine what any of them contained.

"Diana mentioned you'd recently come out of a long-term relationship." Louis handed her an empty plate as the server left. "I know how tough that is."

Frances could have killed her sister. *Recently?* It was going on a year since Ethan had ended things. Her transfer to Montreal had actually come as a relief. Ottawa was a small town, and she'd grown tired of bumping into Ethan at places they'd frequented while together.

She loaded tiny portions of food onto her plate, not because she was interested in eating them but more as a thing to do. "It was pretty amicable. We had different ambitions."

Ethan's had been to get married and have babies, little girls he'd already named Poppy and June. Hers had been to make superintendent by the time she turned forty. In a way, the timing worked out perfectly. His leaving freed her up to take on the Quebec investigation, which put Frances one step closer to a promotion. They never could have made it work while they were together. She'd have turned the opportunity down and quietly resented Ethan for the rest of her career.

"How long were you guys together?"

"Eight years," Frances said as though it wasn't a big deal. It had been—still was.

She'd met Ethan one morning after leaving a security briefing at Parliament Hill. He'd been part of an antiwar protest that had turned violent, and Frances had helped rinse the tear gas out of his eyes with her water bottle. He'd looked up, face red and eyes streaming, and flashed her that disarming smile of his, like he figured it was as good a moment as any to hit on her. They were together by the end of the week. He'd loved telling that story to people they met at parties.

Now it was like time had skipped forward and she had nothing to show for it. While Frances had always been lukewarm about the idea of a family, Ethan was the only man she could imagine having one with. Getting back out there was supposed to feel empowering, but instead, it brought into sharp focus just how good she'd had it.

"Wow, I can't imagine," Louis said, shaking his head sympathetically and scooping what looked like a fake crab cake onto his plate. "Skylar and I were together for two, and that felt like a lifetime."

Frances almost rolled her eyes. Two years was foreplay.

They made uncomfortable small talk through the rest of the meal and parted with an awkward hug. It had been clear from the outset that they were poorly matched. She didn't know what Diana had been thinking.

Fortunately, Frances had far more pressing concerns on her mind. That was the beauty of a demanding job—it left little room to mull over the other things in her life that weren't working.

9

Mathias sat at the bar and watched the line of people queuing for drinks. For a crumbling joint, it was surprisingly busy at two thirty in the afternoon. *Does anyone have a job in this fucking town?*

Gurin had called the previous evening and asked to meet with him to discuss what he'd uncovered about Inspector Allen. Mathias had made the trip out to Hamilton that morning, knowing he couldn't stay long as there were pressing things to be dealt with back in Montreal. He glanced down at his watch. Granted, he was early, but Gurin would have to haul ass if he expected to make it on time. They'd agreed to meet at the same piece-of-shit bar in North Glanford where they used to trade intel when Mathias was stationed in the city.

During his brief stint in Hamilton, he'd grown to appreciate Gurin's practical efficiency, along with his capacity for discretion. Even back then, he'd trusted the Russians more than he had the bumbling head of the Reapers. The Bratva had been in the game longer and knew the value of caution—keeping your mouth shut and your friends close. He would soon find out whether Truman had forsaken both of those tenets.

"I'm not late," Gurin announced as he sidled up and took a seat beside Mathias at the bar.

"Cutting it close."

Gurin grinned and signaled the bartender with his hand. "Still a stickler for the time."

"Time is money," Mathias said.

"That it is," Gurin agreed. The bartender took his order, and Mathias tapped the edge of his empty glass for a top-up. "Rare to see you in town. Not exactly going out of your way to visit these days."

"You could say that." And when he was here, it wasn't Gurin he came to see.

Gurin waited until the drinks were poured and the barman had stepped away before continuing. "So, your girl's been rather busy as of late," he said, reaching into his jacket and handing Mathias an envelope of photos. "Spent some time in the capital with her sister's kids and had herself a romantic evening out."

Mathias flicked through the collection of shots—Allen leaving the RCMP headquarters in Ottawa, at the park with two young children, seated across from a well-dressed man at a restaurant. Then the last set of images made his hand still.

"She even managed a trip out here to catch a hockey game."

There she was, high in the stands of the Copps Coliseum, two seats down from the easily recognizable bulk of the Red Reapers' head, William Truman. Mathias slipped the photos back into the envelope and tossed it onto the bar. The anger rose, a pressure against his chest.

"So now we know," Gurin said. "Truman's been getting cozy with the Horsemen."

"Or maybe they're both Bulldogs fans," Mathias muttered sarcastically. He took a swig from his drink.

Gurin snickered. "Are you really that surprised, Mathias? He's always been a shifty bastard."

"I figured he had too much to lose to squeal. She must have something on him."

"My money's on that as well," Gurin agreed. "If he's willing to go against you and the family, she has him by the fucking balls."

"Any ideas?"

The Russian shrugged. "With Truman, it could be anything. He likes to throw shit at the wall and see what sticks."

"Yeah, we knew that going in."

So why did I let this happen? There had been plenty of opportunities to sever ties with the man and wash his hands of their whole joint venture. Mathias didn't want to dwell on the reason he hadn't—which had nothing to do with Truman.

"It seems he's outlived his usefulness. Now might be a good time to cut him loose." Gurin raised his drink to his lips and swallowed, then he placed the half-empty glass back on the bar between them. "Want me to see what I can find out?"

Mathias nodded. "Any trouble he's in, anything the cops have on him, I want to know about it."

"I can do that," Gurin said, absently twirling his glass on its coaster. "I hear you're due a favor."

"You have a better memory than your boss."

Gurin chuckled. "His is selective. Belkov doesn't like owing people."

"Then he should stop asking for help. But quiet, yes? The last thing I need is for Truman to get wind of the fact that I'm looking into him."

"Please," Gurin said with a smirk. "He's so far up his own ass I'd be surprised if I registered." He downed the rest of his drink. "How's business in Montreal? Margins as crippled as ours with the increased border scrutiny?"

Fortunately, the family had always made efforts to diversify its income streams. When Narcotics took a hit, one of the other divisions picked up the slack. The Bratva's Hamilton activities were almost exclusively tied to their cross-border drug trade, which made them particularly susceptible to recent government crackdowns.

"Piper has a lot to answer for," Mathias said. "You have my sympathy."

"I'll need more than that if things don't pick up soon," Gurin grumbled and signaled the barman for a refill.

After Gurin had left, Mathias dropped a couple of notes down on the bar and slipped the envelope of photos into his jacket. He stood and looked again at his watch, his resolve buckling. The pull was frightening, calling to him with a power that made Mathias want to neglect his duties and throw caution to the wind. He was so close it seemed almost cruel not to.

It would be tight, but there was time.

When Rayan opened the door to his apartment, he found Mathias sitting on the sofa in the living room. His jacket was draped over the back cushions, and he had Rayan's thesis proposal in his hand. The folder lay open on the coffee table, where Rayan had left it that morning.

"Where have you been?" Mathias asked, his voice betraying a hint of agitation.

"The library." Rayan hung up his coat and dropped his bag to the floor. "Not so fun, is it?" he teased, moving to the sofa. "Waiting around for someone to show."

Mathias arched an eyebrow, and Rayan plopped down beside him with a grin. "When did you get in?"

"I'm not staying," Mathias said. "I had something to discuss with Gurin."

"About what?"

"This is what you're working on?" Mathias asked, ignoring his question and flipping through the pages in his hand.

"It's a study of moral luck. Nagel's a big proponent."

Mathias gave a snort of laughter. "Moral luck?"

"The idea that we're morally assessable only to the extent that we're assessed for factors under our control."

"Open to interpretation," Mathias said with a shrug.

Rayan hid a smile. Naturally, that was how he viewed things. "Somewhat. It's more an argument that we can be judged for our intentions, just not the results of our intentions."

Mathias tossed the proposal down on the coffee table and turned to him with a cynical look. "You realize who you're talking to."

Rayan's eyes dropped to the signet ring on Mathias's right hand. "I'm sitting in lectures with kids whose biggest moral dilemma is whether to buy free-trade coffee beans."

"And you think you're more qualified to weigh in on the subject?"

"I wonder," Rayan shot back.

"No one will take you seriously in that fucking thing. You look like a frat boy at football practice."

Rayan laughed, glancing down at the oversized sweater he'd thrown on before leaving the apartment. He'd picked it up at the bookstore one rainy day after getting soaked on his way to class. It bore the school's name and a white coat of arms—tasteless but surprisingly warm. Perhaps on some level, it had been an attempt to blend in with the hordes of carefree students who roamed the campus, pretending that he was one of them and not an entirely different beast.

"I'm sure there's one in your color." He pulled himself onto Mathias's lap, his legs astride the man's muscular thighs. The feel of Mathias beneath him sent a spike of heat through his insides. Rayan reached for the hem of the sweater and yanked it over his head to reveal his bare chest. "Better?"

"Getting there," Mathias murmured, running his hands down Rayan's back to grip his ass.

Rayan lowered his head and kissed him hard. Mathias parted his lips, heady and soft, and the rest faded into nothing, time slowing to a crawl.

"Miss me?" Mathias snickered when Rayan emerged, his breathing shallow.

"Maybe." Rayan ground against him, rocking his hips as the blood surged between his legs.

Mathias wasted no time removing Rayan's cock from his jeans, and it sprang, insistent, into his hand. Suddenly impatient, Rayan tugged at the front of Mathias's slacks, unbuckled him, and pulled his hardening cock from his fly. Mathias spat into his palm and gripped their shafts together, easing his wrist up and down in long, deliberate strokes.

"How about now?" Mathias ran his mouth along the underside of Rayan's jaw and nipped the flesh of his earlobe.

This time, Rayan didn't answer, managing only a low moan. He wrapped his arms around Mathias's neck and bunched his fingers in the back of his shirt. He always felt overwhelmed when they once again found themselves together. Rayan's arousal lurched forward, untamable, threatening his ability to hold back.

Mathias rubbed the pad of his thumb along the slit of Rayan's cock, already leaking, and Rayan groaned. Mathias began to quicken his movements, squeezing and releasing in a way that made Rayan's head spin. He tried to fight it, but the entire world had been reduced to the sensation of them pressed against each other, the warmth of Mathias's hand as he drew it along the length of him. Rayan wanted to make it last—prolong this coveted closeness—yet at the same time, he did not want the man to stop.

When Rayan finished far too quickly, Mathias gave a soft chuckle, tracing a finger through the streaks of white across his stomach. "The stamina of a frat boy as well."

"Fuck off," Rayan muttered, burying his face in Mathias's neck as he caught his breath. "It's been weeks since I've seen you."

"There's three million people in this city. I'm sure someone can help with that."

While Mathias's tone was flippant, his gaze was watchful, like he'd laid down a trap and was waiting to see how Rayan would maneuver. Rayan remembered the way Noah had jumped him in the bathroom and how much he'd hated the feel of the cocky kid's mouth.

"I don't want anyone else," Rayan said, trying to keep his voice light despite the depth of feeling that fact evoked. "What about you—full dance card?" He spoke casually, as if he hadn't mulled the possibility over a hundred times, turning his jealousy over like a stone.

Mathias studied him. "You're enough trouble as it is."

A warmth flooded Rayan's chest. He ducked his head, not wanting the satisfaction to show on his face. Shifting his weight, he pushed Mathias's hand away so his alone was wrapped around the man's cock and began to move—quick, tight jerks, fingers slick with his own come. He yanked open the buttons of Mathias's shirt with the other hand and lowered his mouth to his nipples, feeling Mathias swell in his grip. Rayan curled his wrist and ran his palm across the head of Mathias's cock in slow, circular strokes. Mathias's fingers dug into Rayan's waist, and his chest rose rapidly as he closed in on his release. He came with a short growl, his forehead furrowing before a wave of pleasure washed over his face, momentarily smoothing the hard lines. It was Mathias at his most defenseless, and the sight always made Rayan's throat constrict.

After releasing Mathias's spent cock, Rayan reached for the discarded sweater and used it to swipe away the remnants of their encounter. "It's good for something."

Mathias smirked and pulled Rayan to him. The kiss moved from Rayan's mouth to his jaw then the hollow of his neck and down to his shoulder blades. Rayan stroked the man's hair, savoring the ease of Mathias's hands on him, not wanting to break the spell.

"A woman was caught trying to scatter her husband's ashes from the top of the CN Tower," Rayan murmured as Mathias slid a hand along his chest.

"They found a man in Boucherville housing fifty raccoons in his basement," Mathias returned, tracing Rayan's ribs with his fingers.

Rayan laughed. "You win."

"We seem to be giving the Anglos a run for their money." Mathias brushed his nipple with a thumb, and Rayan—still on his lap—arched against him.

"How was the wedding?" Rayan asked in an attempt to keep him there if only for the moment.

Mathias grimaced. "Which one? They all bleed together." It was no secret that Mathias despised the more socially taxing aspects of his new role. He'd never been one for appearances.

"What else is happening in the city?" Rayan missed the place, the language, and the culture, which felt so distant from his life in Toronto. He could almost picture what the mountain looked like this time of year.

But mention of Montreal made Mathias's face harden, and he dropped his hands. "I have to get back."

"Don't." The word came out before Rayan had the sense to swallow it.

Mathias gave him a stern look. "Don't ask for things I can't give you."

Rayan sighed, defeated, and eased himself off Mathias's lap.

"So, you and my mother..." Mathias stood and began buckling his pants. "You really are a sucker for punishment. She said you came by every month while I was in Hamilton."

"Right." Rayan gave a quiet laugh, refastening the front of his jeans. After meeting her that first time, he'd been compelled by a strange sense of pity. "She seemed lonely."

"She is lonely," Mathias said with a frown. "Always has been. It's her defining characteristic."

Rayan recalled the way the woman's face would startle when their conversation reached a natural lull, as though dreading the space that rose in between. "That must have been hard."

"I know what you're doing."

"Then I shouldn't have gone?" Rayan pivoted.

"You need a hobby," Mathias said, reaching for the top button on his shirt. "You obviously have no idea what to do with your time."

"I can think of a couple things." Rayan looked up, catching the man's eye.

Mathias's fingers stilled. "You're pathetic, you know that?" But his mouth tweaked, and he lowered his hands, letting his shirt fall back open.

Rayan tried to keep the stupid smile from his face. "You have no idea."

With how hard it was proving to get dirt on Mathias, Frances had reached out to Transport Canada and added his plates to their automated recognition watch list. This way, if he crossed provincial lines, she'd know about it. Truman was still playing hard to get, so she figured she'd try to gather her own evidence of the two of them working together.

The opportunity presented itself sooner than expected. Earlier that week, she'd received an alert that Mathias's car had left Quebec and later been clocked through the toll on Highway 407, heading into Hamilton. She'd called in a favor with Stan Redford, a former colleague who had started his own PI firm after leaving the RCMP and was only too happy to take a stab at tailing Mathias. Granted, it was a little unorthodox, but Ontario was her old stomping ground. Out there, she had a greater selection of resources at her disposal, while in Montreal, she had a sneaking suspicion that she was being deliberately left in the dark.

Stan managed to locate Mathias's car parked outside a dump of a dive bar on the outskirts of the city. It wasn't a location Frances recognized from the list of known Reapers establishments. Before Stan had a chance to get out of his car, Mathias emerged from the bar, so there was no way of knowing who he'd met with. Stan followed Mathias as he drove out of the parking lot and onto the highway. But instead of heading back in the direction of Montreal, he'd crossed Burlington Bay and continued north to Toronto. Not one to back down from a challenge, Stan tailed him to a sleepy neighborhood downtown, where Mathias had pulled his car into an underground lot beneath a block of apartments. From there, Stan lost track of him.

When Stan had relayed all of this to her over the phone, she'd been certain they'd stumbled onto something. Perhaps Mathias kept a woman in the city. It was common among the mafia elite and had proven many a man's downfall. In her experience, these women were the ones the men confided in—certainly not their wives or, as Mathias had made painfully clear, the interchangeable girls who worked at the clubs. Mathias had built his life carefully, leaving very little in the way of open doors, but this had the potential to be that opening. If they could find the woman, Frances could start putting pressure on her. She'd instructed Stan to return the following morning and spend three days photographing everyone who entered and exited the apartment building.

Frances sat at her computer—the Montreal office was deserted on a Friday evening, since everyone had gone home to dinner with their families or out with friends—and scrolled through the file of images Stan had sent her. She was looking for a younger woman, polished and beautiful with expensive taste. She'd narrowed it down to a few candidates when she clicked through to the next photo and paused.

The shot was of a man of ambiguous ethnicity, in his early-to-mid-twenties, with tousled black hair. He looked Hispanic, or possibly Middle Eastern, and was athletic in build but dressed casually. She flicked through a few more photos and found him again, this time arriving back at the building in the evening, the collar of his winter coat pulled up against the cold.

Why does he seem so familiar? He wasn't on her map and hadn't been plotted out among the ranks of family soldiers. But she had an eye for faces and couldn't shake the feeling that she'd seen him somewhere before. She flipped through the folder on her desk, not finding him among the stack of printed bios. Then she strode down to the filing room and pulled out a box of images from Giorgio Russo's funeral. HQ had sent over a photographer to capture everyone in attendance so as to assemble an updated record of the group. Much had been speculated about the men at that funeral and what had happened afterward.

She scoured each photo. There were over a hundred of them, with names and known ranks recorded on the backs of the images. When she came to Antonio Giraldi, she stopped, her eye catching on the blurry profile of a man standing behind him. She held it up to her face. He was out of focus, the target of the image being the old man in front, yet the resemblance was unmistakable. She trawled through the remaining archive of figures, from lowly drivers all the way up to Giovanni Bianchi himself, but the dark-haired man hadn't been categorized—he'd been omitted from the record. Or he'd been removed entirely. Purposely erased.

Frances reached for another box, which was dated several years prior to the funeral, when Mathias Beauvais was only just beginning to come up on the RCMP's radar. She scanned the index and then thumbed through it, finding images, documents, and whole sections missing.

"The fuck...?" she muttered.

Someone had done a number on this—a full-scale clean-up job. She picked up the box and hauled it back upstairs to her desk, where she took everything out and went through each piece of paper with a fine-tooth comb. People were fallible. If the mob had someone on the inside, they were bound to have removed the evidence in a hurry to avoid getting caught. And when someone was in a hurry, mistakes were made. Her hand fell on a photo of Mathias in discussion with a large, gruff-looking man, and there, almost cropped out of the frame, was the young man from outside the building. Gone were the tousled hair and the casual clothes. Here was a slicked-back soldier in black, his face a blank mask.

That's right. Before Jacques Laberge, there was someone else... After she'd accepted the transfer to Quebec, Frances had dived deep into the records of the family's purported activities in Montreal and remembered coming across a mention of another subordinate who had worked with Mathias. *What was his name?* For the life of her, she couldn't remember. And it seemed someone else wanted to ensure he was forgotten.

But why? Frances took the photo and held it up beside the image on her computer screen. Then she picked up the phone and called Stan. She hadn't found the woman Mathias was seeing, but this coincidence was too jarring to ignore. She would have Stan follow the man in the photo and find out who he was.

10

Frances watched as the young man shoved his hands into the pockets of his jacket and strode across the icy quad at the University of Toronto's downtown campus. Rayan Nadeau. The admissions office had him registered as Rayan Ayari. She hadn't found any record of that name in her subsequent searches, but the name Nadeau had brought up a plethora of information in the system that seemed to stop dead right around the time the man had turned eighteen.

She knew about the numerous group homes he'd cycled through and the foster family who'd backed out after Rayan refused to be separated from his brother. He had no living relatives except for an estranged father who'd been deemed negligent by the courts and stripped of his parental rights. She'd seen the photos that child protection services had taken of Rayan as a young boy, detailing his bruised face and lacerated neck, which had accompanied the petition for divorce filed by his mother. The divorce was never finalized—several years later, the woman had committed suicide in the apartment where she lived with her two sons. There was a clinical psychologist's report prepared before the custody hearing for the boys, which described Rayan as suffering from post-traumatic stress disorder and dissociative tendencies. The assessment also noted he was hyperlexic and an autodidact, intelligent beyond his years. Then there was his criminal record, which detailed a handful of summary offenses committed in his teens and one auto theft conviction that was later dismissed before trial.

Frances followed Rayan with her eyes as he passed by where she stood outside the student union building and headed toward the gates on College Street. From the information the admissions office had sent through, he maintained a 4.0 average and had condensed a four-year degree into five semesters. But he was also the man who appeared in photos with key figures of the Montreal mafia. Now that she'd seen him in person, there was no denying it.

Her guess was that Mathias was using Rayan as a free agent and banking on his erasure from police records to fly under the radar and break into the Toronto crime circuit. Mathias had done something similar in Hamilton several years prior—a city with virtually no mob presence was turned into a hotbed of family activity almost overnight. Perhaps Rayan had never stopped working for Mathias but had simply been stationed elsewhere to establish a new market for the family's expansion into Ontario, his appearance as a dedicated student nothing more than a ruse.

Frances waited several beats before stepping out. She kept her distance, staying a block behind Rayan as he continued down the street. She hadn't been following him long when he stopped abruptly in the middle of the sidewalk and turned to her, his brown eyes narrowing.

"Mr. Nadeau." As she approached, a flicker of recognition crossed his face. "I'd like to speak with you, if that's all right." She'd spoken in English, but he gave no indication that he'd heard her request. "Would you prefer Quebecois?" she asked, this time in French.

"I'd prefer if you kept walking," he said quietly in English, stepping to one side to let her pass.

She didn't move. "I believe we share a mutual acquaintance. Tell me, how do you know Mathias Beauvais?"

Rayan's expression didn't change. He stared at her with a blankness that disguised his obvious intelligence. "Sorry, I can't help you."

"Then maybe you can help me with something else," she said, undaunted. "Nothing official, just a few quick questions. There's a coffee shop around the corner. Why don't we get out of the cold and have a chat?"

Rayan turned and continued walking, pulling the strap of his satchel higher up on his shoulder.

"Or I could come by one of your classes instead," Frances called out to his retreating back. "Tomorrow morning's lecture on divergent thinking sounds like a real barn burner. I don't mind stopping by your apartment, too, if that's easier. It's a nice building. Summerhill's a great neighborhood."

Rayan stopped. When he looked at her, she could see that he knew he was cornered. "Fine," he said in a voice devoid of polite sentiment. "Lead the way."

They took a seat in the far corner of a nearby Second Cup, which was teeming with students tapping away at their laptops. Rayan sat across from her at the table, refusing to remove his jacket. He looked like he was seconds from bolting.

"Quite an interesting life you've had," she said, cracking open the lid of her takeout cup and tipping in a packet of sugar. "Can't seem to catch a break." She blew across the lip in an effort to cool the molten liquid.

"I don't know what you're talking about."

"There's a pretty comprehensive record of you on file up until age eighteen, and then you just disappear. And I mean comprehensive—not a lot of government departments you didn't touch. Want to tell me about that?"

"Why I slipped through the cracks, or what a shitty job child protection does looking after the kids in its care?"

"How you managed to disappear."

Rayan gave her a cold smile. "Walk the streets any given night, and you'll see how easy it is for a person to disappear."

"Is that when you started working for the family?" She pulled a folder out of her bag and placed the photos she'd found of him with Mathias and with Antonio Giraldi at Russo's funeral on the table. "Look familiar?"

Rayan's eyes briefly skimmed the images before returning to her. "Seems you've already made up your mind, so why don't you tell me why you're here?"

"How rude of me," she said, taking a card from her pocket and sliding it toward him. "I'm Inspector Frances Allen, with the RCMP Organized Crime Branch. We're taking down your boss, Mathias Beauvais, and we'd very much like your cooperation."

Rayan picked up the card and studied it carefully, his face giving nothing away.

"It's a common tactic. I see it all the time," she continued glibly. "Throwing a subordinate under the bus to escape conviction. Suddenly, everything was your idea. If I were you, I'd stay one step ahead and get your statement in first."

"What makes you think I have anything to say?"

Frances took a sip of her coffee, biding her time. "Don't you think it's strange the cops never pursued your brother's murder?" She saw Rayan's eyes widen in surprise. "I mean, looking through the police report, it's clear they could have done more."

Rayan crumpled her card in his fist, and Frances suppressed a triumphant grin. It had been a shot in the dark, but she'd found it—the man's exposed nerve.

"Didn't that make you angry? Or maybe..." She paused deliberately. "You were relieved they didn't look too closely into what happened."

This time, Rayan wasn't able to hide the horror from his face. "What?"

"In the next-of-kin section on the coroner's report, you're listed as missing. And sure enough, your records seem to drop off right around the same time. Awfully convenient, isn't it? I wonder what else we'll find when we start digging."

Rayan shook his head wordlessly.

"It was lucky the police were able to identify him at all," she remarked. "He was in rough shape when they found his body. Turns out one of the officers remembered taking a mug shot of a kid a couple months before. Had a rather unmistakable tattoo." Frances reached into her folder and slid another photo toward Rayan.

The man stood bolt upright, knocking the table and sending her coffee splashing to the floor. His face had gone slack, his eyes fixed, unblinking, on the image between them. Then he grabbed his bag and pushed his way out of the café.

Several people at the other tables had turned to stare. Frances carefully returned the photos to her folder, which she slipped into her bag. Then she stood.

She stopped by the counter on her way out and pushed a twenty into the tip jar. "Sorry about the mess."

Rayan stared down at the scribbles his brother had made on a grease-spotted napkin.

"Well?" Tahir pressed, beaming like it was a work of art. "Pretty fucking sick, right?"

They were in a booth at the back of Pizza Pizza, with a plate of old slices the owner sometimes set aside for them. If Tahir behaved and business was slow, he let them sit inside like customers and looked the other way as they shook a thick layer of parmesan over the greasy sheen of cold cheese and pepperoni.

"Where are you putting it?" Rayan asked, skeptical. The napkin depicted a crudely drawn snake, its mouth open wide to swallow its own tail.

"Right here," Tahir said, raising a hand behind his ear and bringing it down along the right side of his neck. "It's like creation and destruction in one."

Rayan chewed on the remainder of his crust and gave a shrug. "I guess."

"I already know who's going to do it," Tahir continued, taking back the napkin and folding it into his pocket. "Len has a friend who owns a parlor in the Plateau."

Rayan felt a surge of irritation. "You have the money for that? They're not cheap."

"Let me worry about the money. I've got it covered," his brother said blithely.

Rayan swallowed a bite of stale crust. *If you're not worried about money, why the fuck are we eating day-old pizza?* "She wouldn't have liked it," he said. It was the first thought he'd had after Tahir had shown him the design.

His brother scowled. "It's got nothing to do with her," he snapped. "Christ, Rayan, you're always going on about that shit."

It was a common tension these days, with Tahir thinking they could slough off their history like an ill-fitting coat. Maybe he didn't believe it so much as he wanted to.

When his brother went to the parlor the following day, Rayan tagged along anyway. He stood by the door while Tahir engaged in a heated argument with Len's friend behind the counter. The tattooist agreed in the end, despite it being unclear what had been promised as payment. With how light-fingered Tahir had become with Bastien's profits, Rayan figured the money was something his brother had no business giving away. The tattoo turned out misaligned, the snake's head awkwardly grazing Tahir's jaw—no doubt a token of the artist's reluctance.

Later, as he watched his brother furiously inspecting the botched tattoo in a McDonald's bathroom, Rayan had wondered if it wasn't all some cosmic joke— the idea that creation itself could be destroyed by the corruption of a steady hand. Or perhaps Tahir had just been unlucky. Bad fortune had followed them around like a black cloud, ready at any moment to open up above their heads.

In the photo the cop had pushed across the table toward Rayan, Tahir's face was unnaturally bloated, the skin split and discolored. Not much about his features was recognizable, but the ink remained, the snake curving around his throat, taunting, as though it had been an omen all along—destruction, ceaseless and circular, coming for his life from the very beginning. The image was etched into Rayan's brain. As if it was not enough to have witnessed his brother's last moments, now he'd seen the aftermath—his body abandoned to the elements, a shameful, undignified end.

Back at his apartment, Rayan pulled things out of the wardrobe and stuffed them into a duffel bag. He scoured the room, stacking textbooks and notebooks into piles and quickly realizing that they wouldn't fit.

He looked down at months of work, poring over lofty concepts and theories, and gave a bitter laugh at his audacity. Stupid, to think he could finally be happy. The past two years had been the most content he could remember—possibly the most content he'd ever been. He felt a burning rage blistering in his throat. He had no choice but to extract himself once again, uproot the threads of belonging he'd tentatively cultivated and cast himself back into a world seemingly intent on his punishment.

Once, Rayan had assumed his natural state was a transitory one, but now the thought of leaving brought on a surge of outright refusal. Even as he shoved his life into a bag, his mind rose up to fight, pulling at his hands and challenging his resolve: *No. Not again.*

Rayan recalled the woman's smug face and the shock of terror he'd felt when she'd spoken that name, the one he'd thought he'd shed like an unwanted skin. She was with the federal police, and if they'd found him, who knew what they already had on Mathias?

He froze, the panic solidifying into a cold lump of dread. Perhaps, by finding him, they had also found Mathias, connecting the two of them. Rayan had done it again—he'd become the weak link, the point of pressure they would exploit, leading to Mathias's downfall.

He pulled a hat down over his ears, threw on as many layers as would fit beneath his jacket, and shoved whatever else he could into the duffel bag. Then he pocketed his keys, his phone, and what little cash he had on hand and slipped out into the darkening streets. If they knew where he lived, it was likely they were still following him. Fortunately, Rayan was no stranger to making himself invisible. He would spend the night weaving through the city until they lost his trail. Then he'd get on the first bus out of Toronto.

Rayan had thought that if he avoided Montreal, he would succeed in avoiding his old life. But it was coming for him either way. If he was going to be held accountable for the actions of his past, he wanted to be in the place where it had all begun. He would find somewhere to hole up and get word to Mathias.

As he trudged through the muddy snow, the freezing wind burning his cheeks, Rayan felt the churn of memories he'd long suppressed. Here he was once again, fated to keep reliving the same old nightmare.

11

While having Mathias followed in Hamilton had yielded an unexpected win, when he was back in Montreal, he'd proven difficult to track. On her recent visit to Ottawa, Frances had twisted the arm of a connection at HQ to secure warrantless approval for the installation of cameras across the street from several known family locations, and this had allowed her to piece together an idea of Mathias's movements. She learned that he didn't frequent the same places at the same times and was often absent from conventional family establishments. He was also extremely skilled at moving through the city unnoticed, which meant surveillance had lost him more times than Frances cared to admit.

However, as luck would have it, late that morning, Frances had received word from intel that one of the cameras had picked up Mathias and Jacques Laberge entering Gino's—a deli in Petite Italia often frequented by members of the family. She'd driven straight over and caught a glimpse of him through the window, seated at a table with his subordinate.

She pulled open the door to the deli and stepped inside, watching as Mathias caught her eye. His face darkened, and he said something quietly to Laberge, who turned in her direction and got to his feet. As she walked to where Mathias sat, a cup of coffee steaming in his hand, she and Laberge passed each other, and the man gave her a dirty look before moving outside and stationing himself by the door.

"Friendly," she remarked, pulling out a chair and sitting down across from Mathias.

"You again."

"I thought I'd stop by and introduce myself properly. I think we got off on the wrong foot." Frances slid her contact card across the table toward him.

"Is that what you'd call it?" Mathias said, picking up the card and flipping it between his fingers.

Frances recalled the quiet unease she'd felt after their brief interaction in the parking lot. On the drive back to her apartment, she'd found herself checking over her shoulder, unable to shake the feeling. She cast the thought aside. If anything, Mathias was the one who should be on edge.

"If there's something you'd like to discuss, I'm all ears. You wouldn't want someone else to beat you to it. Cooperation can make all the difference in cases like these." She leaned forward and placed her elbows down on the table. "Funny, I was just saying the same thing to an old friend of yours..." Pausing for effect, she felt a shot of exhilaration. "Rayan Nadeau. Mind telling me what he's doing in Toronto?"

Frances could have been mistaken, but she thought she saw Mathias's mouth twitch. So he wasn't entirely impenetrable. She smirked.

"Now that you've infiltrated Hamilton, figured it was time to break into the Toronto market? And what—he's some sort of scout, sent ahead to lay down the groundwork? What have you got him doing out there?"

Rayan hadn't exactly been forthcoming about his involvement during their brief conversation. She'd wanted to spook him into submission and had assumed that, given enough of a push, he would prove cooperative. What she hadn't anticipated was his complete and immediate disappearance. They'd managed to locate CCTV footage of Rayan returning to his apartment and leaving again shortly afterward, but from there, he'd seemingly ceased to exist. There was no record of his attendance at the university the following day or the day after that, and Frances could only assume he'd gone underground. While that was inconvenient, it was only a matter of time before he resurfaced. Meanwhile, she'd gone ahead and lodged alerts with the TPD and all the major airports so she would know if he attempted to leave the country.

"What are you on about, Allen?" Mathias said, the indifference of his tone not reflected in his eyes.

"I think you know."

Mathias leaned back in his chair. He pulled a silver lighter from his jacket and flipped open the lid. "How was your date?"

Frances felt her blood run cold. "What?"

"Last week," Mathias said, flicking his thumb against the striker and letting the flame spark. "Just your type, too—a cuck who likes talking about himself."

She stared at him, unable to mask her terror. "You've been watching me?"

He brought the lighter to the edge of her business card and waited for it to catch. "I thought I'd return the favor, seeing how interested in me you've been lately."

She stood, her chair scraping loudly against the floor. Her heart pounded in her chest, and she fought the instinct to run. "You think you can intimidate me?"

Mathias held the burning card until the flames reached his fingertips then dropped the charred remnants into his untouched coffee cup. He reached into his pocket, and she recoiled—but he produced only a handful of bills, which he dropped onto the table.

"I also have informants, Inspector. Eyes across the country." Getting to his feet, Mathias towered over her. His eyes glittered like those of a snake closing in on its prey. "And I'm willing to bet mine are a lot more motivated than yours."

Frances stepped backward, losing her footing as she stumbled over her chair. She felt the man's hand on her arm, steadying her. His grip was strong, as though capable of crushing bone or tossing her to the floor like she was nothing. She remembered the photos from the files—body bags and dismembered corpses, men shot through the temple, as clean as an execution.

"Careful, Frances," Mathias said as she righted herself. "We wouldn't want anything to happen to you."

He released his grip and strode past her to the door. Frances stood perfectly still, the chair on the floor behind her. She was aware only of the lingering feel of his hand on her arm and the sinister sound of her name on his lips.

Mathias paced the living room of his apartment as he turned the burner phone over in his hand. His jaw was stiff, clenched to offset a growing panic. Early on, they'd established a way for Rayan to reach him without the man's number finding its way into the web of complicity that was Mathias's world. Mathias had an unregistered phone that he never let leave the apartment. He would check it once a day, usually in the evening, and respond then. The system had worked well thus far, and Rayan was never more than a day away from contact—until now. Mathias couldn't get hold of him.

Mathias recalled the inspector's smirk as she'd thrown down Rayan's name like a prize. It had pierced him, a cold needle slid just beneath the skin. He'd thought they'd been careful and assumed that even if someone came for him, Rayan would be safe. Mathias gritted his teeth at his own hubris. He'd been the one to suggest Rayan return to Canada, and now the Feds had found him.

In his hand, the phone gave a short buzz, and he yanked it up to look at the screen. The flood of relief was palpable. *En vacances*, the message read, followed by a truncated address. Mathias plugged it into his phone, and a boarding house in Montreal's industrial district came up.

He's here? That could only mean something had gone very wrong.

The entrance to the concrete residential building was swathed in graffiti, and the glass door panel was badly cracked, a series of jagged lines creeping across its surface. Mathias entered the shabby lobby to find a young security guard seated behind the front desk, watching an unintelligible show on a tiny television. The residence looked like a halfway house, the kind of place that took cash but no names.

"We're full," the security guard muttered, not looking up from his show.

Mathias slipped a fifty across the counter. "I don't need a room."

The man glanced at him then reached over to take the money and returned his attention to the television screen. Mathias moved to the stairwell and made his way up to the fourth floor. The door's number was marked crudely with black spray paint. Mathis knocked once. He heard the click of a deadbolt unlocking, and then Rayan opened the door and ushered him into a tiny bedsit. The air was as cold inside as it was outside. Rayan stood dressed in several layers, his gloves still on and a hat pulled down over his ears.

"It's fucking freezing in here," Mathias admonished him.

"Heat's broken."

He raised a hand to Rayan's cheek. It was like ice. "Why didn't you go somewhere else—a hotel, for Christ's sake?"

Rayan said nothing. They both knew how easy that would be to track.

Mathias saw the skittish glint in his eyes and the way he hunched forward, hands tucked under his arms. This was the version of the man who'd spent nights sleeping on the street, the rest of him retreating within—a well-worn survival mechanism. Mathias had seen snatches of this person before, when Rayan shuddered awake in the middle of the night, his hands clawing at the sheets.

On the wall, the thermostat had been smashed in and hung by a loose wire. Mathias bent to run a hand along the radiator and found it cold to the touch. "Wonderful. Where'd you find this place?"

"Stayed here sometimes when we had the cash."

Mathias stepped into the tiny kitchenette and turned on the hot tap. He waited, but the water didn't warm.

Rayan sat down at the counter opposite, watching him. "It's changed."

"The city or this hole?" Mathias asked, shutting off the tap.

"The city. I got off the bus and couldn't remember where I was."

Mathias fixed him with a careful stare. "What happened, Rayan?"

"They're watching me, the apartment. One of them ambushed me on the way home."

Mathias swallowed the bitter rush of fury.

"The woman knew who I was, knew everything about me, my—" He stopped abruptly and looked away.

"Frances Allen. She's RCMP."

"You knew about this?" Rayan asked, his eyes snapping back, incredulous.

"I didn't know they'd followed me to you," Mathias said tightly. *How did she figure it out?* He'd made efforts to ensure that all trace of Rayan's involvement in the family had been erased.

"I don't think she knew about..." They exchanged a look. "Only that I worked for you."

That had been Mathias's impression as well. The woman seemed to think he'd sent Rayan as some envoy to spearhead a new family operation in Toronto. It was ridiculous but far preferable to her knowing the truth.

"If they think they can use me to get to you, they can get fucked." Rayan's voice was hard, and his eyes shone with anger. "I'm not afraid of prison."

Mathias knew what Rayan was trying to do. Before him, he saw a kid who'd finally been given the chance to figure out what he wanted and deserved the years that stretched ahead to make up for the shitty ones he'd left behind. He wouldn't let Rayan throw that away—least of all on his account.

"You should be," Mathias warned in a low voice. "But that's not going to happen, understand?"

While Rayan didn't look entirely convinced, he gave a short nod. "Were you careful?" he asked with a pensive frown. "Did you drive here?"

"I'm not an amateur. I took the metro."

Rayan raised his eyebrows. "Things really must be bad."

Mathias snorted, secretly pleased at the smile that flickered across Rayan's face. "Speaking of bad, you're not staying here," he said, glancing at the stained yellow curtains hanging limply from the rod above the window. He reached into his pocket, pulled one of the keys from his keychain, and handed it to Rayan across the counter. "I keep a small apartment off Beaubien."

"This is new."

"This is careful," he said pointedly. "After Piero, I figured it couldn't hurt. Make your own way there. Use the entrance around back. Once you're in, don't go anywhere. I'll stop by later tonight to drop off food."

Before she kissed them goodnight as children, Rayan's mother would say, "I hope you wake up to all the good."

That was her wish for him and his brother—a good life, different from the one of pain and loss that she'd left behind. Rayan wondered if her dogged pursuit of this for them had been at the cost of her own happiness. He couldn't remember much good befalling her in the short time they'd known each other. Maybe he and Tahir had been her good, although even they hadn't been enough in the end.

In the bedroom of the safe house, Rayan lay under a thick pile of blankets. The small, minimally furnished apartment on the ground level of a brick triplex five minutes from Beaubien station was fully stocked with the requisite necessities one might need to remain temporarily hidden. He found the place comforting. Clean, austere, and functional, it had Mathias written all over it.

Rayan had left the boarding house shortly after Mathias came by. He hadn't told Mathias, but the man's offer had been the first decent thing to have happened in the past two days, the key pushed across the counter like a rope tossed into the dark well that Rayan had found himself in after the inspector had flagged him down on the street. Once inside the apartment, he'd gone straight to the thermostat and cranked it up as high as it could go. Still, Rayan hadn't been able to shake the chill, so he'd gathered all the blankets he could find, headed to bed, and heaped them over himself as he lay beneath the covers, fully dressed. The ache in his stomach served as a reminder that he hadn't eaten since the previous day, but getting warm was the only thing that mattered, a singular focus that took him back to those long nights lying on concrete floors and grassy verges, staring at Tahir's eyes in the dark and seeing the same hardened resignation staring back. They'd been awake and exhausted but too cold to sleep.

One winter, not long after they'd abandoned their last group home, when he was maybe sixteen and the drugs hadn't yet found his brother, Rayan had fallen ill. The two of them had taken shelter in the interior corridors of the Guy-Concordia Metro station and curled up together on a flattened cardboard box. Rayan had a raging fever and was trembling with chills, and he found himself falling in and out of dreams that were so real he was sure he was awake. He must have been calling out in his sleep, because Tahir kept jostling him awake and telling him to keep it down. The other people holed up in the corridor had started to grumble, and some were becoming increasingly agitated as his delirious pronouncements kept them awake.

The last train on the Green Line stopped running just after midnight and didn't start back up again until five thirty the following morning. It was the part of the night that Rayan dreaded most—when the stream of people dressed in their winter coats and scarves, chattering to friends as they walked, began to dry up and only the rest of them were left—the ones with nowhere to go.

"Shut him up!" someone shouted.

"Fuck you too!" Tahir hollered back, but he moved to Rayan's side, wrapped the blankets around him, and helped him to his feet. "Come on—we gotta go."

They left the Metro station and trudged aimlessly through the snowy streets. By this point, most of the good spots would already be taken. Tahir had once joked about robbing a nearby *dépanneur* so the police would take them in and they'd have somewhere warm to spend the night.

"I hate her." Rayan swallowed back tears. He regretted his words immediately and was filled with a fathomless guilt. "Sorry, Mama," he whispered.

"She can't hear you, you know," Tahir said viciously and turned to glare at him, his eyes black in the darkness. "Because she's in hell. That's where you go when you do what she did."

Rayan drew back in horror.

"And even if she could, she doesn't care. If she did, she'd have hung around to take care of us," Tahir snarled. "So I wouldn't get stuck having to drag a crybaby like you through the fucking snow."

Rayan didn't have the energy to protest. He could only focus on putting one foot in front of the other as he attempted to keep up with his brother. He must have fallen or simply lost the ability to stand, because the next thing he knew, he was lying on the pavement, his burning cheek cooling against the sidewalk sludge.

Up ahead, he saw Tahir stop. His brother swore, kicking at the drifts of snow piled by the side of the road. He picked up a nearby trash bin and sent it skidding across the sidewalk, litter spilling everywhere. Clenching his hands at his sides, he gave an almighty howl that echoed through the empty streets. Then Tahir made his way back to him, and Rayan felt his brother's hands under his armpits, pulling him up.

"Come on, *akhi*," Tahir said quietly as he hoisted Rayan onto his back. "I won't leave you, no matter how bad it gets."

And Rayan, dizzy with fever, had known in his bones that it was the truth.

Rayan heard a click from down the hall as the front door to the apartment opened, and he stiffened in learned fear. Then came the purposeful sound of shoes on the parquet, and he knew it was Mathias. His shoulders slackened in relief. It was strange to recognize someone from the tread of their feet alone. He knew a lot about the man now—the way he inhaled sharply just before waking, the soft grunt of approval he made when Rayan took him into his mouth.

A paper bag rustled, the fridge opened and closed, and then footsteps came down the hallway toward him. Mathias paused at the entrance to the bedroom, a silhouette in the darkness. Rayan lay facing the door, the blankets gripped in fists by his chin, his jaw clenched to fight the unceasing shiver.

"There's food in the kitchen," Mathias said. "I'll be back in a day or two. Don't go anywhere."

Rayan remained unmoving. If he opened his mouth to speak, his teeth would chatter and give him away.

Mathias gave a sigh. "Still cold?"

The floorboards creaked as he moved into the room. Then came the dull thump as Mathias kicked off his shoes and the swish of fabric as he shrugged out of his jacket. The bed gave a squeak, and he climbed in beside Rayan, still in his clothes. Rayan felt the man's solidness against his back as Mathias's arms wrapped around him and pulled him to his chest. Rayan let out a shuddering breath, and finally, the chill began to recede.

"Go to sleep, Rayan," Mathias murmured into his hair. "Tomorrow it starts again."

Unlike his mother's sendoff, this one made no promise of the good.

12

André Nadeau was nothing like what Frances had expected. She'd driven to Maskinongé to find out more about Rayan and how he'd ended up working for the family, entertaining the hope that she might discover the man hiding out at his father's house. After all, the tiny town in rural Quebec seemed like the perfect place to disappear.

She still believed he was key to the case against Mathias. Not only had Rayan worked closely with the mafioso, but he was also implicated by his own involvement in the family and a string of prior crimes on his record. Then there was his brother's murder. Frances had stretched the truth somewhat when she'd spoken with Rayan in Toronto. There was no open investigation into Tahir Nadeau's death. However, the circumstances were suspicious enough to serve as a compelling weakness to exploit—maybe even convince Rayan to turn on his boss.

"About time you people did something about him," André said after she'd introduced herself. He peered at her through a crack in the front door as she stood on the porch of the run-down bungalow where he lived.

"May I come in?" she asked. "I have a few questions."

André appeared to consider her request for a moment before stepping back and beckoning her into the house. Frances had conjured the image of a man wracked with guilt about what had happened to his wayward son. Instead, she found herself face-to-face with a sour-faced alcoholic. She could smell the beer on his breath at barely ten in the morning. She glanced around the mess of the living room. Filth covered almost every surface, and the distinct odor of mold clung to the air. She didn't feel comfortable sitting, so she remained standing by the door, her notebook and pen in hand.

"He's always been a bad apple," André asserted, stumbling to his easy chair and lowering himself into it with a labored wheeze. "He and his brother."

Frances stilled. "Tahir?"

"That one." He picked up an open can of beer from the end table. "Bunch of ingrates." He brought the can to his lips and took a long swig. "She picked the names. I thought women from over there were supposed to be submissive, obey their husbands and all that. But she made such a stink about it I let her have her way."

"Sir, Tahir Nadeau is dead," Frances said dubiously, not sure whether he was simply confused or truly hadn't known. "I have the police report with me. I was going to ask what you knew about the circumstances surrounding his death. It appears to be a homicide, but no investigation was launched."

André gave a dispassionate grunt and took another pull from the can.

Frances frowned. *He doesn't care if his own kid is dead. But why does that surprise me?* She'd read the custody-hearing transcript and seen the numerous attempts the court had made to contact this man. His definitive silence said everything.

"Tell me more about Rayan. When did you last hear from him? Has he made any contact recently?"

"I don't hear shit." André gave a phlegm-filled cough. "You think he'd bother to call once in a while, help his old man out. I'm on disability—it's all I have."

"He's been associated with certain criminal groups," Frances nudged. "What do you know about that?"

"It doesn't surprise me. He was always following his brother into trouble." André repositioned himself on the chair with considerable effort, his breath rasping as he held the can of beer close to his chest, making sure not to spill. "You wanna know more about the kid? Start writing, lady."

As Frances recorded André's testimony, she grew more skeptical of his credibility. He had plenty to say about his son—how disobedient he'd been as a child, how violent. Yet the details were vague and the timing all over the place, and she had a growing suspicion it was just a story he told himself. She would file it and add it to the case she was putting together on Rayan, but she was pretty sure it wouldn't hold up to scrutiny.

Frances recalled Rayan's expression when she'd addressed him by his family name, the briefest of flinches, as though she'd unearthed something unpleasant. Having seen his state records and now his childhood home, she struggled to reconcile the unwelcome sense of pity that surfaced. His surviving parent was a man convinced of his victimhood, with no comprehension of his own faults, the ripple of hurt forever expanding outward.

Frances left the house, less confident than when she'd arrived. She hurried to her car as a sprinkle of snow began to fall. Once in the driver's seat, she pulled out her notebook and absently flipped through her notes. She let out a frustrated sigh and tossed the pad onto the seat beside her.

Despite her overarching belief in the rule of law, the cynical side of her knew that Rayan was someone who'd been given very few chances in life. She'd encountered many men like that during her time, and they almost always ended up addicts, criminals, or dead. Then there was the fact that Rayan was a student at one of the country's top universities and apparently doing quite well for himself. In the brief overview of his movements that Stan had put together, Frances had been hard-pressed to find any indication that he was engaging in much else besides his studies.

Her theory about him working as a satellite agent for the family might be misplaced. Maybe instead, he'd had his likeness scrubbed from the record so he could leave his old life behind. If that was the case, she needed to figure out why.

"Repeat it back."

Rayan rattled off the number he'd just saved to his phone, his mind already storing it away for future reference.

"Good." Mathias tossed his empty coffee cup into the trash. "That's who you call—no questions. He knows what to do."

Rayan nodded. He'd arrived at the Collections office that morning to find Mathias's Mercedes parked outside, which was unusual. Typically, Rayan sat around for a good half hour before his capo stalked into the office with a sour look on his face. Mathias was not a morning person. The reason behind Mathias's early appearance had something to do with the notable absence of Franco Ricci.

"He's got a semiautomatic stashed in the trunk and picks a fight with the cop giving him a speeding ticket!" Tony's voice had a habit of carrying, and Rayan had been able to piece together the rest as he waited in the hallway for Mathias to emerge from the man's office.

Mathias had been tasked with coordinating a peaceful resolution, and while their interactions with local law enforcement were brief—almost nonexistent—he'd decided to use this moment to impart an important lesson to Rayan. The phone number belonged to Grayson Dubois, a defense lawyer and well-oiled friend of the family. He sat on an annual retainer, the cost of which Rayan could only guess at. And in return, when there was trouble—as the present situation demanded—Dubois was called in to perform his magic.

Rayan drove Mathias downtown to a swanky bistro in the Quartier International. A man in a gray suit and tie was seated toward the back of the restaurant and waved them over. On the table before him were several plates of food—eggs, bacon, sausage, pancakes. He picked idly from the plates with his fork, like a king at a banquet.

"It's been a while, Mathias," Dubois announced. "I know a smart man when I never see him. Now, some of your friends, on the other hand—"

"I have a job for you," Mathias interrupted, taking a seat across from the lawyer. "But we need to move quickly."

"We always need to move quickly," Dubois said, spearing a large chunk of sausage and shoving it into his mouth. He was bulky, with sandy hair parted neatly to one side. The dewiness of his pale skin had the curious effect of obscuring his age. "I'm almost finished here. Help yourselves, gentlemen. Anything you'd like to order?"

Mathias ignored him. "Francesco Ricci. His bail hearing's at noon."

"What are we talking?"

"Unlawful possession, disorderly conduct."

"Rather tame for your lot. I take it you'll cover bail as required?"

Mathias gave a brief nod.

Dubois lifted his cup to take a large gulp of coffee then patted down his pockets for his wallet and tossed down a handful of notes beside the plates of half-eaten food. "Shall we?" he said, standing, and together they made their way outside to the car.

Rayan dropped the lawyer off at the municipal police station and then parked the Mercedes across the street to wait. Beside him, his capo rolled down the window and idly tapped out a cigarette, watching the trickle of people moving in and out of the building. Twenty minutes later, Franco—looking slightly worse for wear—emerged from the station, accompanied by a smug-faced Dubois.

"He sent you," Franco sneered when he reached the car and stopped beside the open passenger window. "Big surprise."

"A little more of that gratitude, and I'll leave you here," Mathias replied stonily, flicking the butt of his smoke at Franco's feet before turning to address the lawyer. "Appreciate the favor, Dubois. Payment will be forthcoming."

"Pleasure doing business with you fine fellows. Until next time." Dubois grinned and raised his hand to hail down a passing taxi.

Franco got into the back seat, and Rayan started the engine. He pulled the car out onto the road and joined the line of vehicles inching through downtown traffic.

"Franco," Mathias said flatly as they made their way past the convention center.

"Yeah, it was stupid," the man muttered.

"It's more than that. You can be stupid without drawing attention to yourself," Mathias scolded. "Caravella should've been enough of a deterrent."

"You had to bring up Angelo fucking Caravella," Franco growled.

"You seem intent on following in his footsteps. Keep this up, and Franco Ricci will be the next name thrown around as a warning."

"All right, all right," Franco said. "What do I owe you?"

"My fucking morning back," Mathias snapped. "You can take the money up with Tony."

"Ah, Christ," Franco said with a grimace. "Do you know what a pain in the ass it is owing that man money?"

"I think our clients have a fair idea." Mathias smirked. "Never been dumb enough to have the privilege myself."

Free from the worst of the congestion, Rayan merged onto Pie-IX Boulevard and headed toward Rosemont.

"Back before your time, Tony never would have trusted anyone with something like this," Franco said. "But now it's all Beauvais this, Beauvais that. You're the closest one to figuring out how he runs the joint."

"Only because he hates getting off his ass," Mathias scoffed. "So he sends me out like a trained monkey."

"Because he trusts you," Franco retorted. "And he sure as hell doesn't trust the rest of us. Even though I've been working for him since you were in fucking prep school. You should know what that means."

Rayan turned the car down a narrow street beside Marché Jean-Talon and shot his boss a furtive glance. Mathias was staring out the window, silent.

"You know he's going to give it to you," Franco continued.

"What?"

"Collections."

"I don't want it," Mathias said curtly.

Rayan had a feeling Mathias's eyes were on a bigger prize. He pulled the Mercedes up outside Franco's house.

"How'd you—" Franco laughed and leaned forward to clap him on the shoulder. "Shit, I always forget this one drove for me. Nadeau, isn't it?"

Rayan nodded.

"He doesn't forget much," Mathias remarked, and Rayan tempered the swell of pride at his capo's indirect praise. "Get yourself cleaned up. Tony's expecting you back at the office."

Franco muttered a string of curses, stepped out of the car, and slammed the door behind him.

"Who's Angelo Caravella?" Rayan asked as they drove back toward the Collections office.

Mathias gave him a sharp look. "At least give the impression you're not listening in."

"Right," Rayan said, averting his gaze.

Mathias let out a reluctant sigh and leaned back in his seat. "Angelo Caravella was one of De Luca's captains a couple years ago. He made a name for himself taking risks, but he got too cocky, and the cops started snooping around. They didn't go to him direct—they came after his contacts—the ones more likely to roll over. Then they started singling out people closer to the family. Word gets to the council then the boss, and soon, Caravella stops showing up. The family acts like the man never existed. The cops can't get a case together, and eventually, they back off. Still, Caravella's nowhere to be found—disappeared completely. That's what happens when you get too much of the wrong kind of attention."

Rayan knew now why Franco had bristled at Mathias's warning.

"You would do well to remember that, Rayan," his capo said, his eyes fixed on the road ahead. "You're part of something bigger than yourself. Like the boss, I won't hesitate to remove a weak link from the chain."

It was late when Mathias let himself into the safe house. Since Rayan's unexpected reappearance in Montreal, he'd found his attention splintered—which was dangerous, especially with so much in the air. He needed his head on straight if he was to figure out how to get them through this mess. But when he'd stopped by the apartment with supplies the previous evening, Rayan had seemed unusually thrown. Mathias had felt compelled to return that night, if only to assuage his own nagging concern.

The lights were off, and he assumed Rayan must have gone to bed. So he was surprised to see a darkened figure in the kitchen when he closed the front door behind him.

"You keep this place well stocked." Rayan's speech was slower than usual, and Mathias spotted an open bottle of Macallan on the counter.

Mathias took off his coat and hung it by the door. "Figured if I ever got holed up here, I'd want the essentials." He walked into the kitchen, prized the half-empty glass of scotch from Rayan's hand, and downed the remainder. "It's late. You should sleep."

"Why? It's not like I have anything to do tomorrow."

"You have work to finish."

"Work?" Rayan gave a short laugh. "That's not work."

"It's not nothing."

"It's pointless bullshit."

They stood across from one another, the light from the window illuminating Rayan's face, tired and hostile. "It doesn't suit you," Mathias said.

"Maybe I've always been a drunk," Rayan said with a lazy half smile. "Just waiting to live up to my potential."

"Giving up," Mathias corrected him. "It doesn't suit you."

Rayan's smile disappeared, and his eyes glinted. "I don't know why I didn't try it sooner. Life has shown me over and over again it's not worth the effort. About time I took the hint."

Mathias placed the empty glass down on the counter, put a hand on Rayan's shoulder, and guided him toward the bedroom. He would deal with this tomorrow when the man had sobered up. They made it to the end of the hall when Rayan reached for him, his hands presumptuous and demanding.

Mathias was in no mood. "That's enough," he said, growing annoyed.

"I don't get to fuck angry?" Rayan retorted. "Hasn't stopped you."

Mathias grabbed his arm, stilling him. "You want to fuck angry?" he murmured, his face inches from Rayan's own. "I'll make it so you can't walk tomorrow."

There was the slightest flicker in Rayan's eyes that gave him away, an almost imperceptible flinch as Mathias called his bluff. Enough to cool the sudden flare of anger. Mathias let him go, and Rayan stepped back, glaring at him.

"Did you know about my brother?"

"About what?"

"The investigation into his death."

"Peripherally," Mathias said, remaining tactful. "Enough to be sure nothing came back to the family."

"Why didn't you tell me?"

"Tell you what?" Mathias asked, narrowing his eyes. "That they found him washed up ten miles down the Saint Lawrence? That the cops launched a half-assed inquiry into how some junkie ended up with a hole in his chest—" He stopped when he saw the look on Rayan's face.

"I saw him," Rayan muttered. "Allen showed me. There were photos."

Mathias understood then. The scotch, the dark smudges beneath Rayan's eyes, the shadow of the man unearthed from the past. He silently cursed the meddling bitch.

"She made it sound like I was relieved." Rayan swallowed hard. "Like I was a suspect."

Mathias snorted in disbelief. "The thinnest fucking case alive."

"Not when I'm on trial for everything else. Then it's not a far stretch of the imagination."

"She was baiting you."

"What else do you know?" Rayan asked. "She said I have a file."

Mathias chose his next words carefully. "Rayan, you spent half your life on the government's radar. You have a file as thick as my fist."

"So, you've seen it?"

"I did my research."

"When?" Rayan asked.

"When you first started. I needed to know who I was working with."

Rayan's lips pulled into a sneer. "And were you disappointed?"

Mathias held his tongue. He would allow him this. Rayan was entitled to a reaction.

"Do you still have it?" Rayan pressed.

Mathias sighed. "Go to bed, Rayan."

"Show me."

"No," Mathias snapped, putting an end to the discussion. He'd reached the limits of his patience. He wrenched open the door to the bedroom. "Now, you can get in there yourself, or I will make you."

Rayan scowled, walking past him into the bedroom and slamming the door in Mathias's face.

13

"Brake. No, the other one's the brake."

Rayan pressed his foot down a little too hard on the left pedal, and the car lurched.

"Jesus Christ!" his brother yelled, one palm splayed against the dashboard to steady himself.

"Sorry." Rayan laughed, buzzing with excitement.

He'd played wingman whenever Tahir boosted cars, and it was finally his turn behind the wheel. There came a series of honks from behind them. Rayan pulled the car over to the side of the road.

"Don't cause an accident," his brother said grimly. "Or we'll really be in the shit."

The SUV was practically new and fitted out with plush leather seats and a touchscreen monitor. Its well-heeled owner was probably wondering where it was by this point.

"Take it easy. Slow to accelerate, slow to stop."

Tahir's eyes were glazed. From what, Rayan couldn't be sure. It was happening more often, the slack features and unfocused pupils making it hard to separate his brother from the person he was when he was high.

Rayan continued down Sherbrooke West, deriving a cheap satisfaction from the powerful pull of the car as it sped forward. "It's not so hard."

"You drive like a granny who escaped the rest home," Tahir jeered.

Rayan eased to a stop at a red light, and a man in faded overalls and combat boots approached them, gripping a bucket in one hand and a dirty sponge in the other.

"No, no!" Tahir called out, winding down the window. "Fuck off!"

Out of habit, Rayan scanned the man's features, shadowed beneath the lowered brim of a baseball cap. As he scuttled away, Rayan's eyes followed his retreat, trying to assemble a face in his mind that he could barely remember.

"Green, it's green!" Tahir snapped, and Rayan flew back to the present, gunning the car and speeding through the intersection. "It wasn't him, you know."

Rayan started and glanced over at his brother, who was staring at him with a guarded expression. "Yeah, I know," he said, covering his momentary lapse with a short laugh.

They continued through the city, killing time to delay the inevitable, the night stretching out before them.

"You knew when he put on his boots it was trouble," Tahir muttered into the darkness of the cab. Every Sunday, their father cleaned and polished a pair of black army-issue boots. He kept them on the top shelf in the hallway closet. "When he was done with us, he used to go after her."

Too many nights to count, they'd lain on their sides in the dark, whipped and shamed after a beating, eyes meeting across the yawning divide between their two twin beds as they listened to the steady thump of his boots down the hall.

"If that had been him," Rayan said, gripping the steering wheel, "I'd have run him the fuck over."

Tahir laughed, turning and socking him hard on the shoulder. "Like hell you would. You're all talk, Rayan. You don't have the stomach for it."

Rayan glared at the city as it sped past through the windscreen. For his father, he would make an exception.

"Head to the overpass—I have to meet someone," Tahir instructed.

Rayan changed lanes and turned onto Saint-Laurent Boulevard. He knew who his brother was meeting.

They were several meters from the turnoff when Tahir leaned forward in his seat. "Here, pull over."

Rayan brought the car to a stop, and his brother jumped out, his head swiveling anxiously before he started to cross the road. Rayan watched as Tahir waited, noting the nervous jerk of his brother's foot and the way he kept crossing and uncrossing his arms. Evan appeared from the shadows, removed a brown paper bag from his jacket, and held the bag out to Tahir.

Rayan looked away. He hated seeing his brother like that—the gleeful shine in his eyes, his hands trembling with anticipation. Or withdrawal. It was hard to tell at this point. Rayan kept his gaze fixed on the shuttered hardware store up ahead, whose sign above the entrance was so faded it was barely legible.

The passenger door opened, and Tahir slipped into the seat beside him.

"*Akhi...*" Rayan began quietly.

"Don't call me that," his brother said, the words curling viciously. "You're just like her—too fucking soft. Now, drive. I want to see how much Lenny'll give us for this ride."

Mathias sat in his car in the parking garage beneath his building, phone pressed to his ear. Through the windscreen, he could see a couple arguing by the elevator. She was young, a redhead, with a designer purse clutched to her ample chest. The man stabbing a finger in her face was much older and should have known better.

Mathias had returned to his apartment the previous evening after mustering enough sense to leave the safe house before he really lost his temper. He'd stood fuming on the other side of the bedroom door, fighting a deep-rooted urge to show Rayan exactly who he was dealing with. But something had stopped him. There had been a rawness to Rayan's pain that he hadn't seen before, and Mathias wasn't sure how to approach it.

"She hasn't got approval from the Crown to tap phones, but you're under intermittent monitoring," Gagnon said on the other end of the line. "There are cameras."

Mathias had been on his way out when the cop had called. He'd known Alexandre Gagnon for years, first as a corruptible rookie with the metropolitan police and now as a sergeant at the RCMP's Quebec divisional office. He'd proven an invaluable resource when it came to intel on the Feds' activity in the province and beyond. Gagnon's biggest flaw had always been easy for Mathias to exploit: the man could not keep his dick in his pants.

"Where?" Mathias asked as the woman by the elevator reached into her purse and pulled out a tissue to stem the blackened streams pouring from her eyes.

Gagnon cleared his throat nervously. "Several of your offices have been targeted. The club. Some of the regular meeting spots. She's trying to put together a schedule of your activities."

That explained how Allen had managed to ambush him at Gino's. "Good luck with that," Mathias said scornfully, irked by the woman's nerve. "And Nadeau?"

"They've lost eyes on him. Either he's holed up somewhere in Toronto, or he's left the city. But he's still in Canada. Allen has alerts set up. She'll know if he tries to leave the country."

Mathias rapped his knuckles against the steering wheel in agitation. "She's building a case against him?"

"It's likely—she's looking into everything. Went to talk to his father yesterday, to find out what he knew. Came back with a pretty damning character reference."

Mathias snorted, incredulous. "His old man? What would he know?"

"Seems he had a lot to say, actually. I'll send you a copy of the write-up. It's a common tactic. She puts a case together against Nadeau, scares him enough to get him to roll over, and then she uses his testimony against you."

"And if he doesn't roll over?"

"Then she'll probably trial him anyway," Gagnon said. "Allen is ruthless. She has something of a reputation."

Does she? Mathias seethed.

The cop swallowed audibly, and when he spoke again, his voice was strained. "I may have to keep communication brief in the next few days. There's additional scrutiny with HQ involved, and they're keeping a close eye on the office."

"Brief?" Mathias mocked. "You'll answer when I call, Gagnon. Unless your wife would like to know about the apartment I bought for your new mistress." He hung up and absently tapped his phone against his knee. Allen was going after Rayan. At least she didn't know that he was here in Montreal, hiding out under her very nose.

In his hand, his phone gave a short buzz, and Mathias pulled up the file Gagnon had sent through. He scanned the document on the screen, a spike of anger lodging in his throat. Then he dropped his phone onto the seat beside him and gunned the engine, startling the couple by the elevator as he squealed out of the garage. He had an errand to run.

Maskinongé was just over an hour's drive from Montreal. The landscape changed rapidly the farther out of the city Mathias got, buildings giving way to long stretches of empty farmland punctuated by the occasional gas station. He didn't often venture this far into the province. He'd always found rural Quebec more dreary than idyllic.

The town itself consisted of a main street lined with weathered-looking stores housing an array of local businesses: grocer, drug store, butcher. Farther down the street was a small school with a rusted jungle gym out front. From there, the road led out of town, and the houses became more spread out, set on blocks of empty land speckled with the odd piece of farm machinery or the remains of a stripped-out car.

Several miles along this road was where André Nadeau lived. Mathias pulled the Bentley into the gravel driveway beside the house as spatters of rain crowded the windshield. The place was a dump. The paint had long since peeled off the cladding, and the front yard was littered with all manner of trash and debris. Both of the windows facing the road were covered with what looked like black plastic. He tried to imagine a young Rayan growing up here, a boy slipping through the broken slats on the porch railing and dodging the minefield of glass bottles strewn across the snow-dusted lawn. But try as he might, he couldn't.

Mathias got out of the car, fastening his coat against the increasing downpour, and made his way up the path toward the house. He sidestepped the holes in the rotting wooden steps and raised a gloved hand to knock loudly on the front door. From inside, he could hear someone shuffling about, the creak of floorboards, and the methodical unlatching of locks.

A man eased open the door. He looked older than he should, his sagging face crisscrossed with angry red spider veins, his skin a jaundiced yellow. And the smell—it was enough to turn Mathias's stomach, as though the man were being pickled from the inside.

"Who're you?" André Nadeau glowered. "I don't want nothing to do with Jesus, you hear?"

He began to close the door, but Mathias put his foot across the threshold, pressing his weight against the panel, and found it gave way easily in André's grip. "Trust me, he wants nothing to do with you," Mathias said, forcing the door open and stepping into the house.

Beside him, André stood impotently, his hand still clutching the doorknob. Mathias took in the surrounding dimness, the covered windows shutting out all light from the outside. The place smelled of unwashed bodies and decay, the odor sticking to the back of his throat.

"You had a lot to say to the police about your son," he said, his eyes flicking to the cans of beer lined up along the coffee table. In the corner, the TV was on at a low murmur. "Funny, since you haven't seen him in the better part of twenty years."

"I know his character," André said gruffly. "He was always up to no good, no surprises there."

"Especially considering his gilded childhood," Mathias scoffed. "Did you tell them what a doting father you were?"

He felt the anger then, white-hot, simmering in his chest. The intensity caught him off guard. André Nadeau was no one to him yet summoned a hatred reminiscent of what he'd felt for his own father. Rayan didn't speak much about his life before they'd met, but Mathias knew enough. He knew what it was like to have the odds stacked against you by your own family.

His gaze returned to André standing by the door, shriveled and diminished. "He doesn't look anything like you," Mathias remarked, cocking his head. "That must have been a disappointment—two sons and not a glimmer of resemblance. I'd say they both got off lucky."

André scowled. "They got her coloring, that's for sure. Her rabid insolence. Mongrels through and through."

Mathias moved into the kitchen, not sure what propelled him, both curious and repulsed. It was an eternal mystery how two strangers possessed the ability to create someone so different from themselves. He'd always thought that about his own parents and felt the same thing now. He couldn't imagine how the man who'd come to mean so much to him had sprung forth from this creature.

He took in the filth—the unwashed dishes stacked by the sink, the trash spilling from an overflowing bin in the corner of the room. On the fridge, a single cream-colored business card was held fast with a magnet. Mathias knew whose name he would find printed on the front of that card.

André had followed him into the kitchen and stood watching, his arms crossed. "So, what—you're with the cops too? I already told that woman all I know."

"Do I look like a cop?" Mathias's eyes dropped to the counter, where a carving knife lay abandoned on a plastic cutting board. He picked it up and turned to André. "He might not have taken after you, but you made sure to leave your mark."

André stumbled backward as Mathias advanced.

"What's it like, slicing a little boy's throat?" Mathias shoved him against the wall, bringing the knife to André's neck. "How old was he—six, seven?" He pressed the point into the withered flesh, slowly increasing the pressure. Something in him itched to pierce the skin. "Must have been a real rush, watching him squirm."

André's bloodshot eyes widened in recognition, mouth opening and closing like a fish. "Who are you?" he wheezed.

Mathias thought of that first night at the safe house, how dull Rayan's eyes looked in the dark. Rayan had shuddered when he'd climbed into bed beside him and Mathias felt the weight of something there with them, a part of the man he'd never truly known.

Making André Nadeau pay wouldn't change a damn thing. It couldn't undo what had already been done. Mathias released him, stepping back and tossing the knife into the sink. André slid to the floor, panting. Mathias took the inspector's card from the fridge and flicked it down at the man's feet.

"Call your friend, and tell her you're a pathetic old man who makes up stories," he said in a hard voice. "A lying drunk who left his kid for dead and hasn't seen him since."

André nodded his head vigorously, scrabbling for the card on the floor.

"Fortunate, in the end," Mathias murmured, almost to himself. "In spite of you, he turned out a decent man."

He headed back toward the front door, and his gaze was caught on the framed military commendations hanging from the living room wall. Not a single photo of his wife and children but a veritable shrine to his glory days. Mathias walked over to peer at the yellowing service certificates trapped behind glass. From the corner of his eye, he could see André standing meekly by the entrance to the living room.

"You've seen it, then—how much blood a dying man can spill." Mathias turned to fix him with a steely glare. "I've seen it too. Buckets of the stuff. You think they're done, but it keeps on flowing."

The old man shrank against the wall. Mathias took down the frame declaring him the recipient of a Medal of Bravery and shook his head at the irony.

"The only thing you need to know about me is this," he said, letting the frame drop from his hand and smash to the floor. "If I have to come back here, I will slit you ear to ear and watch until there's not a drop left."

14

Rayan woke well past noon with a pounding headache. His mouth felt dry, and flashes of the conversation he'd had with Mathias the night before filtered into his brain. Rayan had been unfairly upset, his own feelings of futility running up against his fear of Mathias's intolerance for weakness. But Mathias's reaction had been surprisingly measured. In fact, he'd said far less than he deserved to say under the circumstances. Rayan felt a sting of humiliation at his behavior, recalling Mathias's expression when he'd closed the door in his face. He knew the liquor was a mistake, but he'd spent the day stuck in his head and had been desperate to erase the image of his brother from his mind.

Attempting to sit up, Rayan found his limbs uncooperative, pinned to the bed by a looming dread. The feeling transported him back to those isolated days in his apartment, waiting for the wound in his shoulder to heal. Then, he'd been trapped by his own physical limitations. Now he couldn't leave for fear of being seen—not just by the Feds but by the family as well.

Rayan had to remind himself that he wasn't alone and this time was different. He ordered himself up out of bed and walked to the bathroom to wash his face. The room had an enormous clawfoot tub—ornate and indulgent—that seemed out of place among the rest of the modern fittings. Rayan assumed it had been an original feature and was too cumbersome to remove from the apartment. It stood against the wall, empty with promise.

He stepped into the living room and peered out the window at the deluge falling outside. The sky above was an ominous swathe of dark-gray clouds. Rayan went about gathering the notes he'd brought with him and laid everything out on the dining table. Mathias was right—while his work was pretentious and ultimately meaningless, it was still something. Sitting, he began to go through what he had. There were gaps—books and readings he'd left behind—but possibly enough with him to push through. He tried to focus and get his mind to clear, only to discover that his words had turned to hieroglyphs in his notebook. The chill was still there, having settled against his bones, his body stubbornly refusing to warm.

Rayan tossed the notebook down onto the table and strode back to the bathroom, where he filled the clawfoot tub with scalding water. Then he undressed and lowered himself in to his chin. The heat permeated his body, seeming to cross the threshold of his skin and silence the jangle of noise in his head.

Rayan lay still and found his thoughts straying once again to the file. Ever since Allen had brought up his state record, he'd wrestled with an intense need to know what it contained. Perhaps because it wasn't just the inspector who was well acquainted with the minutiae of his past but Mathias as well. They had been there all this time—the missing parts of his life that he'd tried to piece together. Rayan had lost faith in his ability to tell which of his memories were real, and it was possible that what he knew about himself and his experience growing up was riddled with self-deception. Now that he'd seen what had become of his brother, he could no longer rely on the fantasy of denial.

Rayan hadn't been in the tub long when Mathias appeared in the doorway to the bathroom. He stepped into the steam-filled room, his dark hair damp from the rain, and stared down at Rayan with a quizzical look on his face. "Don't tell me you're drunk again."

Rayan shook his head, chastened. "About that. I—"

"Save it," Mathias cut in. "I'm not in the mood for woeful excuses."

Rayan swallowed the empty words. Not sure what else to say, he raised an arm instead, woozy with warmth, and beckoned. "Join me."

Mathias raised an eyebrow, and Rayan waited for the snide remark. But there was a reluctance about him—Rayan had felt it the previous evening as well—as though Mathias was handling him carefully. Rayan felt a prickle of shame. *The last thing I want is his pity.*

Then Mathias was reaching for his Rolex, snapped it off his wrist, and placed it on the large marble vanity. He began to undress slowly, methodically, as though aware of Rayan's eyes unabashedly appraising his body. It was magnificent, as though chiseled from marble, and Mathias inhabited it with the confidence of someone who knew exactly that.

Mathias lowered himself into the water, and it rose to the very brim, threatening to spill over. Rayan drew up his knees, and they sat across from each other, Mathias's feet brushing the outsides of his thighs. "Reminds me of being a kid," Rayan said.

"How so?" Mathias asked, cupping his hands and bringing the water to his face.

Rayan smiled, curious. "You didn't take baths as a kid?"

Mathias slid down so his chest was submerged. There was a splash as the water tipped over the edge of the tub and down to the floor. "Used to clean my clothes in the bath until I figured out how to work the washer."

Rayan stared at him and he looked back, impassive. "You were alone a lot, growing up?"

"I learned English from watching hours of television," Mathias said, turning his hand beneath the water. "You read books. I got stuck with a little black box for company."

"And your mother?"

Mathias snickered. "Suffocating or absent entirely. Once she disappeared for a week when I was eight. Turned out she was in Paris, visiting a friend."

Rayan frowned. "Weren't you afraid?"

"No," Mathias said, gray eyes snapping to his. "And if I was, you think I'd have told her?"

Rayan recalled the photo of Mathias he'd seen in his mother's entranceway. He knew now why he'd felt the need to take it. He'd wanted to get him out of that apartment and away from her. "I'm sorry," Rayan said into the quiet of the room.

"Please," Mathias scoffed. "Your family wasn't exactly the Bradys."

"No, but my brother looked out for me. You had no one."

Mathias pulled himself up and leaned back against the edge of the bath. "Kids are soft. They like to make up stories."

Rayan studied him, the weight of things left unsaid filling the space between them. Mathias's gaze dropped to his chest, to the raised white dimple just below the clavicle. "Does it still give you trouble?"

"Sometimes," Rayan admitted. "It's not so bad." There was a soft trickle from the tap and the faint echo of water lapping against cast iron. "I kind of like it now. This way, I won't forget."

Mathias was silent for a moment then placed his hands on both sides of the bath and drew himself up. "My skin's about to peel off." He stepped out and took down a towel, a small puddle of water appearing on the floor at his feet.

Rayan moved to follow, goose bumps breaking out across his skin as his body hit the cold air. He raised himself from the bath, feeling flushed and wobbly. Mathias reached toward the rack for another towel and handed it to him.

Rayan brought it to his head and rubbed it through his wet hair. "Has the rain let up?"

He lowered the towel to find Mathias looking at him with a bemused expression. Rayan realized they were inches from each other, completely naked, the heat rising from their steadily cooling bodies. And he'd asked about the weather.

He lurched forward, and Mathias's arms encircled his waist as Rayan kissed him. Mathias pushed him backward until he bumped against the vanity, and then the man was lifting him up onto the edge, spreading his thighs as he ground his cock against Rayan's. Since leaving Toronto, Rayan had felt neutered, an emptiness snatching away any trace of feeling. Now it surged back to life. Mathias's hands on him and the feel of his warm, wet skin beneath Rayan's fingers stoked a fire he hadn't realized had gone out.

He suppressed a moan as Mathias nipped his ear with his teeth and ran his mouth down the side of his neck. Mathias's hand moved between Rayan's legs, capturing his cock and running it through his fist. Then Rayan was pushing him back and getting to his knees on the bathroom floor. He looked up at Mathias as he brought him to his mouth. Mathias let out a hiss as he took him in to the root, one hand reaching out to grip a fistful of Rayan's hair. They moved together, Mathias guiding him with his hand while Rayan gripped the back of the man's legs. Rayan refused to touch his own cock as it curved upward toward his stomach, his head buzzing as Mathias slid back and forth between his lips. The pace was at first steady and restrained then abruptly quicker, with a growing urgency to their movement. Rayan dug his fingers into the taut muscle of Mathias's thighs, a hum of pleasure rising in his chest.

"Rayan," Mathias warned, his voice thick.

But Rayan would not relent. He wanted Mathias's release—wanted it sliding down the back of his throat. He felt the clench of fingers in his hair, and then Mathias was coming, his face clouded, teeth bared. Rayan swallowed and let him slip from his mouth.

Mathias stood unmoving, breathing hard. Then he reached down and pulled Rayan to his feet and wordlessly led him into the bedroom, where Mathias doubled him over on the bed, hands pressing down on the backs of Rayan's knees. Mathias brought his mouth to the base of Rayan's cock then slowly, achingly, moved it lower.

Rayan made a sound that wasn't his own, something bestial tearing from his lungs. Mathias held this card close to his chest. He'd discovered, after the first time, that it had the power to annihilate Rayan—get him from nothing to coming in a matter of moments. It was mostly the thought of Mathias holding him down while he ate him out that rendered Rayan completely fucking senseless.

Wait. The word was close to Rayan's lips despite his entire body crying out *please.* Fortunately, he was no longer capable of forming intelligible words. He thrashed his head to the side, almost biting through his lip, the feeling both too much and not enough at the same time. Mathias moved his tongue languidly, undaunted, reducing him to an incoherent mess. Unable to fight the overpowering urge, Rayan reached desperately for his cock, managing only a few short jerks before he came with a force that blurred his vision, a guttural howl wrenched from his throat.

Mathias released him, and Rayan slumped back on the bed, his body deadweight. After moving to lie beside him, Mathias kissed his shoulder as Rayan returned to himself. "Look at you, all wrung out," Mathias said.

Rayan curved into him, pressing against the heat of Mathias's naked body. The heaviness had lifted momentarily, allowing him to see past the darkness that had descended. "I haven't given up," he said into the man's chest.

"Good. Because this could go any number of ways, and I need you to keep a clear head."

"You don't think I know that?" Rayan said, smarting at the familiar reproach. That had always been his problem—feeling too much.

Mathias pulled himself up and leaned back against the headboard with a sigh. Only then did Rayan notice how tired he looked. He'd been so addled the past few days that he'd no idea what Mathias had been contending with.

After a moment, Mathias spoke. "He wore a white shirt and had your eyes."

A hot jolt seized Rayan's stomach, and he sat up. "Stop," he said forcefully.

"You wanted to talk about him, so here we are." Mathias turned to look at him. "He was coming down from something. It must've been a decent hit because I noticed the twitches."

Mathias had never spoken about what he remembered from that day. Somehow, it made it more real after all those years existing only in Rayan's mind. "He was manic," Rayan muttered. "I hadn't seen him in days. It had been getting so bad he barely recognized me anymore." He noticed he was gripping the sheets and stared down at his hands.

"He told me no matter what happened, he wouldn't leave me." It was the first time Rayan had said it out loud—not realizing, until he'd spoken the words, how tightly he'd held onto them.

Mathias's face softened. "It was a doomed promise, Rayan," he said quietly. "One you keep until you can't."

"I know," Rayan said with a half smile. "I just didn't realize how much I believed it until he was gone."

Mathias was getting dressed in the bathroom when his phone began to ring. Still in bed, Rayan listened as he picked up. There was a long pause.

"I'll be there," Mathias said, the words coming out muffled through the half-open door. Mathias stepped into the bedroom shortly afterward and slipped on his jacket. "I brought food." He gave Rayan a pointed look. "Hands off my booze."

A flare of heat rose to Rayan's face. Then he felt Mathias's hand on his neck and the press of his lips against his hair before the man turned and strode out of the room. The sound of the front door closing always left a hollow ache in Rayan's chest.

He threw on some clothes and wandered out to the dining table, where he'd left his books. Beneath the pile of notes was his laptop. He opened it absently to discover an email from Professor Hofstein. Rayan paused, his finger hovering over the trackpad, unwilling to open it. He stared at the subject line. It was a reminder of that other life and how arrogant he'd been to call it his own.

Frustrated at his own indecision, Rayan clicked open the message and skimmed through the professor's friendly greeting. In the remainder of the email, Hofstein expressed his concern for Rayan's increased absence from class and their appointed meetings.

Rayan thought about his thesis—almost complete—sitting in a folder on his computer. He'd told Mathias he hadn't given up, but it was naive to think there was still a place for these things. Why should he be allowed to start over? The world didn't owe him that. The world owed him nothing.

He reread the professor's kind words and then moved the cursor to the top of the email, which he swiftly deleted. After closing the lid of his laptop, he stalked into the kitchen. On the counter were a brown paper bag of groceries and a fabric tote containing something else. Rayan reached for it and pulled out a lacquered wooden chess set. The lid of the box opened to reveal a board and two rows of beautifully carved pieces, black on the right, white on the left.

It had started as another lesson, one more thing he'd never learned. While visiting Rayan during his first year in Toronto, Mathias had discovered he didn't know how to play. Rayan had gone out and bought a set and made Mathias teach him. They would leave the game set up in his living room, with a silver quarter on the table beside it. Every time Mathias was in town, he would make a move and flip over the quarter so Rayan knew it was his turn. He was heads, Rayan tails. Their games would last months, a sporadic flurry of movements giving way to nothing, marking the time together and apart. So far, Rayan hadn't succeeded in beating him. Mathias had a knack for anticipating potential moves before they appeared and planned his victory several turns in advance.

Rayan took the board and set it up on the side table in the corner of the living room, where he placed each piece in its assigned square. He picked up the white pawn and moved it two spaces forward. Then he retrieved his wallet, extracted a silver quarter, and left it beside the board, heads up.

This time, Mathias went alone to see Belkov. A thick-jawed Russian soldier escorted him into the office at the back of Château Suzdal, where he found the Bratva boss with his feet up on the desk.

"You're going to want to sit down for this, Beauvais."

Mathias scowled and pulled up a chair.

"Gurin called," Belkov said with a smirk. "With some more information about our Hamilton associate."

"You seem awfully pleased."

"Pleased, not pleased—that's not important." Belkov waved a hand dismissively. "The point is, you, my friend, are in trouble."

As if I didn't already know that.

"Gurin looked into what the cops have on Truman. The Reapers have been gunrunning, working with other chapters across the country, only to find themselves tangled up in a Border Services investigation. Not trivial, either—we're talking a national sting operation."

Mathias felt a pounding in his head as his anger unfurled.

"And that's just the start. They've caught Truman personally handling product. He's staring down the barrel at jail time—has a trial date coming up in the next month or two."

"So, what—the Feds have promised him immunity for handing me over?" Mathias asked.

"The Feds have promised him something—that's for sure." Belkov spread his palms. "Looks like you've found yourself in quite the predicament."

Mathias narrowed his eyes. "Why do I get the feeling you're about to try and strike a deal?"

Belkov chuckled. "Always thinking the worst of people, aren't you, Mathias? Thing is, shortly after the whole business with Russo, when Truman and I parted ways, I figured it wouldn't hurt to get my hands on a little insurance policy in case the man ever decided to misremember the particulars of our short-lived alliance. The Reapers and the Bratva have a... how would you say? Tumultuous history."

"Where are you going with this?"

Belkov swung his legs down and bent to open the top drawer of his desk. He took out a small brown envelope, which he placed between them. "Leverage. I no longer need it now that he's come after you instead. And it'll only go to waste if Truman ends up in one of our fine correctional institutions."

Mathias lifted the envelope from the desk and opened the flap to find a small stack of black-and-white photos.

"All sorts of surprises came up when my men started digging," Belkov said with a waggle of his eyebrows.

Mathias pulled out the stack and peered closely at the faces in the first shot, tempering his astonishment. "Is that—"

"You'd better fucking believe it."

Mathias looked up at the Bratva boss, whose mouth was stretched into a cocky grin.

"Bet you're glad for all those favors now, Beauvais. I just gave you a chunk of solid gold."

Shaking his head in disbelief, Mathias stared down at the images in his hand. "He can't be this fucking stupid." He inspected Truman's profile in the next photo and the slackened grin of the man beside him. "You've really captured his good side."

"Always knew having dirt on Truman would come in handy. Take it. Use it as a bargaining chip with the Feds. They hate us, but they hate an inside job even more. Stings when it's one of their own."

Mathias felt an immediate kickback at Belkov's mention of collaborating with the RCMP. The photos were damning—and he didn't doubt they had the potential to bring Allen to the negotiating table—but the idea pushed up hard against the reputation he'd built for himself. If he was to demand respect in this world, his word had to mean something. Mathias wasn't a rat. The thought of going to that smug woman to plead his case and giving her the satisfaction of knowing she'd gotten to him was just as impossible as handing himself in.

"And I'm to believe you're doing this from the goodness of your heart?" Mathias sneered.

Belkov shrugged. "Let's say I have a shared interest in Truman going down. Our Hamilton operations have been stifled as of late. I could use the breathing room."

Mathias thumbed through the photos absently. He'd been strangely undecided on how to proceed with Truman. It wasn't as simple as confronting the Reapers' head. He had to try to figure out exactly what Truman had given Allen first.

"So, you'll stand to gain no matter which way this falls," Mathias remarked.

The Bratva boss couldn't hide his glee. "And that, Beauvais, is where you'd be right. That man has been a thorn in my side for years. Your can of worms happens to be my lucky break."

15

Truman appeared considerably more agitated when Frances met with him a second time. Following pressure from the RCMP, Border Services had come down hard with their gunrunning charges and issued a freezing order, which prevented the Reapers' head from accessing assets for several of his establishments. A summons had been issued, and he was due in court the following month. It was enough to propel Truman to seek her out and grasp at the possibility of a plea. Not that it made him any more gracious in his dealings with her. He'd been pushed hard into a corner, and it was clear he wasn't happy to find himself there.

They'd arranged to meet at a deserted Hamilton movie theater that was screening a matinee of a recent action film nearing the end of its run. Frances had arrived first and seated herself in the back row to wait. After the opening credits had started, she saw Truman slink into the darkened cinema.

"Nice choice," she said sarcastically as he squeezed his considerable bulk down the aisle toward her.

The movie was about a cop called out of retirement to hunt down a serial killer— at least that was what she'd gathered from the first few painful minutes. As someone who worked in the profession, she'd always found cop movies hard to stomach. The blaze of guns and glory obscured what was, in reality, a tedious push and pull of dead leads and paperwork.

Truman came to a stop and lowered himself into a nearby seat with an audible grunt. "Creaming your panties already?" he shot back.

"I see you've changed your tune. Something to do with the impending trial date?"

Truman glared at her in the darkness, and Frances held his gaze. He'd need more than a sour look to ruffle her. In truth, she'd been relieved to get word from her go-between that Truman wanted to meet again. Since her fruitless visit with André Nadeau, she hadn't made much in the way of progress.

Rayan still hadn't resurfaced, which didn't bode well. If he'd been concerned about saving his own skin, he would have made contact by now. She'd thought his initial reluctance to divulge anything about his boss had been typical family bravado, but if he would rather spend his life on the run than roll over on Mathias, that threw her strategy out the window. Fortunately, Truman had sweetened the bitter taste of disappointment. Of the two possible informants with the potential to bring Mathias down, he was the more promising choice.

Truman shoved a hand holding a crumpled manila folder into the empty space between them. She leaned over and took it then pulled her phone from her pocket to illuminate the contents. At first, Frances wasn't sure what she was looking at. The initial few pages were Hamilton-Oshawa Port Authority documents that detailed fees paid for scheduled shipments from the Hamilton port to the ports of Montreal. Someone had circled the name of the company addressed in the invoices: Laurent Importations. The following pages were customs seizure notices listing the shipment identification numbers and sailing times. She flipped back and forth between the pages, noting that the ID numbers on the port authority invoices matched those of the shipments that had been seized.

"What is all this?" she asked, growing annoyed. Truman had said he had something connecting Mathias to the cross-provincial drug trade that would substantiate the original tip-off.

"Christ, lady, I gotta do all your work for you?" Truman snapped, shifting in his seat. "You've got a whole office of pencil-pushers at your disposal. Look up the holding company. I think you'll find that it links directly to our friend."

Frances flipped back through the pages in her hand. Laurent Importations didn't appear anywhere in the sender or recipient details for the seized shipments. There had been a handful of different names and addresses listed on the customs forms that the Quebec office had looked into, only for the trail to go cold. But that was because they hadn't thought to link the shipments to port authority fees, a connection that could only have come from someone on the inside, someone who knew they were being paid off.

"It's a start," she said, keeping her voice even so as not to let on how pleased she was. "But I'm going to need more than this to put him away. And you're going to have to up your game if you want any chance at a plea."

Truman slammed his fist against the back of the empty seat, causing the row of plastic chairs to shudder. "What the fuck are you playing at? You said you needed info. Here it is. Don't go changing the rules to suit yourself."

Frances let out a short laugh and got to her feet. "Not fair enough for you, Truman? I make the fucking rules. And if you want a snowball's chance in hell of walking away from prison time, you will follow them." She tucked the folder under her arm and strode out of the theater.

When she emerged into the lobby, Frances took out her phone and called the office's head of research. "I need everything you can find on a Quebec-registered holding company, Laurent Importations." If what Truman had said was true, and they could link the company back to Mathias, she would have enough for a warrant.

"Come here—let's have a look at you, then," Freddie Mancini announced from the living room.

Mathias came to a stop in the hallway, only steps away from the front door and mere moments from freedom. It wasn't often that he saw his father. As Mathias had gotten older, the visits began to occur less frequently. When his father did come by the apartment, it was never to see him, and Mathias knew to make himself scarce.

Mathias was barely thirteen and still growing into himself, his body different from one day to the next. He turned around for his old man's assessment, hating the hope that leapt to his throat, as though his father would suddenly bestow upon him years of abandoned praise.

"You're a tall one, aren't you?" Freddie chuckled. "And those eyes. You sure he's mine?"

He glanced over at Mathias's mother, who was standing by the sofa, and she gave him a small smile. A joke, but it set the fury burning in Mathias, making what he was even more sullied. After all, it was a special kind of bastard who didn't know his father. Mathias, on the other hand, saw too much of the man in himself. When he looked in the mirror, it was his father who looked back—the dark hair, the wide shoulders, the rise of his forehead.

"I've got something for you," Freddie said.

That came as a surprise. Mathias couldn't remember ever receiving anything from his old man. Freddie reached into his jacket pocket and pulled out a cheap watch with a blue plastic strap, like something you gave a kid who was learning to tell time.

"Man's got to have a watch. Don't leave home without it." He folded his arms, displaying the gold band of his Rolex. "Listen carefully, kid. Ain't nothing more important than being on time. That's how you get ahead in life."

Mathias stepped forward and took it.

"So, you play sports—part of a team?" Freddie asked. "Can't be good for a boy to spend so much time with his mother."

Mathias turned the shiny face of the watch over in his hand. *Whose fault is that?*

"He's always so busy at school, leaving early and staying late. What is it you practice again?" his mother asked, her tone vague.

Mathias was amazed she'd even noticed. He hadn't had to come up with an excuse because she'd never taken an interest in where he was. *That's what she thinks I'm doing—making the most of the school's extracurriculars?*

Mathias sold pills—Adderall, Ritalin, Klonopin—behind the gymnasium before and after school, sometimes during lunch if he was feeling entrepreneurial, though that ran a higher risk of being discovered by the faculty. A fellow student, Philippe Bossé, bused in from the South Shore and stole the pills from the back room of his parents' drugstore. He and Mathias divided them into baggies and sold them to the rich kids at their private school. They were making a killing, selling them for far more than street value, because when Mommy and Daddy were the source of endless pocket money, who gave a shit what things cost?

Philippe was skinny and a good head shorter than Mathias. He'd attempted the enterprise before only to end up with a black eye and his stash stolen. Philippe had come to him because everyone at school knew Mathias could deal a decent punch and had no qualms about handing them out. He cut Philippe extra for sourcing the supply, and they split the remaining profit.

"I run track," Mathias lied, if only so his mother wouldn't look like a complete idiot.

Freddie let out a rasping laugh. "No point training to run away from things, boy. Got to meet life head-on."

Mathias wondered what other kernels of truth his father felt generous enough to lay on him. But Freddie had already lost interest and had turned away without another word. Instead of heading to the door, Mathias walked back to his room and tossed the watch into the trash bin by his desk. Then he took down the tin from the top shelf of his wardrobe and retrieved a handful of cash.

A man needs a watch, does he? Well, Mathias would have to go out and buy himself something decent.

Mathias sat at Tony's desk in the Collections office. He still thought of it as Tony's desk—the man had occupied it long enough. Compared to his old boss's tenure,

Mathias's time as division head was merely a blip. Since inheriting the role, he'd considered himself more of a placeholder and figured it was just a matter of time before someone relieved him of the inconvenience. Because of this, he'd left the office mostly unchanged. If Tony happened to stroll in one day, back from the dead, he would find things as he'd left them, with fewer dirty coffee cups but retaining the ever-present whiff of cigar smoke.

Mathias studied the figures on the latest contract remittance sheet while Jacques sat across from him, smoking absently. "They don't add up."

His second nodded. "That's the problem—I can't figure out why."

Mathias dropped the sheet onto the desk. "And Lucio prepared this?"

"Based on the numbers Franco sent through."

"Either Lucio's made a mistake, or Franco's fudging the numbers." Mathias got to his feet. "I need to speak with Lucio about month end anyway." Jacques stood to follow, and Mathias gave a curt shake of his head. "Stay here," he instructed, a common refrain in recent months. "Sonny's late dropping off his takings, and I need someone in the office to lock up."

"Sure thing, boss."

Mathias pulled open the office door, stepped into the hallway, and made his way to the stairwell. With Collections, it was always one step forward and two steps back. Now he knew why Tony had been such a grumpy bastard—managing the division was like herding cats.

Lucio could usually be found at the office, but he'd been called in by the Betting division that morning to help his former team with an emergency. It was late Friday afternoon, and Mathias knew, heading into the weekend, with paychecks hot in people's hands, the place would be inundated. As he reached the bottom of the stairs and strode out into the parking lot, Mathias saw the car first—an unmarked silver Ford Explorer looking out of place idling behind the building. Then he saw the cops. Both plainclothes, they waited to one side of the car as he stepped through the door. Mathias let it swing closed behind him and watched as they approached.

"Mathias Beauvais?" the younger of the two asked, sounding peppy and sporting a bright smile, like they were fucking friends.

"What's it to you?"

The older cop beside him scowled and folded his arms. Despite being familiar with several of the regular players that covered their beat, Mathias didn't recognize the man. "Let's not make a fuss, Beauvais."

"Let's not," Mathias said and moved to pass. "Excuse me, gentlemen."

"Afraid we can't let you do that," the glowering man said, and the young cop pulled out a pair of handcuffs.

Mathias arched an eyebrow. "What's this, then? Show me the warrant."

The older cop handed him a sheet of paper, and Mathias scanned it carefully, seeing his name printed clearly in black ink at the top of the page. The charges were deliberately vague, which was good. It meant they didn't have what they wanted on him—something to put him away for a long time. He suspected this was Allen flexing her muscles. She was sending him a warning, hoping he would spook.

"Come quietly now," the older man warned, eyeing Mathias warily as though he expected him to go down guns blazing.

Mathias gave a snort of laughter. "What do you think I am, a fucking animal?" He held out his wrists, and the young cop cuffed him then steered him by the elbow toward the Explorer. Mathias pulled back pointedly. "Don't need my hand held, kid."

On the drive to the station downtown, Mathias ran through his options. His phone burned a hole in his pocket, but with the cuffs on, there was no way of getting to it and letting anyone know he'd been pulled up. He would have to wait until he was booked before he made his official phone call. Mathias only hoped the man was available—for what the family paid him, he'd damn well better be.

A group of officers gathered behind the glass screen of the processing room when he arrived, no doubt relishing the sight of one of the family's elite detained in custody, the ink still drying on his fingers. Mathias stared right back, swallowing his pride, which stung like acid going down. He was relieved of his phone, his watch, and the ring taken from the little finger of his right hand. Mathias watched as the young officer slipped the ring into the clear plastic bag with the rest of his possessions and wondered if he registered its significance. Mathias counted himself lucky he didn't take to carrying a weapon these days. That would have caused a raft of additional problems. It had been a necessity when he'd spent his time chasing down clients. Now he had people to do that for him.

After being booked, he was led through a series of sterile corridors before being shoved into a holding cell. The door slammed closed behind him, with no mention of the call he was entitled to. Mathias sat down on a metal bench bolted to the wall and took in his surroundings.

The room was an off-white box of concrete, empty save for the homeless man stretched out across the green linoleum floor, snoring loudly. Graffiti was scrawled across the walls—previous occupants had taken it upon themselves to inform the world of such truths as *NIQUE LA POLICE!* The booking officer must have had some latitude when it came to what was confiscated going into the cells—his Rolex was deemed far more dangerous than some scumbag's pen. Or perhaps they got a kick out of parting him from his spoils.

He figured the fanatical police interest, those sneering faces pressed up against the glass, wouldn't be the exception going forward. Looking down at his cuffed wrists, Mathias tried to ignore the cold sense of dread they conjured. He'd never been afraid of a fight and was confident in his ability to hold his own. But this was different—this was no place for retaliation, only submission.

He focused on pulling air slowly through his nose to squash the panic. If Mathias was honest, he'd always harbored a secret belief that he was more likely to be shot down by some disgruntled lackey than get pulled in by the pigs. He'd gotten where he was by deftly navigating the legal system's many incompetencies, yet here in the belly of the beast, Mathias was beginning to feel the creep of foreboding.

It must have been evening by this point, though it was impossible to tell in the windowless cell. Above, fixed to the ceiling in cages, the fluorescent lights flickered away with unnatural intensity, creating an artificial, unending daylight. His gaze kept returning to the thick metal door, which set off an unsettling hum in his brain, a callback from the past that kept slipping through his memory, refusing to be caught.

Mathias's head began to throb, and he knew he would have to keep his wits about him if he was to win this round. He assumed the denial of his legal rights was simply an extension of Allen's flex. It was reckless—unlike his world, this one had clear rules, and if she didn't follow them, it would be to her detriment. So far, he'd demonstrated nothing but compliance. He just had to wait her out.

Despite his ability to rationalize the unfolding situation, the feeling was still there—a low drone in the back of his mind. Mathias shifted on the bench, the metal cutting into his wrists, and his pulse began to race. Then it came to him, a flash of memory almost belonging to someone else, like a story he'd heard and not lived himself—the lock on his bedroom door. It had been fixed to the outside so she could keep him in when his father visited—as if he didn't know what the man was there for. Sometimes, she forgot to unlock it after he'd gone. As a child, Mathias would sit on the floor in the room, all distractions exhausted, and stare at the door. He'd imagine what would happen if his mother never let him out, how long he could survive without food or water. But he didn't call out or bang on the door. He refused to give her the satisfaction. And when, hours later, she would finally appear—voice keening with apologies, hands fluttering about his face—he would brush her away so she couldn't tell how relieved he was to see her and how afraid he'd been.

Stiff within the shackles, Mathias turned over his left hand, an instinct years ingrained, only to be confronted by his bare wrist. An hour might have passed or only five minutes—there was no way of knowing. Trapped in a cage devoid of space and time, Mathias leaned back against the cold concrete wall and waited.

16

Rayan stood by the chessboard in the corner of the living room and rolled the white knight between his thumb and forefinger. He gripped his phone in the other hand, but it remained silent, the screen dark. For the second time in two days, he'd called, and Mathias hadn't picked up. He tried to be careful about his expectations. Between Mathias's family commitments and the growing urgency of the situation with the Feds, it was understandable that his visits would become more sporadic. But after two days with no word, Rayan couldn't shake the feeling that something was wrong. While he knew Mathias's other number by heart—filed away since those early days, a number that had always sent a flutter of anticipation in his stomach when he'd seen it appear on the screen—there was no way he would take the risk of calling it, especially with things as they were.

He thought of how the inspector had confronted him in Toronto and all the ways in which Mathias might find himself similarly ambushed. That first night after arriving in Montreal, when Mathias had come to find him at the boarding house, he'd given Rayan a brief rundown of the investigation and the tip-off that had launched it. But Rayan had worked with the man long enough to know Mathias was deliberately withholding certain details. While Mathias's unwillingness to confide in him pained Rayan, he understood his reticence. Rayan hadn't exactly been acting like he had things together.

Rayan deliberated at length before making his move, vaulting over Mathias's bishop to capture one of his pawns. He placed the black piece in the box and flipped the coin on the table so that it once again sat with the Queen's profile face up. Then, as though his play on the chessboard was merely a proxy for the real move he'd been considering, he strode to the dining table and pulled out his notebook and pen. He began to scribble, the numbers spilling from his mind—reluctant, hazy after having been buried so long. The last two he struck through and flipped. Only when they were out on paper could he be sure of the order.

He stared down at the number and scanned his brain for confirmation. It was as close as he was going to get. He picked up his phone, dialed, and held the receiver to his ear before realizing it was a Sunday afternoon.

That didn't seem to matter to the man who answered. "*Oui?*"

It was impossible to tell from his greeting whether he was who Rayan hoped he would be. "Dubois?"

"That's me," Grayson Dubois rumbled. "Who's this?"

Rayan knew he had to be cautious. Here he was, in a city where he was no longer supposed to exist. "I need your assistance," he said, dodging the question. "Am I right to assume you still have an agreement with Mathias Beauvais?"

There was a pause. "That would depend on who's asking."

"Someone looking out for his interests," Rayan hedged. "If the arrangement no longer stands, I'll facilitate one of my own. Name your price."

What did Mathias say about getting creative? Rayan would use every last cent if he had to. Through the earpiece, Rayan heard the rustle of fabric and then the sound of a door closing.

"The arrangement stands," Dubois said.

"I need to know if he's been detained and, if so, how to get him out."

"Easy enough. Give me a few hours. Not everyone's so cooperative over the weekend. I'll find out what I can and call you back on this number," Dubois said. "But I'll need a name and half up front. I'm not a fan of the whole anonymous thing. I like to know who I'm dealing with."

A name, Rayan thought. *Easier said than done.*

After he hung up, Rayan wired the lawyer the agreed amount and waited, the hours dragging by as he paced the safe house, unable to think of anything else.

Dubois called him back that evening, as promised. "He's being held at the station downtown. They picked him up Friday."

Friday? Rayan ground his teeth in frustration. *He's been there since Friday?*

"I can't do anything until they schedule his bail hearing, and that won't be until tomorrow at the earliest. The judges don't work weekends."

"They can't hold him that long without a hearing," Rayan protested, trying not to imagine how Mathias had spent the past few days.

"I suspect that's why they timed it the way they did. This has got the Feds written all over it—the paperwork is a mess, deliberately complex to drag out the process. Has Beauvais got some heat on him?"

"The RCMP have an investigation open."

Dubois sucked his teeth. "Well, there you have it. The charges themselves aren't overly concerning, but they're bucking procedure—that's for sure. Wanting to send a message. I'll bet the bail's set high too. Might be hard to meet."

"I'll meet it," Rayan said.

"All right, then. I'll head in first thing in the morning and see what I can do."

Rayan stood and raked his eyes across the darkened apartment. He felt powerless stuck within the confines of its four walls. No longer able to do anything to help Mathias, he could only sit tight and wait.

Mathias spent the first night in the holding room before being moved to a small single cell the following morning. Only then were the handcuffs removed. His wrists stung where the metal had cut into his skin over the course of a long sleepless night. Still, he was not permitted a phone call. Twice a day, a metal tray of food was pushed in through a slot in the door, which he barely touched. While his hunger had all but dissipated, he was desperate for a cigarette. The need gnawed at him with a ferocity that made his fingers itch.

After two more nights, Mathias was once again cuffed and escorted by an unnamed officer to one of the station's interrogation rooms. He had a crick in his neck from sleeping upright against the wall. There was no way he was getting near the discolored mattress that lay across the rusted bed frame in the corner of the cell.

He wanted nothing more than a hot shower to wash the filth off him. It hung in the air and covered every surface, a feculence that permeated every pore. The room was bare except for a table and two chairs. He was led to a chair and instructed to sit.

Several moments later, Allen appeared at the door, her mouth pulling into a smirk when she saw him. "Comfy?"

The woman's face conjured a word in Mathias's head, as though there existed a flashcard with her image on one side and the letters CUNT on the other. "The kind of hospitality I'd expect from your kind," he retorted.

"Now it's my turn to be intimidating," she said, sitting down across from him and reaching over to activate the switch on the recording device in the center of the table.

"That'll be hard for you to pull off."

"I thought a couple nights in the cells would've taken the wind out of your sails."

"Then you don't know a fucking thing about me."

She leaned back in her chair and crossed her arms. "Well, then, tell me, Mathias. What are you all about?"

He gave a short laugh. It was ridiculous, like some surreal job interview. He stared back at her, silent.

Allen continued, unfazed. "We're going to take someone down, whether it's you or Bianchi or one of your other friends on the council. My advice? Keep an eye out for yourself. There are some very generous deals on the table, provided you cooperate."

"You really haven't done your homework," he said scornfully. "You think I'll roll over for a plea? I'd sooner chew through my tongue."

"That kind of blind loyalty won't save you from prison."

The thought of returning to that filthy cell brought back the crushing darkness of the past few days. Mathias had been forced to use every trick in his arsenal to stop himself from being pushed to the brink. "I want my phone call."

"So you can contact some smarmy lawyer and try to wiggle your way out of this?"

"I'm well within my rights to do so."

"Rights?" she jeered. "Did you think about rights when you decided to break the law?"

"Did you?" he said, raising his shackled wrists, which were an angry red from having been rubbed raw. "I've seen the arrest warrant, and there's not a concrete thing on there. But this, on the other hand, is pretty compelling evidence."

The woman's smug look disappeared.

"You're not fooling anyone with your schoolgirl French," Mathias said, mimicking the lilt of her accent on the last word, like an American on holiday. "If you were from here, you'd know Quebec has a soft spot for the less enfranchised— the squatter over the landlord, the accused over the prosecutor. You think taking a hard line will get results? That may have worked on your other cases—and I've done my reading. I know all about your other cases. But here, it will get you nowhere."

The door opened, and a rush of sound flooded the tiny room. Grayson Dubois strode in with two flustered-looking cops following at his heels.

"What's this?" Allen snapped, furious.

"We tried to stop him," one of the officers offered meekly.

"Stop me from what?" Dubois announced. "Seeing my client, whom you have denied legal representation? Refused access to adequate facilities and..." He tutted, taking in the state of Mathias's wrists. "Subjected to physical intimidation?"

Allen's face darkened. "This is a federal case under my jurisdiction. We deemed it more important to—"

"We're not in Ottawa, sweetheart."

The inspector flushed at the lawyer's condescending tone.

"And if you're conducting police business in Quebec, you follow provincial laws. Or I start proceedings for a human rights violation."

"Come on," she scoffed.

"Why is my client still handcuffed?"

"He's a safety risk."

"Is he? But you have him in for..." Dubois raised the piece of paper in his hand and held it up to his face. "'Holding shares in a company allegedly benefitting from the proceeds of criminal activity.' Doesn't sound like a violent offense, now, does it, Inspector? And by the looks of the treatment he's received under your care, it seems my client is the one who should be concerned about his safety."

Allen clicked her tongue and gestured to one of the uniformed policemen. "Uncuff him."

"You can do more than that," Dubois said snarkily. "I've spoken with the magistrate, and he's dismissed the charge without conditions." He opened his briefcase and placed a stack of paperwork down on the table as the officer removed the restraints from Mathias's wrists.

"The bail hearing's not until noon," Allen countered.

"He approved my request for expedition, considering that my client has been unlawfully detained for the past sixty-five hours," Dubois said. "Mr. Beauvais's shares are held in a purely custodial role, and he has no connection to the management or activities of the company in question. Not to mention, as a silent shareholder, he's legally exempt from prosecution."

Allen picked up the first document in the stack and began to flip through it, a deep line forming across her forehead.

"Don't worry—I'll be sure to have my secretary send additional copies through, along with a civil claim for wrongful arrest and detainment without sufficient evidence."

It was Mathias's turn to smirk when he saw Allen's reaction.

"Now, if you don't mind, Inspector, I'd like to speak with my client in private," Dubois said, pointing at the recording device sitting on the table. "With that turned off."

After the cops had retreated from the room, Dubois tossed his briefcase and plopped down on the chair Allen had vacated. "Hell, I'm never up this early."

"You're not getting extra for that, Dubois."

"Even locked up, you drive a hard bargain," the lawyer quipped with a shake of his head.

They went back years now, yet the number of times he'd had to engage Dubois's services could be counted on one hand. "First time I'm happy to see your gold-plated ass," Mathias remarked, masking his relief.

"Worth every penny." Dubois chuckled. "A little birdie told me you might be in trouble with the law. I see you still have loyal friends, Mathias."

Mathias blinked. He scanned his memory but couldn't think of anyone at the office who might have sounded the alarm, what with Tony gone and Jacques not the sharpest tack in the drawer.

"It was tricky to find you. They pulled you up on a federal charge, had an Ontario judge approve the warrant, and buried the case in paperwork. You could tell it was weak because they kept it quiet, didn't make a big splash in the papers. Thought they'd take advantage of the weekend lull to hold you as long as possible. No doubt, they're trying to scare you." Dubois reached into his pocket, pulled out his phone, and raised it to take pictures of the marks around Mathias's wrists. "Against protocol—it all helps. If we can show mistreatment in a white-collar case like this, it doesn't matter what the fuck you did."

Mathias knew why they'd kept him in cuffs. It was how they liked to see him— the infamous mafia captain shackled like the criminal he was.

"Anything else? Broken bones, missing teeth?"

"I'm fine," Mathias said flatly. "Get me the fuck out of here."

In the back of Dubois's car, as his driver peeled out of the parking lot beneath the station building, Mathias absently rubbed his wrists, the feel of the restraints lingering. He looked down at his watch and took a strange comfort in seeing it returned to its rightful place. The farther they got from the station, the less his chest ached. Mathias stared out the window and found himself drinking it in—the skyline, the people, the freedom.

"Who called you?" he asked, turning to Dubois, who sat beside him in the back seat, tapping away at his phone.

"Said his name was Angelo Caravella, though he didn't sound Italian."

Mathias snorted, shaking his head in astonishment.

"Where should I drop you off?" Dubois asked.

"Here," Mathias said suddenly. He wanted nothing more than to get out of the car and on his feet and disappear into the crowd of commuters converging on the street. The driver pulled the car over to the side of the road. "What do I owe you?"

114

Dubois shook his head. "Already taken care of." Then he gave Mathias a serious look. "I have a feeling this won't be the last of it. Do you know what they're after?"

My complete and utter destruction. "Allen wants to take me down."

Dubois made an ominous sound in the back of his throat. "It starts getting tricky when the RCMP get their teeth in."

At least now Mathias knew without a doubt that Truman was behind it—not just the tip-off but this latest leak to the Feds as well. It was no coincidence that the charges they'd arrested him on were directly related to their joint venture, the particulars of which Truman was very well acquainted with.

"Keep me informed of any developments," Dubois said.

Mathias pulled open the door and stepped out of the car into the frigid air. It stung his throat and made his eyes water—a welcome jolt of clarity. He stood and lit a cigarette from the confiscated pack the officers had returned to him, the first lungful of nicotine planing down the jitters as he watched Dubois's car disappear into the distance. His building wasn't far from here—a few blocks' walk through the bustling downtown center. He imagined the emptiness awaiting him back at the penthouse, the cold gray walls not unlike the cell he'd just escaped. Mathias longed for a shower. He wanted to lie down and close his eyes, but the thought of the eerie quiet of his home unnerved him. He brought the cigarette to his lips and took a long pull. Then he turned in the opposite direction of his apartment and began to walk.

17

Rayan was rinsing dishes in the kitchen when the front door opened and Mathias strode into the apartment. It had been three days. Three days in which his mind had run through every possibility, mining them for their potential likelihood. None of the scenarios he'd envisioned had involved Mathias simply reappearing, clothes disheveled, hair mussed, his face a mask of stone.

He walked past Rayan as if he weren't there and closed the bedroom door behind him with a thud. Moments later, Rayan heard the hiss of the shower as it turned on. Still, he didn't move, not quite sure that what he'd witnessed wasn't an apparition.

Rayan waited until after the shower had been turned off, pacing the hallway to curb his impatience, before finally cracking open the door to the bedroom. He found Mathias freshly changed, his wet hair slicked back, standing by the window, smoking. Rayan hung back. He could feel the swirl of hostility emanating from the man and see it in the stiff angles of his body.

"They let you out," he said flatly.

Mathias exhaled a thin stream of smoke through his nostrils. "Took them long enough."

"I didn't think you'd come here." Rayan had assumed in the event that Mathias was released, he would immediately launch into an aggressive counteroffensive.

Unless it's not retaliation he's preoccupied with...

Rayan's gaze dropped to the red marks around Mathias's wrists. He could only imagine what the past few days had been like for him—stripped of his respect and paraded about like a prize. He felt a swell of sympathy for Mathias, who, usually in complete control, had found himself in uncharted territory.

Rayan moved carefully into the room as though approaching a wounded animal: unpredictable and prone to lashing out when cornered. "What do you need?"

Mathias stubbed out his cigarette in the ashtray on the windowsill. "I don't need anything," he said stiffly and headed for the door.

116

Rayan stepped into his path, stopping him. "What do you want, then?"

Mathias's eyes narrowed. He shoved past, but Rayan caught his arm and held firm. Mathias yanked it free. "The fuck does it matter?"

"So I can give it to you," Rayan murmured. He stepped forward and softly brushed Mathias's mouth with his own.

This time, Mathias didn't pull away. Instead, he parted his lips, the subtlest of gestures yet all the intimation Rayan needed to take him into his arms, desperate to blunt the force of his outrage, which threatened to swallow the man whole. They moved fast, Mathias tugging roughly at Rayan's pants. *Here's something he can control: me.* And Rayan would submit himself freely. But Mathias stilled, his grip slackening, arms falling to his sides. They stood, momentarily fixed in place, before Rayan realized it wasn't control that he wanted.

He raised his hands to the buttons of Mathias's shirt and undid them one by one. Rayan slipped his thumbs beneath the fabric and slid it off his shoulders. He reached down to unbuckle Mathias's belt, unfastened his pants, and let them drop to the floor. Rayan shed his remaining clothes and led Mathias to the bed, where he lowered him down on his back. Rayan moved so he was above the man and trailed his lips across Mathias's bare skin—stomach, chest, shoulders, neck—feeling the rise and fall of each breath beneath his touch. He stroked the smoothness of Mathias's cheek, freshly shaven, breathing in the familiar scent of his aftershave. Finally, Rayan reached his mouth, kissing him gently as he waited for Mathias to work loose. He felt Mathias's arms loop around his waist, bringing Rayan to him and holding him close. They lay flush, mouths together, the heat transmitting through their skin until Mathias began to stir, as though Rayan had breathed life into him, pulling him back from the depths.

When it came to understanding the inscrutable nature of Mathias's feelings, Rayan eschewed words and instead relied on the man's body as an indicator of what was roiling beneath the surface. That could take the form of a fist clenched in anger or—like now—the forceful, purposeful grip of Mathias's hands as he guided Rayan onto his back beneath him. There was an intentionality to the way Mathias commanded the muscles in his arms and legs to pin Rayan to the mattress, a conscious recentering, his body regaining the clarity his mind had momentarily lost. Finding himself once again.

Mathias held him down by the wrists, and Rayan's arousal sprang into the gap between their bodies, demanding attention. Lowering his head, Mathias brought his lips to the tip of Rayan's cock. His tongue teased along the slit, making Rayan groan and push against his iron grip. Where Rayan was eager, Mathias was deliberate. He intended to bring Rayan close to the edge while simultaneously pulling him back. And he was fucking good at it. Mathias took his cock deeper into his mouth, changing the pace, taking his time, sending Rayan spiraling. But before Rayan could lose himself, Mathias released him, hard and taut, from between his lips.

"Please..." Rayan protested weakly.

Mathias drew himself up, his cock curving toward the muscular lines of his stomach, and stared down at Rayan with a knowing look. "Why don't you tell me what you want?"

Flushed, Rayan held his gaze. "You. Inside me."

Without another word, Mathias flipped him onto his stomach. Rayan heard the nightstand drawer glide open and the snap of a lid. Then Mathias's palm was on the small of Rayan's back, sliding down his ass, a slick finger pressing against him to curve inside, finding just the right spot. A moan escaped Rayan's clenched teeth. It was his fault—he'd shown Mathias how easily he could be trained. Mathias continued stretching him, two fingers now, deliberately slow, so Rayan reared against him, willing him deeper.

When fingers weren't enough, Mathias pulled back and used his knees to spread Rayan's legs from behind. He moved so the head of his cock rested against Rayan's opening. Rayan could hear the thunder of his own breath in his ears. He felt Mathias's eyes on him, making him wait. Then Mathias drove forward, and Rayan's back arched as he was filled, a shudder spreading from his hips to his toes.

There was something intoxicating about giving himself over to Mathias, relinquishing himself to his will. Rayan had done so for years as his second, handing over his life for Mathias to do with it as he pleased. But this was different. Back then, Rayan's devotion and desire to please had only run one way. Even now, it came as a surprise when Mathias demonstrated that those intentions were in fact reciprocal.

A hand curved around his neck, turning his head, and Mathias leaned down to kiss him, his chest pressed against Rayan's back. They moved in tandem, an established familiarity between their bodies. Mathias lowered his forehead to Rayan's shoulder, his arms straining as he held himself aloft, hips slamming into Rayan with each measured thrust.

Rayan's fingers curled into the sheets—the heat, the fullness, the weight of Mathias bearing down on him was overwhelming. Mathias began to move faster, rising to press down on Rayan's hips, forcing his legs wider and deepening the angle in a way that left him gasping. Rayan didn't dare touch his cock, which was beading beneath him. He wanted only for this annihilation to continue—to remain in this version of reality in which only the two of them existed.

Rayan could tell Mathias's reserves were low, his self-control depleted. The man was close, his movements no longer controlled but raw and untamed as his restraint began to crumble. Mathias circled an arm around Rayan's chest and pulled him up on his knees. His other arm dropped between Rayan's thighs, and his hand moved to jerk Rayan's cock.

Arching his back, Rayan tilted his chin to press his mouth against the line of Mathias's jaw. "Come for me," he murmured.

With a sharp grunt, his breath cut in two, Mathias crushed Rayan to his chest and shuddered against him as he came. A wave of pleasure shot down Rayan's spine, and he made a noise in the back of his throat, discovering he was closer than he'd realized. He grasped Mathias's hand, still around his cock, and eased it along his shaft. Mathias, still hard inside him, rocked his hips, grazing the spot that made Rayan's mind blur. He gave a low growl and spilled, hot and wet, through their entwined fingers.

They remained fused for a moment as Rayan caught his breath, before Mathias gradually extracted himself, his residual warmth sliding down the inside of Rayan's thigh. Lying with Rayan on top of the sheets, Mathias's eyes closed, and Rayan greedily searched his face for clues. Mathias opened them suddenly, catching him in the act.

"Angelo Caravella?" he asked, the corners of his mouth curving upward. "Is that your idea of a joke?"

Rayan recalled Dubois's insistence on a name and how the memory of the two men was intrinsically linked in his mind. It had come out before he'd registered the ominous parallel. "More of a coincidence."

Mathias shook his head, mystified. "You don't forget a fucking thing, do you?" He let out a snort of laughter and rolled onto his back. When he next spoke, his voice was quiet. "Thank you." The words registered like an electric shock, and Rayan's eyes widened. "Don't look so surprised," Mathias admonished him. "I'm not incapable of gratitude."

Rayan hid a smile. It seemed his former capo was capable of a lot more than he'd given him credit for. "What did Dubois make of it?"

"They couldn't get these charges to stick, but it's only a matter of time before there are others. Everything points to Truman. Turns out he's kicked up a lot of dirt, and the Feds have him over a barrel. Now he's singing like a canary." Mathias struggled to dispel the fury from his face. He turned to Rayan, his eyebrows drawing together. "It gets murkier. Belkov has intel that Truman's in bed with Wainwright."

"Wainwright?"

"Roger Wainwright, chief of Hamilton PD. There are photos of them together—with hookers, money, blow, you name it. That's the problem with a cocky bastard like Truman—he's been greasing the wheels in all the wrong places."

Rayan blinked as he realized what this could mean. "That kind of information... Couldn't you use it to—"

"I'm not giving her shit," Mathias snapped, throwing him a sharp look. "I'd rather face jail time than cut a deal with that woman."

Rayan knew better than to challenge him. Mathias was paradoxical like that. Certain lines he had no trouble crossing. Others he upheld with a noble sort of integrity. And if there was one thing he despised above all else, it was a rat.

"Back then, what you said about Caravella," Rayan said carefully. "The Feds start investigating, and he disappears. That was the family, wasn't it?"

Beside him, Mathias pressed his lips together, frowning.

"This is a lot of attention," Rayan continued, attempting to silence his own misgivings. "What will the family do?"

Mathias exhaled slowly, and there was a shadow of doubt in his eyes that Rayan hadn't expected. "I don't know."

Mathias stood in the kitchen, boiling water for coffee. Two showers hadn't been enough to forget the crawl of filth from the jail cell on his skin. Despite the fact that he'd been released, Allen had succeeded in rattling him. He'd cornered her on his turf, and she'd turned around and done the same—giving him a taste of things to come if she got her way.

Mathias poured the water from the kettle over the ground coffee in the press and eased down the handle. Rayan appeared next to him, silent on bare feet, and took down two cups from the cabinet, which he placed on the counter. Mathias filled them both with coffee and slid one in Rayan's direction before taking a frying pan from the drawer and placing it on the stove.

After Dubois had dropped him off, Mathias had made his way to the nearest metro station and taken the train to Beaubien. From there, it was a short walk to the safe house. When he arrived at the apartment, he wanted only to scour himself. He stepped into the shower without waiting for the water to warm, convinced the cold, not the memory of that empty cell, was making him shiver. He stood under the water for a long time, letting it thunder down on his shoulders as he tried to clear the fog from his head. It wasn't until Rayan had taken his arm and he'd felt the warmth of the man's skin against his own that Mathias had realized how deeply he'd retreated into himself.

While Rayan drank his coffee at the counter, Mathias took eggs from the fridge and punched bread into the toaster. He fried the eggs with one hand while sipping his coffee with the other. Then he set the toast onto two plates and piled the eggs on top, sprinkled with a dash of salt and pepper—simple, unembellished. Mathias viewed cooking as he did most of life's obligatory tasks—not to be enjoyed, merely to be completed.

He pulled up a stool beside Rayan and placed the plates down on the counter, surprised to discover he was famished. As they ate, Mathias noticed Rayan was wearing one of his T-shirts. He'd brought so little with him from Toronto. Slightly too big, the shirt hung low around his neck, revealing the line of his collarbone. He must have found it in the bedroom dresser. It was unsettling how much Mathias enjoyed seeing him in it.

The safe house had been the easiest place to disappear, at least temporarily, but it wasn't the real reason he'd found himself here. The gravity of what Rayan had done by contacting Dubois wasn't lost on him. He'd extracted himself from his old life at a great personal cost, only to throw himself back in for Mathias's sake.

Here it was again: the impossible situation. Their lives were fundamentally incompatible but inherently intertwined. Whereas before, Mathias had attempted to cut himself off, now the prospect was unthinkable. He was in far too deep, his grip on Rayan unable to be prized open. He didn't know how to unravel what they had without unraveling himself.

"Are we going to pretend you didn't spend the last three days in jail?" Rayan said finally, pushing away his empty plate. His voice was measured, as though he'd been waiting to bring it up.

"High chance I'd end up there eventually," Mathias said blithely, unwilling to touch on the fear that lurked in his mind. He stood, reached for the frying pan, and spooned the remaining eggs onto his plate.

"Different when it actually happens, though," Rayan said, staring back at him.

That look was dangerous, the way it cut through everything else and aimed right for the jugular. It made Mathias want to confess to things he'd never uttered aloud.

Mathias placed the pan back on the stove. "I went to see your father."

Maybe he said it to turn the lens back on Rayan—distract him from his calm observations, which hit a little too close to home. Rayan's eyebrows shot up. He stood jerkily.

"What?" He practically spat out the word as his fists clenched at his sides, angrier than Mathias had ever seen him.

Mathias shrugged. "You and my mother seemed awfully close—I thought he and I could be pals."

"Don't fuck with me, Mathias!"

Mathias relented, seeing how affected he was by the news. He hadn't expected Rayan to take it quite like this. "Allen tracked him down. As it turns out, he had several choice things to say about you to the police."

Rayan shook his head, his face furrowing in confusion. "About what? I haven't seen him since I was a kid."

Mathias hesitated, realizing the nature of what the old man had said. But Rayan had a right to know—it was his father, after all. He took out his phone and pulled up the document Gagnon had sent him. He handed it to Rayan. Rayan's eyes darted across the screen, and he grimaced then placed the phone face down on the counter.

"It's a crock," Mathias said. "Not that it matters. I convinced him to reconsider his testimony."

"Did he...?" Rayan spoke haltingly. "Was he...?" He gave a ragged sigh and ran a hand through his hair. "I don't care."

Mathias was struck by how young he appeared in that moment, as though mention of his father had revealed something of the boy within. "Why don't you go ask him yourself?"

Rayan tilted his head, and his mouth curled into a half smile. "What for? I have nothing to say to a stranger." He rubbed his palms across his cheeks, smoothing something that wasn't there. "I've always been half a fucking stranger."

Mathias recalled the dilapidated house and the old man's yellowed eyes, his biting commentary. He thought of the inscription etched carefully in the book from Rayan's mother, black ink in a steady hand: *I can already see the man you will become, noble and kind. Someone to be proud of.*

"You're nothing like him," Mathias said. "You must be all her."

Rayan's eyes, wide and unblinking, flew to Mathias's face. Then he turned and walked to the window, concealing his expression. Outside, the snow was falling once again, floating silently from the sky and muffling the noise from the street. Mathias stared at Rayan's shoulders, broad beneath the plain white T-shirt, and the curve of his neck as his head angled toward the window. He could see Rayan's face reflected in the glass, his brown eyes shining.

"You were right, though," Mathias said into the silence. "Maskinongé's a shithole. Lucky you got out when you did—plane or no plane."

Rayan gave a short laugh and brushed the back of his hand beneath his nose. When he turned back, the sheen in his eyes was gone.

18

The deputy commissioner's here," Sabine said at the front desk when Frances showed up late to the office that morning. "He wants to see you." Frances nodded, still smarting from the events of the previous day. She'd suspected the family was accustomed to wiggling its way out of police scrutiny, but to have someone as prestigious as Grayson Dubois on their payroll... Dubois was legal royalty in Montreal and had recently acquitted a trio of municipal councilors in a high-profile embezzlement lawsuit. After scanning the civil claim Dubois had handed her in the interrogation room, she'd had little choice but to release Mathias.

Missteps had been made—she could admit to that. But Frances had wanted Mathias to feel in his bones what the next few decades of his life would be like. Yet he'd walked away unaffected—albeit slightly less put together. At least she'd succeeded in dulling that immaculate facade of his.

Deputy Commissioner Thomas Gill was waiting for her in the boardroom. "Morning, Inspector," he said, offering out his hand.

"Deputy Commissioner," she said as she moved to shake it. "I didn't know you were in town."

She'd worked with Gill on several cases over the years. He was nice enough, a barrel-chested man in his late forties who looked more tired every time she saw him. His wife had some sort of autoimmune disease, and he had two teenage boys in Ottawa but spent a considerable amount of time traveling between the provinces as he assisted in overseeing the RCMP's C Division, which included Quebec.

"It was somewhat of an unplanned stop. I wanted to speak with you about the investigation," he said, pulling out a chair.

Frances took a seat at the table across from him, keeping her face neutral. "Progress has been slower than I'd hoped."

"I received a report on Friday that we had Beauvais in custody."

124

She felt a spike of anger. After they'd released Mathias, she'd stood outside the booking room and watched him retrieve his personal effects with an arrogance that set her teeth on edge. "He's been released."

"Released?"

Frances looked past the deputy commissioner to the curling poster on the wall, which featured two uniformed Mounties holding their hands to their hearts. *Maintiens le Droit*, it read. "His lawyer contested the charges."

Gill made a reproving noise with his tongue. "If Beauvais is proving difficult, why not focus on the other key figures? At this rate, we only need one to justify continuing the investigation."

"They're relics, figureheads. Beauvais has been the most active player in the province for years. He's said to have orchestrated the expansion of the mob's construction sector lending and is widely believed to have played a key role in Bianchi's takeover."

"You know, or you suspect?" the deputy commissioner asked carefully. "If there wasn't anything to hold him long enough for a hearing, I'm not sure what you're going off here."

"Statements, evidence," she replied, flustered. "I have William Truman of the Hamilton Red Reapers as an informant. He's proven very helpful."

"Not helpful enough." Gill fixed her with a judicial stare. "I hate to have to do this, Frances, but we're almost a year in and have nothing to show for it. HQ needs results to continue the funding. Otherwise, it will be shifted elsewhere."

"They'll pull the funding?" she asked, her voice rising. "We're working against decades of entrenchment here. The family's influence stretches as far as the mayor's office, maybe further."

Gill glanced down at his watch. "It's out of my hands. Launching this investigation in Quebec was already a showy move. There are other cases that need the money, and HQ's looking to repurpose some of it. It's about optics at this point—"

"Otherwise what?" Frances challenged him. "We leave the province with our tails between our legs?"

"If it comes to that, HQ knows how to spin it. Throw the divisional office under the bus—Lord knows they're finally due for some scrutiny. The Montreal branch has always been a weak link. I sent you out here to show them how it's done, and when you eventually step away, and they don't follow through—which we both know they won't—it's not on us."

She narrowed her eyes. "To be frank, Deputy Commissioner, that benefits no one."

"Who it benefits is not my problem. I just need to worry about where the money goes."

There was a knock at the door, and Sergeant Gagnon poked his head into the room. "Sorry to interrupt, sir. Inspector, I've got legal on the phone about the civil claim."

Frances could have kicked the man. Across from her, Gill raised his eyebrows. "Civil claim?"

"Beauvais's lawyer is citing human rights violations," Gagnon supplied almost eagerly.

To his credit, as someone more familiar with the Quebec legal system, he'd cautioned Frances about her tactics. However, he'd appeared unduly amused when the whole thing had ended as a bust. She'd procured the warrant for Mathias's arrest from an Ontario judge she was on friendly terms with, bypassing regular proceedings in Montreal, only to find that the local magistrate was less inclined to side with her and had promptly thrown out the charges.

"Sergeant, have legal call back. I need to speak with Inspector Allen a moment longer," the deputy commissioner instructed.

Frances steeled herself as Gagnon left the room. The door clicked shut behind him.

"I've known you almost your whole career, Frances. You're tenacious, with an impressive track record, but you should know by now this job isn't that simple. Not everything can be categorized neatly in terms of success and failure." Gill folded his arms. "When you get too hung up on results, you make stupid mistakes. When you make stupid mistakes, you give the wrong people all sorts of opportunities."

"I know," she relented. "But come on, Thomas. We've done this so many times—we put the pressure on and pounce when they crack."

The deputy commissioner frowned. "You said it yourself—the mob is entrenched here. This isn't some two-bit street gang. They rub shoulders with the city's elite. They have powerful friends in high places, and they will be looking to exploit any vulnerability you give them. We need everything to be aboveboard, by the book. You can't afford to play fast and loose. And we can't afford a legal battle—a fucking civil claim, Allen? Do you want the funds meant to put this man behind bars lining a bunch of lawyers' pockets?"

She shook her head, chastened. "Point taken, sir."

"Good. And on that note, I saw in the case file you have alerts set up with Transport Canada. Remove them. The last thing we need is for him to go after us for surveillance without probable cause."

"Noted," she replied tightly.

Gill gave a sigh. "It's not like you to let a case get under your skin. I sent you out here for results, Inspector, so get your proverbial shit together. We're running out of time."

After the deputy commissioner left, Frances remained in the conference room until she'd managed to get a handle on her frustration. The last thing she needed was for the rest of the office to catch wind of her not-so-subtle rap on the knuckles. *Seeing how dedicated they are to the investigation,* she thought dryly.

When she stepped out into the hallway, she found Gagnon waiting by the elevator. "What did the deputy commissioner want?" he asked as she approached.

Frances suppressed a derisive snort. The sergeant had been gunning for her failure since she'd first arrived at the Montreal office. "Results. They're looking to repurpose the funding if we don't make progress soon," she said, pressing the call button on the wall as the elevator whirred to life. "The suits at HQ have no idea what we're up against, how things are out here."

"Hate to say I told you so," Gagnon said. "Ottawa's only a few hours away, but it might as well be another country. Things work differently in Quebec."

"So I keep hearing," she said, trying to keep her voice even. The elevator doors opened, and they both stepped inside.

The sergeant waited until the doors had closed before turning to her. "While you were out earlier, surveillance called. Said they've been asked to pull back on Beauvais and can no longer approve the use of cameras. I think it might have something to do with—"

"Thanks for letting me know," Frances cut in, well aware of what he thought.

First the funding and now the surveillance. How am I supposed to get results with no resources? It was as though HQ had lost faith in her ability to turn the investigation around after the bungled arrest and was preemptively retreating.

Seething, Frances returned Gagnon's self-assured gaze. "You know, I was going through some of the old boxes in the filing room and discovered the strangest thing." She studied his face for clues, but Gagnon simply stared back at her, undeterred. "Documents and photos missing. It looks like Beauvais's former subordinate, Rayan Nadeau, has been wiped from the record entirely. Seems odd, doesn't it?"

Gagnon shrugged. "Those boxes get passed around a lot of different departments. We're working on a better system to ensure everything is accounted for when they come back."

Frances hit the emergency-stop switch on the wall, and the elevator lurched to a halt. "If we're being candid, Sergeant, it looks like an inside job. Like the mob had their reasons for wanting that information erased. I wonder what else may have slipped through the cracks in your system."

Gagnon gave her a steely glare. "What exactly are you implying, Inspector?"

Frances stepped forward. "I thought that was pretty clear."

"Are you accusing me and my department of disposing of federal evidence for the mafia? Just wanting to be sure you knew exactly how dangerous your insinuations are."

"Well, you would know, right, if someone was tampering with evidence?"

"I would know," Gagnon retorted, defiant.

"My mistake. I thought that was just another thing you did differently here."

Gagnon leaned over to release the switch, and the elevator once again began to whir. "I'd be careful if I were you," he warned quietly.

Frances gave a short laugh. "You sounded like Beauvais there for a second. So I'll tell you what I told him: you don't scare me."

The doors opened with a ping, and she strode out of the elevator and into the office.

Mathias had known the call was coming, but that didn't make it any easier when it did. The boss wanted to see him. No longer at his home—a privilege that had clearly lapsed—instead, he would meet Giovanni at Vol de Nuit, a club on the outskirts of Hochelaga. While the fall was to be expected, it was no less jarring, and Mathias tried not to draw parallels to the time Giovanni had broken the news of his impending transfer to Hamilton.

The club was unaffiliated, which made meeting here safer than one of the family's own establishments. There was no telling what the Feds had eyes on at this point. Mathias walked in and slid the bouncer a fifty to gain access to the darkened passage behind the stage. Henri stood outside the door to a small room in the hallway and gave Mathias a short nod as he approached. He opened the door, and Mathias stepped into the room to find Giovanni seated at a table with a bottle of whiskey and two glasses.

Mathias pulled out a chair and sat down across from him, and the boss poured a generous amount into both glasses. "Drink," he instructed.

Mathias took a swig, and Giovanni did the same then placed his glass down on the table with a dull clink.

"Lose the shirt," the boss said.

Mathias balked. "Are you fucking serious?"

Giovanni fixed him with a hard stare.

Exhaling loudly through his nose, Mathias stood and shrugged off his jacket. He undid the buttons of his shirt and held it open to expose his bare chest. "Satisfied?" he snarled.

The boss nodded and reached into his pocket for his smokes. "It's simply a precaution. You've got a lot of heat on you. Naturally, my first thought was whether you'd made some sort of arrangement."

Mathias finished rebuttoning his shirt and tucked it back into the waistband of his slacks. "If you think I'd come here with a wire," he said in a low voice, pulling on his jacket and once again taking a seat, "then quit wasting my time, and get Henri in here to finish me off."

Giovanni chuckled, placing the cigarette between his lips and flicking his lighter. "No need to be dramatic."

Mathias scowled. "Or better yet, do it yourself."

The boss let out a slow curl of smoke and studied him carefully. "For whatever reason, the Feds have latched onto you. It seems your time is up."

Mathias felt a drop in the pit of his stomach. Since being released, he'd managed to downplay the danger of his predicament. But coming from the boss's mouth, the situation took on a whole new meaning.

"As long as they're digging, we're all in the line of fire," Giovanni continued. "The way I see it, you have two paths going forward. One, stay and see what you can wriggle out of with that impressive Rolodex of contacts you keep—all the while knowing that prison is right around the corner. Or two, leave."

Mathias struggled to hide his disbelief. "Leave? And betray my oath? I've given my fucking life to the family."

The boss snorted. "Jesus, kid, you're not even forty. Let me tell you about life, Mathias. It's longer than you think."

What the fuck am I supposed to do if not this?

"I'm not going to run like a coward," Mathias snapped.

"And what would you do here? Your name is mud. I can't have you involved in establishing a new direction for Collections—the RCMP will tear it to pieces.

When you've got the smell of the Feds about you, everyone keeps their distance. I know you, Beauvais—you can't sit still long enough to blow your fucking nose." Giovanni reached for his glass. "Think about it. Plenty of men have left when the heat got too much, when they were looking at ten, fifteen years in the hole. Some of them come back. Others don't." He took a pointed sip.

"And the ones that don't?" Mathias asked, his eyes narrowing. "Like Caravella. What happens to them?"

The boss stared at him across the table. "When someone gets too much attention, we cut them off. You know that. It's nothing personal—think of it as self-preservation. Even now, I'm taking a risk meeting with you like this."

During Mathias's time, a few faces had quietly disappeared. Or taken the fall—exactly what had happened was never entirely clear. He shook his head, refusing to let the man spook him. "The charges they held me on were paper-thin. Allen talks a big game, but she's got nothing. If they had something concrete, this would be over already."

"So it's just a matter of time. That doesn't make you any less radioactive."

"Giovanni," Mathias cautioned sharply, breaking rank. He'd known the old man longer than he'd been boss. "Don't write me off yet."

Giovanni sighed, and they exchanged a look. "The runaround you've given this girl means ongoing funding could be a sore spot. The new government wants to pay for results, not dead ends. But she's got her eye on you—that's for sure. Doesn't look like she'll give up easy."

Mathias hated that he was right. Allen was proving far more tenacious than a stone he could simply shake from his shoe. "Truman's behind this. He's on the hook with Border Services, so he's passing on information to Allen in exchange for leniency. I'm heading to Hamilton to set him straight and cut ties—that is, with your sign-off."

Giovanni shrugged. "Your tower. You built it—you can tear it down. Can't say I'm not glad to be rid of him. I'd be happy to wash our hands of the Reapers. Though I do recall warning you not to trust the man. Looks like what we're offering is no longer tempting enough."

Mathias bristled. That had been the reasoning he'd offered Giovanni back then. He'd made the mistake of assuming the Reapers' head was rational enough to predict. But Truman's recent actions might as well have come from the mind of a petulant child.

"The way I see it, it'll only delay the inevitable," the boss said, his mouth pulling into a frown. "Even if you can silence Truman, you're just waiting around for the

Feds to find something strong enough to put you away. I wouldn't take the gamble, but I'll give you some runway with this. That being said, don't think for a second I won't cut you off if I have to. That's just business. You're no use to me if you're too dangerous to have around."

Mathias downed the last of his whiskey to quell the resentment that gripped him.

"There's an art to knowing when to leave," Giovanni said, leaning back in his chair. "If you can't make that call, you might find someone does it for you."

19

fter A Belkov confirmed the scope of Truman's involvement with the RCMP, Mathias had intended to travel to Hamilton to confront the Reapers' head. Then two plainclothes cops had appeared in the Collections office parking lot, and he'd lost days to righting the mess.

Within the span of a week, Mathias had become better acquainted with the prospect of his chickens coming home to roost. It wasn't as though he'd never considered the possibility. From early on, he'd put arrangements in place. It was an occupational necessity—money scattered in foreign exchange accounts, assets held abroad under different names. There had always been an escape plan, a rip cord to pull should he need to leave the country in a hurry. But Mathias refused to run at the first sight of trouble, so he would have to wade in deeper if he wanted to make it out the other side.

Mathias stared at the bleak winter landscape through the passenger window as Jacques drove them across the provincial border into Ontario. He struggled to reconcile his growing sense of apprehension with the confidence that had fueled his ambition. For as long as he could remember, Mathias had viewed the world as a simple dichotomy between what he had and what he wanted. How muddied it had all become.

His second pulled up outside the Hamilton office, and the two of them got out of the car. Mathias had contacted Truman before leaving Montreal and instructed the man to meet him here. He wouldn't risk engaging with him on Reapers territory—not this time. Truman had been surprisingly accommodating. Either that was more of his signature nonchalance, or he was as stupid as Mathias had always believed.

Paulo Bilotti, the new regional head, met him at the door to the building. "Good to see you, Mathias," he said, shaking Mathias's hand as he ushered him inside.

They made their way up the stairs to the office, and Mathias received a series of nods from the assembly of men who dotted the room, most of whom he'd installed during his tenure.

"Let him in when he gets here," Mathias instructed Jacques and followed Paulo into the corner office, leaving his second to wait with the rest of the Hamilton team. He turned to Paulo as the man shut the door. "Have the arrangements been made?" Mathias had called ahead to enlist Paulo's help.

Paulo nodded. "We got our hands on the shipment this morning, and it's now at the bottom of Lake Ontario. I've assembled the full team, some here, some stationed around the building as backup."

"Good."

Mathias glanced idly around the room. It brought up an unwanted nostalgia, a callback to a different time. Paulo hadn't changed much in Mathias's absence—the place was as pared back as he'd left it. He sat down behind the desk and pulled out his cigarettes. He'd barely lit one before the door opened and Truman strode in. Mathias indicated for Paulo to leave, and the regional head stepped out, closing the door behind him.

"Changing it up, are we?" Truman announced, hooking his thumbs through his belt loops. "I haven't been here since Moretti. Sure spruced up the place."

He'd done more than spruced it up. Mathias still remembered how his skin had crawled the day that old hack had led him and Rayan up to this dump. He exhaled a stream of smoke through his teeth. "I thought I made myself clear when we first met."

The air in the room shifted. Since carving out their unconventional alliance in the lead-up to Russo's death, they had remained on relatively amicable terms. That was no longer the case.

"Clear about what?"

"How I conduct my business."

"Nothing's changed there."

It had always been a gamble, relying on such an erratic personality. On some level, he'd known that ever since he'd first asked Gurin for an introduction. Mathias had made it this far by being careful who he trusted, and Truman wouldn't have made the cut if necessity and circumstance hadn't drawn them together. Truman and the Reapers had been an asset at the time. The family wouldn't have succeeded in taking down Piero without them, but his usefulness had clearly run its course.

"Hasn't it?" Mathias brought his smoke to his lips.

Truman cocked one eye. "What're you going to do—pull out your gun?"

"I've done it before."

"I believed you that time." Truman shook his head, his expression almost reflective. "Back then, I knew you were gutsy enough to do anything to get ahead. Now you've already got what you wanted. There's nothing in it for you."

"Why don't we talk about what's in it for you? There must be something you're getting by cutting a deal with the Feds."

Truman gave a low chuckle. "Look, that's something else. They've got me against the wall for some stuff Border Services caught us shifting for the West Coast chapter."

"Stuff?" Mathias echoed. He knew exactly what Truman had been shifting.

"Guns, ammo," Truman admitted grudgingly.

Mathias rested his cigarette on the edge of the ivory ashtray sitting on the desk and got to his feet, attempting to suppress the flash of fury at the man's casual tone. Truman had no idea the risks he'd been taking—what he'd put in jeopardy—with his carelessness.

"Are you a fucking moron?" Mathias muttered. "Gunrunning's far too conspicuous with what we have going on. It's the basics in this business— compartmentalize, stagger activities, distance yourself."

Truman shrugged. "What can I say? I'm greedy. I like a finger in a few pies. You know how it is—it's not always about the money. Sometimes we do it for the hell of it, because we can."

"No, I don't know how it is," Mathias said, astounded by Truman's idiocy. He stepped away from the desk and moved to face the Reapers' head.

Truman rocked back on his heels with a smirk. "Come on, Mathias. They've always been after us. One by one, eventually, we'll fall. It's just a matter of time. I'm not afraid to go down in a bloody mess. Better than slinking off to prison—"

Mathias smashed his fist into Truman's face. A spurt of blood flew through the air, and Truman staggered back, stunned. Mathias cracked the knuckles of his right hand, surprised at the sting. It had been years since he'd done his own dirty work. Maybe he had grown soft, as Truman had said, now that there wasn't anything left to want.

The Reapers' head gave a gurgle of laughter and wiped the blood from his mouth with the back of his hand. "I probably deserved that. Heard you spent some time in the slammer."

The second blow hurt less, Mathias's body getting back into the swing of things—a violent sort of muscle memory. Truman doubled over and spat a hock of red onto the office floor.

"Okay, okay, enough," he declared, squinting in anger as he straightened. "I wanted to give you the benefit of the doubt, but I'm not dumb enough to come here alone. I've got ten guys outside with a pretty decent mob complex. They'd be happy to take you on. Even you, Beauvais, aren't fucking invincible."

"Let's see you try," Mathias snarled. "The men behind this door were trained by the Bratva. They'll tear your hobby bikers to pieces."

"Look, I didn't give them anything," Truman said. "The pigs put two and two together and caught on to our little arrangement."

"An arrangement that is, as of this morning, dead in the water—along with your last shipment. You're welcome to recover what you can from the bottom of the lake."

Truman's face flushed red. "That was half a mil worth of product!"

"So run and tell that bitch from the OCB you were chatting up. Like you have about everything else."

"I didn't sell you out," Truman growled. "She came to me with this gunrunning charge, trying to twist my arm, all right? She wanted dirt on you, and I told her to fuck off."

"And she just happened to know about the holding company, the agreement with port authority?"

"Shit, she's got the whole RCMP at her disposal. If the shipments are getting seized, the Feds are going to start sniffing around to see what else they can find." Truman gingerly brought his fingers to his split lip. "But in spite of all that, I came here, to your turf, to meet with you—someone I would consider a reasonable man—"

"Reasonable?" Mathias repeated, looking down at him with contempt. "You're more deluded than I thought."

"I'm helping you out here, trying to smooth things over," Truman said, holding up his hands. "From what I've heard, this broad won't let you out of her sights. I figure I can help with your little problem and solve one of my own in the process. Who knows? If we play our cards right, all of this might just disappear."

Mathias felt a flicker of warning. "The fuck are you talking about, Truman?"

"Allen. She's the one pushing hard for this," Truman said, lowering his voice. "She's also the one whipping Border Services into a frenzy and siccing them on my ass. She goes quiet, and what do they have? With no one to lead the investigation, they're back to square one. The government's fighting a war on multiple fronts. You think they wanna bleed resources on a little provincial spat?"

The implication slid like ice down the back of Mathias's neck.

135

"All I'm saying is, I ain't no stranger to spilling a bit of blue blood to get the job done. As far as I'm concerned, if someone's in my way, I take them down, badge or no badge. She's been at me to meet again, so I figured it's about time I took another trip to Montreal." Truman chuckled. "You know how I like the women in Quebec."

This was an unexpected development. Mathias brushed the blood from his knuckles on the leg of his pants. He reached for his still-smoking cigarette, brought it to his mouth, and took a slow drag.

Mathias knew that he shouldn't, but upon returning to Montreal, he'd forgone his own apartment in favor of the safe house. With his world closing in around him, it was the only place he felt calm enough to think, and after his meeting with Truman that afternoon, there was a good deal to think about.

By the time he arrived, it was late in the evening. Mathias sat at the dining table while Rayan made coffee in the kitchen. Spread out before him was the series of photos tracking Inspector Allen's movements. He wasn't sure what he was looking for—justification? Mathias had mulled over Truman's proposal the entire drive back to the city, unsure why it had hit a nerve, like a splinter lodged beneath the skin.

Rayan appeared at his side, placing a steaming mug down on the table. His hand reached out to pluck a photo partially obscured by another in the pile. It was Allen at the playground, pushing a little girl with pigtails on the swing. "She has a kid?"

"Her sister's."

Rayan put the photo down and pushed several of the images around on the table with his fingertips. "What are you going to do about her?" he asked cautiously.

Mathias hesitated, recalling how flippantly Truman had thrown down his gambit—a simple solution. "There are things that can be done," he said, and Rayan's gaze flicked to his, a look of warning in his eyes. Mathias sat back, thrumming his fingers against the table. "Truman's under the impression it would be a relatively easy problem to solve."

"She's not some dealer who's stepped out of line," Rayan said sharply. "She's a police officer. This is her job."

"And this is mine."

Mathias didn't say that he, too, had found himself unsettled by Truman's proposition. Rayan was right about one thing—Frances Allen hadn't ventured into their world for a share of the promised bounty. She was there because of a sense of duty, as cheap and misguided as that was.

"You're better than that," Rayan muttered.

First philosophy, now charity—as though the man had emerged from a state of stasis and was only now determining where he stood. Mathias felt the fury rise like a wave. It was new, this power Rayan had over him and the way his words pierced Mathias to his very core.

"Am I?" Mathias sneered. "You think a couple of college papers make you an expert on right and wrong? You don't have a fucking clue." He stood and reached for his jacket where it hung on the back of the chair. "And I don't recall this righteous sense of justice before."

Rayan couldn't hide the shadow of a grimace. "You know that was different."

"Was it? Or maybe you don't remember how fallible you are."

"I remember," Rayan said, looking away.

Of course he remembers, Mathias admonished himself, thinking of all the times he'd awoken in the night to find Rayan gone from bed, sleep eluding him.

"I told you I couldn't give you what you wanted," Mathias said in a low voice. "You know what I am. Your newly adopted moral code doesn't apply where I'm concerned." He pulled on his jacket and strode toward the door.

"People change," Rayan said to his retreating back.

"Spare me the shrink talk—"

"You have."

Mathias stopped.

"I used to marvel at your ability to walk headfirst into any situation, no matter the stakes," Rayan said. "I thought it was superhuman, wished I could be the same. But nothing ever scared you because you didn't care what happened either way."

Mathias clenched his jaw.

"Now you do."

Mathias reached for the door handle and gripped it in his palm. He thought of the pale-green linoleum in the holding cell, smelling of piss and bleach. Then he yanked open the door, stepped out into the cold night air, and slammed it closed behind him.

20

Rayan could no longer stand the four walls of the safe house. He felt himself bouncing against them like a rubber ball—or worse, a crazed man in a straitjacket. Here he was again, tossed about on a whim as his life spiraled out of control. If it had come to this—if Mathias was being forced to consider that—then things were coming apart faster than he'd realized, and Rayan could not hang back and relinquish his part in it all.

He dressed warmly, wearing a sweater beneath his winter coat, and laced up his shoes by the door. The urge resurfaced the same as before—the only way to shake free from the tumbling mess in his mind was to take to the streets. When he stepped out of the apartment and into the freezing air for the first time in almost two weeks, Rayan felt reborn, and his feet took over without him having to think.

The day he'd arrived on the bus from Toronto, Montreal had appeared to him like a foreign land, the neighborhoods he'd once known unrecognizable. Now he moved through streets carved with memories, returned to their familiar state. Compelled by nostalgia, Rayan let himself be led through the city, his body buzzing with the taste of freedom. He hadn't realized how much he'd missed it.

Rayan didn't know what to do about the unfolding situation, only that he had a hunch that Mathias's stony response hadn't been the full extent of his feelings on the matter. Why else would he have reacted so defensively when pushed? There'd been a shift in Mathias since his release from jail. He'd returned that day, humbled and disheveled, his conviction knocked. Rayan knew Mathias was protecting him, but in doing so, he was shutting him out. Mathias couldn't do this alone—it was already taking its toll. Rayan had to stop him from making the situation even more impossible to walk away from.

In Toronto, Allen had come to him for information. Perhaps there was something he could give her that would help shift the direction of the investigation away from Mathias. While Rayan had fewer scruples than Mathias when it came to collaborating with the police, the danger lay in the very real chance of turning the man he loved against him.

Rayan found himself downtown, standing on the corner of a street he knew well and staring up at a building he knew even better. This was where his feet had taken him. He didn't go through the lobby, instead slipping into the parking garage and taking the elevator from the basement. The code was the same, and the elevator launched him up to the top floor, where he was released into a familiar entranceway. He moved to the door at the end and brought his hand to the buzzer.

Rayan's mind blanked as he waited for the door to open. The excuses that had sounded plausible in his mind, the infallible lines of reasoning for why he was there—when he'd so clearly been instructed otherwise—abandoned him. Instead, he stared at the man who appeared in the doorway before him, shirtsleeves rolled up, his sharp features set in a scowl.

"You shouldn't be here," Mathias cautioned quietly.

Rayan said nothing. He stepped forward, reaching for the front of Mathias's shirt as the door closed behind them. Rayan pushed his lips against him like a drowning man, and Mathias raised a hand to grip the back of his neck, deepening the kiss.

Then Mathias pulled away, his face rippling with fury. "How fucking reckless can you be?"

Rayan shrugged off his coat and shoved Mathias against the wall in the hallway. "You're going to call me reckless in the face of what you're considering?"

Mathias knocked his hand away and stalked down the hall. Rayan caught his arm at the door to the bedroom, and Mathias whirled around and threw him onto the bed. After climbing on top of him, Mathias sat on Rayan's legs and pinned his arms to the mattress, the iciness not leaving his eyes.

"Is this a game to you?" Mathias asked.

"I was careful."

"I told you not to leave."

"But you can come and go as you please?"

"You think showing up here will make me change my mind?"

Rayan threw his weight to one side and rolled Mathias beneath him. "I don't think you've made up your mind."

Mathias glared at him, his expression darkening. "Stay the fuck out of my head."

"It's too late for that," Rayan said, cavalier despite the ramifications, wanting to push him that little bit further.

Mathias, stronger than him, tossed Rayan back onto the bed and lowered his face so it was inches from his own. "Careful, Rayan." His eyes glinted dangerously. "You're getting ahead of yourself."

Rayan raised his head and brushed his mouth along Mathias's neck. Then he sank his teeth into the skin below Mathias's ear, and the man pulled back sharply, bringing his fingers to the mark Rayan had left behind.

"Make me regret it," Rayan said.

Mathias gave him a look that would have set the fear of God in any man but flooded him with an arousal so intense his cock strained against his pants.

"Oh, I will," Mathias said, his voice deadly serious.

Mathias stood on the balcony, a cigarette perched between his fingers, the smoke curling from its tip as he stared out across the city below, a tapestry of tiny lights in the darkness. Rayan was inside, asleep.

Mathias had been furious to find Rayan at his door, knowing just how dangerous it was for him to be seen in Montreal. But Rayan had wanted to make his protest clear, and the only way to do that—with the little agency he currently possessed—was to go against Mathias's direct instruction. He was beginning to see that Rayan had grown tired of being sidelined in his own life. As infuriating as his actions were, it was difficult for Mathias to fault him.

What followed had been reminiscent of earlier times—rough and ruthless, a mutual frustration fueling their arousal. Mathias had fucked him face down on the mattress, one hand gripping Rayan's wrists behind his back, the other clenched around his throat. Rayan's usual reticence disintegrated as he pleaded in a low murmur for Mathias to let him come. But Mathias remained true to his word. Only when Rayan was moments from release did Mathias reach for the man's cock, slick and arching, to finally provide him relief. He envied the way Rayan gave himself over completely, wielding his submission with a strange power that was both thrilling and frightening, like free-falling.

Mathias sucked in a lungful of smoke and exhaled, his mind replaying the conversation afterward. They'd been splayed out, the bed a mess of twisted sheets. Rayan lay beside him, his skin still flushed from their exertions.

"It's strange being back here," Rayan said, taking in the room, which hadn't changed much since he'd last been in Montreal. "I used to think if I went through everything in this place, I'd somehow figure you out."

Mathias's mouth twitched, amused. "Nothing's stopping you. But you won't figure out shit."

"Yeah, that would be too easy." Rayan frowned pensively, as though the subject hadn't been far from his thoughts. "What happens when the cop investigating both of us turns up dead?"

If they weren't under enough scrutiny as it was, they would be then. "Now's your chance, Rayan," Mathias said soberly. "You can disappear for real this time. I won't stop you."

"That's where we're at?"

Mathias recalled Giovanni's thinly veiled threat. "It's not good. Any more heat, and the boss'll cut me off."

"What exactly does that entail?"

"I'm not in a hurry to find out." He'd tried to keep Rayan out of this, but the larger implications of the investigation were coming for him, which was one reason Mathias had found himself entertaining Truman's suggestion, as unhinged as it was.

"And if you end up in prison instead?"

"That's not going to happen."

Rayan gritted his teeth. "What was it you said about doomed promises?"

"It's not a promise—more a prediction."

Rayan's eyebrows pulled together, and his lips flattened into a grim line. "I'm tired of losing everything. I can't lose you too."

He looked at Mathias, his eyes betraying the depth of his feeling. No one had ever looked at Mathias like that. The sheer weight of emotion pressed against his armor, causing it to crack. Unable to hold his gaze, Mathias turned away.

"So you're just going to stay here and take your chances?" Rayan asked.

Mathias didn't see what other choice he had. Run like a coward? Abandon everything he'd spent his life building? But the thought niggled: *what have I really built?* Once he took his foot off the city's throat, someone else would just take his place.

"Disappear with me," Rayan said softly.

"I can't do that."

"Then I'm not going anywhere," Rayan had said.

On the balcony, Mathias pulled out his phone. He punched in a series of numbers and raised it to his ear. There was a click as the line connected, and Mathias spoke into the receiver. "I want in. Your takedown of our little friend—I want a piece."

Truman chuckled. "I knew you'd come around."

"What are we looking at?" Mathias continued. The stream of smoke from his cigarette contrasted with the black sky.

"She's meeting me tomorrow night at the auto-parts warehouse on Chantier Naval Road, around eight. Don't worry—I'll take care of preparations."

"Tomorrow?" Truman was moving fast. Allen must really have lit a fire under his ass.

"Figured the sooner the better. What, prior commitments?"

"No, I'll be there. This is personal."

He hung up, pocketed his phone, and turned to find Rayan standing by the door to the balcony. Mathias hadn't heard the man approach, but by the look on his face, he'd overheard the conversation with Truman.

"Don't look at me like that." Mathias brought the cigarette to his lips and took a drag.

"What are you doing?" Rayan asked, his voice rising in anger.

"Stopping some dumb cop from getting herself killed," Mathias snapped, and Rayan's expression changed as realization dawned on him.

Desperation had a way of simplifying complex decisions. When a person was in a panic to make a move, it was easy to lose sight of the larger picture. A decision like this, half-baked and hastily executed, had the potential to lead to disastrous consequences. Mathias was not desperate—not yet.

"I'm coming with you," Rayan said.

Mathias snorted and turned his gaze back to the flickering lights. "You'll stay here."

"You know as well as I do Truman won't come alone. You'll be outnumbered. I'm not letting you go without backup."

Mathias's eyes snapped to his. "Stay here," he repeated sharply.

"You don't give me orders anymore, remember?" Rayan countered, holding steady.

Mathias clicked his tongue in frustration. "I swear to God, Rayan—"

"That's what this is now," he cut in. "I don't stand back and do what you say."

Mathias took in the defiant jut of his jaw. He could still feel the sting along his neck where Rayan's teeth had cut into his skin. "When did you get so fucking stubborn?"

"I learned from the best." Rayan gave a shrewd smile and moved across the balcony to him. He placed his hand beside Mathias's on the railing, the touch of his skin a shot of warmth in the cold night air. They stood like that while Mathias finished his cigarette, and then Rayan spoke.

"The file. Is it here?"

Mathias felt a twinge of unease. "And if it is...?"

"I want to see it."

As far as Mathias was concerned, some things were better left buried. But who was he to try to protect him? If Rayan wanted to relive the turmoil of his past, fine. He was welcome to it.

Mathias stubbed out his smoke and pulled away from the railing. He strode into the apartment and down the hall to his study, aware of Rayan following silently behind. Mathias bent to open the lower drawer of the cabinet against the wall. He removed a thick manila folder and dropped it down onto the desk.

Rayan stood in the doorway, watching. Slowly, he made his way over to the desk. He remained standing, one palm resting against the desk's surface as he flipped open the cover. He turned each page methodically, his face unmoving as his eyes scanned the contents. He didn't look like a man uncovering the minutiae of a life riddled with abuse and neglect, all the painful details distilled into a case worker's clinical notations.

Turning the next page, Rayan froze. "Christ..." he hissed and lurched back from the desk as though struck. He brought a clenched fist to his mouth, making Mathias wish he'd lied. Rayan shook his head in disbelief. "It's been here all this time? I've spent years wondering what happened..." His face twisted in anger. "And you never thought to tell me?"

"This isn't about me." Mathias stepped forward, glancing at the report—a series of grisly images laid out on the page—before closing the folder.

When he looked up, Rayan was staring at him, his eyes hollow. "It doesn't even say where she's buried."

"Laval or Longue-Pointe," Mathias said. "That's where the city takes them when there's no family."

"I'm her family," Rayan whispered, slumping against the wall. "What kind of person lets his mother rot in an unmarked grave?"

"You were a kid."

"I'm not a fucking kid anymore."

"Then decide what you're going to do about it," Mathias said quietly. "Because it's not going to get any better if every time you press against it, it bleeds."

21

"I want you armed." Mathias slid on his holster and removed his gun to check the chamber. "The Reapers aren't much for subtlety."

It was the following evening, and they stood in the living room of Mathias's apartment, readying themselves to go and extract Allen. While Rayan felt nothing but disdain for the federal inspector and would have preferred if their paths had never crossed, it didn't mean he wanted her dead.

"I don't suppose you have your old gun," Mathias said archly, reaching for his jacket and pulling it on.

Rayan shook his head. "Long gone." He'd made careful arrangements when he'd first left the country, ensuring that whatever remained of the weapon would never be found.

"Figures. Get one from the safe."

Rayan made his way down the hall to the bedroom, his mind once again crowded with thoughts. After seeing the contents of the file and the clinical summary of his mother's death, he hadn't trusted himself to return to the safe house. He'd slept here instead, waking bleary and disoriented in the late morning with Mathias pressed against his back. He'd been naive to think he could access that part of his past with the cold detachment of a stranger. Instead, it had all come back—the eerie silence that had swallowed their apartment, the locked bathroom door, the way Tahir had curled into himself, rocking from side to side at the end of his bed.

Why did I want to know? It hadn't made anything easier. The feelings were still there, just as raw as before.

Rayan walked over to the closet and crouched before the safe. He spun the dial back and forth, the numbers still engraved in his mind. The door gave way with a sturdy click, and he eased open the handle to find two pistols and a box of ammunition stacked on the lower shelf. He reached for the 9mm and loaded it carefully, his fingers propelled by habit. Standing, Rayan stared down at the gun in his hand. It felt heavier than he remembered and looked out of place in his grip. Pushing the thought aside, he tucked the pistol into the waistband of his pants and moved to close the safe.

He wasn't sure why it caught his eye—a small brown envelope wedged in tight on the top shelf, the seal open slightly to reveal a sliver of glossy photo paper. Rayan reached for it and let the photos slide out of the envelope and into his palm. He flipped through the first few images, the dots connecting rapidly in his brain. He'd been looking for a chance to shift the course of the investigation, desperate to do something besides stand idly by as their futures hung in the balance.

Before Rayan could reason with himself, before he could truly consider what a grievous breach of trust it was—a trust so precious and painstakingly cultivated—he shoved the envelope into the pocket of his coat. Then he slammed closed the door of the safe and went to join Mathias.

They drove through the darkened city toward the shipyards and turned onto a street dotted with industrial buildings. Mathias backed the Bentley into a narrow distribution alley across the road from the warehouse, where Truman had arranged to meet the inspector. They waited in the car, staking out the place, with a full view of both sides of the street. Before long, two men on motorcycles rode into the empty concrete lot outside the warehouse then disappeared along the side of the building. Several minutes later, a silver sedan pulled up at the curb, and Frances Allen got out.

"You'd think she'd have more sense," Rayan muttered as the woman walked toward the warehouse door.

"She's getting antsy," Mathias observed. "Taking unnecessary risks. The Montreal office isn't backing her, so she thinks she has to do everything herself."

Rayan turned to Mathias, giving him a pointed look.

"Fuck off," Mathias retorted.

Rayan snickered. "Maybe you're more alike than you think."

"I'm glad this is so amusing to you," his former capo said, eyes narrowing as another figure on a motorcycle pulled up outside the building. This man was bulkier than the other two, the patch on the back of his jacket more prominent. Rayan guessed that he must be William Truman.

"We're clear?" Mathias asked, his gaze still trained on the man in the leather jacket, who dismounted his bike and headed to the warehouse entrance.

"I get to Allen and pull her out while you deal with Truman. Then I get back in there before he goes nuclear."

For a moment, it was as though they'd stepped back in time, transported to any one of the innumerable Collections jobs they'd found themselves on over the years.

He felt a swell of pride at how well they worked together, bolstered by the patchwork of their shared past.

But then Mathias turned to Rayan, hesitation in his eyes. Things weren't the same. He didn't want Rayan here. "Things get hairy, and you're out. Got it?"

Rayan nodded, hoping he looked convincing. There was no way he was leaving without Mathias.

The thud of their shoes on pavement broke the stillness of the deserted street. When they reached the door to the warehouse, Mathias pulled it open, and Rayan stepped ahead into the cavernous space. The overhead lights were on, sending pools of yellow down onto the exposed concrete floor. The large man Rayan had seen outside earlier was speaking with what appeared to be his subordinate. Inspector Allen was nowhere to be seen—neither was the other man they'd seen ride up.

Rayan was immediately on guard. *Are we too late?* Surely, the Reapers weren't that efficient.

The bulky man, his motorcycle jacket laden with inscrutable stripes of some rank or another, looked up as they approached. "Mathias, glad you could join us."

"Truman... where's the cop?" Mathias asked, as though sharing Rayan's thought.

Truman smirked. "Waiting for me out back. Figured we could use the chance to compare notes." He inclined his head toward Rayan. "Who's this?"

"He's with me." Mathias turned to Rayan, his face void of all expression. "Go and see how our friend is doing."

"Tell my guy to go easy on her," Truman called out as Rayan ventured farther into the warehouse.

Rayan spotted a dimly lit corridor that led to a series of back rooms, and he felt his adrenaline surge. It had been a long time since he'd put himself at risk like this. Once, danger had been part of the job, so normal it barely registered. Now his heart slammed against his rib cage as he strode down the corridor, hyperaware of the fact that he'd left Mathias alone and outnumbered. He had no idea what he was walking into and could only hope Allen was still alive. Otherwise, all of this would be for nothing.

Rayan hadn't realized how much he'd been conditioned against fear until he'd spent time living in a world where he rarely encountered it. With his resistance gone, he was at a grave disadvantage. He understood Mathias's look of hesitation—the man could see what Rayan had been too afraid to admit.

Then he brushed against it—a familiar resolve buried deep but not gone. Rayan felt his breathing slow as instinct took over. There was no going back, only forward. He reached the closed door at the end of the corridor and heard voices behind it.

This was nothing. Compared to everything he'd done, everything he'd seen, this was just one more job. All he had to do was get it done. Rayan wrapped his hand around the cold metal door handle and pulled.

Frances had shown up at the place she'd arranged to meet Truman only to find herself face-to-face with two of his lackeys.

"He's on his way, got held up," the taller one said with a wide grin.

That wasn't the only concerning thing about this particular rendezvous, news of which had initially given her the smug satisfaction of knowing she'd gotten under Truman's skin. The location, which had been relayed over the phone as an associate's business, was instead a deserted auto parts warehouse strewn with mechanical debris. Frances chided herself for being too complacent, her smugness replaced by a creep of nerves as her gut attempted to assert itself.

"When's he supposed to get here?" she asked, glancing around the building while attempting to hide her disquiet.

"Not long now. He said to wait for him in the back room."

The man who'd spoken indicated for her to follow, and she walked behind him through the junk-filled space to a narrow corridor at the back, his friend remaining by the entrance. She had her agency-issued weapon strapped to her chest beneath her jacket and, despite the Reaper's size, was confident in her ability to take him if provoked. The room at the end of the corridor was completely bare, in stark contrast to the mess of the warehouse. The man closed the door behind them and stood to one side as they waited, lighting a suspiciously pungent cigarette.

After the deputy commissioner had laid out just how close the investigation was to getting pulled, Frances found herself possessed by a heightened sense of urgency. When Truman called to set up the meeting, she'd grasped onto it like a lifeline, perhaps her last chance to get her hands on the evidence she needed to nail Mathias. In her impatience, Frances had downplayed the risk. After all, she'd emerged from their last meeting with a clear advantage, Truman's blustering coming across not as ominous but more like the desperation of a man beat.

Yet unlike with Mathias, there was no artful deception where William Truman was concerned. He had an unpredictability that to Frances—alone in an empty room in some run-down warehouse—suddenly felt sinister.

"I'll wait outside," she said tightly, changing tack and moving toward the door.

"Not so fast, sweetheart," the man said, standing in front of her and folding his tattooed arms. "I like the look of you."

Frances widened her stance, conscious of the one button she'd left open on her blouse, as if it were a neon sign. She wasn't a delicate flower. She'd handled herself in difficult situations, but she'd always had backup. Since arriving in Montreal, she'd had to contend with the icy front of her fellow colleagues at the divisional office and their reluctance to pursue a group that was somewhat accepted as part of the city's natural landscape. Without fully realizing it, Frances had begun to distance herself, viewing the investigation as her own personal crusade.

Stupid. Because it was clear she needed help, and as each second crawled by, she was becoming less confident that she had the skills needed to get herself out of this.

Truman's lackey took a toke from his spliff and advanced toward her. "Awfully straitlaced, aren't you?" he observed with a leer. "It's always the good girls that are into the real nasty stuff."

Frances had once taken part in an investigation alongside Vancouver PD, in which they'd succeeded in embedding a female officer in the West Coast Reapers chapter. The officer had gained access to the group by posing as a stripper at one of their private clubs and had been close to getting all the information they needed to start issuing warrants when she'd tapped out. The woman had left the force shortly afterward. Nothing had ever been spoken of officially, but Frances had heard rumors about the things she'd been subjected to.

This was different, though. Frances had clearly identified herself as a federal officer. Truman wouldn't be that brazen. Still, it didn't stop her from recalling the photos she'd seen—women dumped, crude symbols tattooed onto their bodies, arms shredded with track marks. Truman not only dealt in the importation and trafficking of women across the country but also seemed to take personal pleasure in their destruction.

"Back the fuck off," she snapped, as if her words might erect a barrier between her and the roaming reach of his gaze. "You know who I'm with. I'd be careful if I were you."

The man laughed, revealing a set of yellowing teeth. "You think I'm scared of the pigs? You're about as frightening as that pout on your face."

Frances reached into her jacket for her gun, but the man was quicker, grabbing her wrist and pushing her back against the wall.

"And a little piglet like you?" He grinned, and the rankness of his breath was enough to make her gag. "I think I'd like to hear you squeal—"

The door to the room swung open, and Frances started. Rayan Nadeau stood in the frame, looking nothing like the young college kid she'd ambushed outside the university in Toronto. With eyes cold and shuttered, his face was set in a hard mask as he glared at Truman's lackey. No, this was someone else entirely. This was the man from the photos.

"She's coming with me," Rayan instructed, his voice low.

The Reaper straightened up, still holding her wrist, and scowled. "Who the fuck—"

Rayan moved quickly, stepping forward and slamming the side of his hand into the man's throat. He doubled over, retching.

"Come on," Rayan said, beckoning her with a tilt of his head.

Frances lurched toward him, and he led her swiftly out of the room and toward the barred fire door on the other side of the corridor. She threw a glance over her shoulder, expecting the Reaper to come charging after them, but he remained kneeling on the floor, red-faced and wheezing. Rayan lifted the metal bar that had been wedged across the door and dropped it to the floor at his feet. He attempted the latch, and the door shook slightly but wouldn't give, appearing to be stuck. He muttered a string of curses in Quebecois before stepping back, turning on his side, and ramming the full force of his shoulder against the door. It shuddered open, and they burst into the freezing night air. Rayan picked up the metal bar and jammed it through the handles of the door from the outside.

When she'd first seen him, Frances had been confused by the flood of relief she'd felt. Rayan was likely just as dangerous as the man they'd left behind in that empty room, yet he'd appeared to her as a savior. For all she knew, he could be taking her to Mathias to meet a similar fate. *So why aren't I afraid?*

They strode along the side of the building and toward the empty lot out front. There came a loud thud from behind them, and her hand shot out and gripped Rayan's arm. It was the door, still held fast, refusing to buckle. Frances released her grip.

"What are you doing here, Nadeau?" she said finally.

"Making sure you don't end up dead," he said, the slight hint of an accent pulling at his English. He walked her to the road where her car was parked under a nearby streetlamp. "You all right to drive?"

"Of course I can drive," she hissed, raking a hand through her hair to hide the shake. She must not have looked all right, if he'd asked the question. "Truman... what was all this? What did he have planned?"

"What do you think?" Rayan replied stonily. "You've got dirt on him, and you're trying to exchange it for complicity. It won't work. If Truman's cornered, he'll go down kicking."

Her eyes flicked to his face. "And you came to make sure that didn't happen?"

"No," Rayan said, looking back at the warehouse. "He did."

"Mathias?" Frances scoffed. "He wouldn't do anything that's not for his direct benefit."

"Maybe," Rayan said cryptically. "But wouldn't he benefit more if you disappeared?"

A chill ran through her.

"You're in too deep, Allen. Dig any further, and you won't make it out."

Frances didn't want to imagine what might have happened if Rayan hadn't stepped through that door. She swallowed hard. Mathias Beauvais had saved her fucking life.

Rayan moved to go but stopped. He turned, his expression conflicted. "You need someone to go down, right? What do I do to make sure it's not him?"

"Believe me, if Mathias wanted to throw you under the bus, you'd be locked up already," Frances said, still perturbed by that particular fact. If that wasn't confusing enough, Mathias's interference in that night's scheduled activities had really thrown her for a loop. "He's shielding you. I'd take that and run."

Rayan shook his head. "I can't do that."

"Look, Rayan," she said with a sigh. "If we're being honest—and hell, after tonight, I owe you that much—you're a ghost. Try as I might, there's little I've found with your fingers on it. It'll be hard to tie you to anything substantial."

He reached into his coat pocket and pulled out a small brown envelope. "I want to make a deal."

"I told you, you're not a priority."

"Not me. I have something of value to the RCMP. But in exchange, I want you to back off Mathias. Find someone else to sink your teeth into."

He held out the envelope, and she took it, shaking her head as she reached inside to pull out a stack of photos. "There's nothing that'll get him off that easy—" Frances stopped when she realized what she was looking at. "Holy shit..."

"I know Piper's staunchly anti-crime, but I'm pretty sure what the public hates more is a dirty cop," Rayan said. "And not just any cop—a police chief."

She flicked through the photos, each one more incriminating than the next. And what was worse, by viewing them, she had now implicated herself. Because if she were to shrug and hand them back, she'd be willfully ignoring a gross breach of professional conduct. She would be placing her investigation above what was potentially a more concerning crime—one that came from the inside.

"I'd need to bring this to my superior before agreeing to anything," Frances said, the consequences fanning out before her.

"No," Rayan said, his mouth a flat line. "I want your word now, or I take them and leave. Then we'll see what happens when it gets out that the Feds knew about this and tried to sweep it under the rug. My guess, you'll be out of a job."

Frances glared at the man, silent.

"The way I see it," Rayan continued, and there it was again—that flash of quiet intelligence—"you can keep trying to catch the one that got away or actually land something."

It would be a huge case, on par with bringing in one of Montreal's notorious mafiosi. Rayan was right—she was no closer to pinning Mathias down, whereas this had been handed to her on a silver platter. She thought of the funding, already at risk. If she didn't act, there was a high chance both opportunities would slip through her fingers.

"Or maybe I should take you back in there," Rayan said, his tone suddenly menacing. Like a switch had flipped, the sincerity from before having vanished. "We wouldn't want to keep Truman waiting."

Frances gritted her teeth. There was the matter of whom she had to thank for standing here, having moments ago assumed the worst. "Fine," she said, the word forced from her mouth.

"Your word," Rayan pressed.

"I'll pull the investigation off Mathias—but just this once. If he comes up again, if he finds himself drawn into any other case—and believe me, with what I know about him, he will—all bets are off."

"I'll take it." Rayan glanced back again at the warehouse.

She frowned. "Why are you doing this?"

"I owe him."

"For getting you out?"

Rayan stared at her, his eyes unreadable.

So he'd left the family and attempted to start over. And if that were the case, there was no way Rayan had accomplished that on his own. Now she knew who'd helped him, despite that fact going against everything she'd assumed about Mathias.

"While we're being honest," Rayan said, "what's happening with my brother's investigation?"

Frances thought about lying, about putting the screws to the master manipulator. Then she remembered the look on Rayan's face when she'd shown him that grisly photo, the pain so raw she'd felt a sting of shame. "That was a tactic to get you to talk," she admitted. "It's a cold case. We're not reopening it."

"Some tactic," Rayan muttered, his brown eyes flashing. He turned without another word and headed back the way they'd come.

"Rayan," Frances called out stupidly, struck by a sudden concern for him that leapt in her chest.

But he didn't look back. She was already forgotten.

22

Mathias watched Rayan disappear down the corridor and toward the back of the warehouse. If Truman suspected anything, he didn't show it. Mathias reached beneath his jacket, fingers brushing his gun, and pulled out his cigarettes. He placed one between his lips, flicked his lighter, and held it to the tip then pocketed everything before taking a long drag.

"He's going to take her with him," Mathias announced. "I don't need pig blood on my hands—not now."

Truman's lackey glanced in the direction of the corridor then turned to his boss. "Should I—"

Truman raised a hand, silencing him. "Don't tell me you've lost your nerve."

"I haven't lost shit," Mathias said. "But unlike you, I'm not an idiot. When the heat's on, it's better not to light a match."

"Or what?" Truman baited. "They'll lock you up? The mighty Mathias Beauvais, afraid of prison. That's where they'll send us anyway if we sit on our hands."

"I'm tired of your shit, Truman." Mathias clenched the cigarette between his fingers as he stemmed the roiling in his gut. "I was tired of it years ago—hell, I was tired of it the minute I met you. It was only a matter of time before you did something to fuck us both over. And now you're going to knock off a federal cop?"

"Ah, come on," Truman protested. "I was led to believe you, of all people, weren't afraid to do what it takes."

It was as though they'd returned to that fateful first meeting, the man having learned nothing. There was an art to this, whether one was conducting business or bloodshed. Both relied on a certain finesse—the ability to approach the situation with a level head, anticipate the potential complications, and act accordingly. Shooting first and thinking later almost always led to far greater trouble, a lesson Truman had still not grasped. The sudden disappearance of a federal inspector might well compel the government to open the lid on the provincial Pandora's box that was Quebec and flush them all out for good.

"And this coming from the man conspiring with the Feds. The first hint of trouble, and you rolled, belly-up," Mathias shot back.

"I told you I didn't give them nothing," Truman spat.

"You handed them my name and the details of our arrangement wrapped up in a nice little bow."

Truman frowned, his pale eyes narrowing. "They had your name before they came to me. They were already looking into you."

"Because your tip-off launched the whole fucking investigation," Mathias growled, tossing his smoking cigarette at Truman's feet. "All hush-hush, too, getting them to strike your name from the record."

"What the fuck are you talking about?" Truman exclaimed.

Mathias felt a sliver of reservation at the baffled expression on Truman's face. It was a performance, more of the man's bullshit, but for a moment, it looked pretty fucking convincing. "I had you followed—I know you've been meeting with her," Mathias snapped. "You think it's a coincidence they discovered the link to the holding company right after you and Allen were seen together?"

"Why would I make a tip-off to the Feds?" Truman thundered, his neck flaring red. "I'd be shooting myself in the foot. I'm just as tied to the shipments as you are."

"They already had you against the wall. You're just trading one felony for another. This way, you can pass the buck, and who better to pass it to than me?"

"Look..." Truman rubbed his chin with the back of his hand, lowering his voice. "The company—I'll admit, that was me. I have a fucking trial date. I was desperate. But I swear to God—"

"You've been desperate for a while now, Truman. The mess with Border Services—that's a year in the making. You expect me to believe when you got word of it brewing, you didn't send a friendly message up the chain to try and see what you could get out of? The trouble with the Feds is that one bit of information is never enough—they'll always want more. And then you end up where you are now, spilling your fucking guts. Once a rat..."

He didn't need to finish. A silence fell over the warehouse. Above them, the overhead lights flickered.

"So, what are we starting, Mathias?" Truman said, a hard glint in his eye. "We gonna have ourselves a little shoot-out? As you can see, you're a man down." Beside him, Truman's lackey gave a slow grin and shoved his meaty hands beneath his armpits.

"You forget where you are," Mathias said. "This is my city. Here, I'm never outnumbered." He saw the Reaper's face slacken as he processed the fact that he was now in enemy territory. "And we aren't starting shit." Mathias slid his hands into the pockets of his slacks. "I'm finishing it. This alliance was built on trust, and you sold me out. The family is done with you, Truman. We're pulling port access and wiping our hands of the shipments. See how far you get when the door closes in your face. You think after what you tried to pull tonight, Allen's going to come back for more? You blew your chance at a plea, and in a month, whatever's left of you will be finished off in court—I won't even have to lift a finger."

"You're making a mistake, Beauvais," Truman warned.

"My only mistake was not pulling the plug earlier," Mathias said. "Fortunately, that oversight has now been rectified."

"There's more hands on this than you think," Truman said viciously, spit forming at the corners of his mouth. "Someone else is looking to bring us down."

There remained an inkling of a feeling—something that didn't quite add up. Yet Truman had already admitted to lying, and what was this but more smokescreen?

"You would say that, wouldn't you?" Mathias sneered. "How is it that you have a trial date, but I'm the one who found myself in the hole? I won't stand around while you play me, Truman. I'm taking the girl, and I'm leaving. You're not my problem anymore."

As Mathias walked to the warehouse doors, he slipped a hand beneath his jacket to grip the handle of his gun, readying himself for the man's reprisal. But Truman remained quiet, letting him leave.

No sooner had Rayan removed the metal bar from the door than the lackey who'd been in the room with Allen burst from it, blocking his path.

"There you are," the man said, flushed and furious, his hoarse voice a lingering reminder of Rayan's blow to the throat. "What do you think you're doing?"

"Who's asking?" Rayan hadn't planned on striking him, but something about the way he'd gripped Allen's wrist and the fear in her eyes had pulled him back to another time, sending a surge of violence through him.

"You little shit!"

He saw the man coming. The old Rayan would have ducked and smashed a fist beneath his jaw. But in the time it took Rayan to grapple with the resistance that thought brought on, a set of knuckles made impact with his cheek, and he hit the ground, dazed. His muscle memory had deserted him, his conscience too fractured to fight back.

He felt the metal barrel of the pistol dig into his lower back. Rayan had only to reach for it, and the man would be finished. But he couldn't do it. He couldn't get his fingers to move.

"Finally figured out where you belong," the man jeered, standing over him. "Down on your ass—"

There was an audible crack as Mathias struck the Reaper clean on the side of the head, teeth bared, his face twisted in fury. Rayan hadn't witnessed his former capo's particular shade of brutality in a while, and the sight sent ice down his spine.

The man tottered, almost able to recover, but Mathias was faster, a fist to the guts sending him crashing against the warehouse wall. "We're done here," Mathias instructed Truman's lackey. "Take it up with your boss inside."

The man glowered, managing to heave himself up and stagger to the front of the building. Rayan got to his feet as Mathias approached.

"You let that ape lay hands on you," Mathias snarled. He reached out to grip Rayan's chin and turned his head to inspect the bruise throbbing along his cheek. He clicked his tongue. "If I taught you one thing"—his voice was lower now, his grip softening, gray eyes revealing a flicker of concern—"it was how to defend yourself." Mathias dropped his hand. "Come on." They walked back to the car, and Mathias got in behind the wheel, pulled out of the alley, and sped down the road. "Of all the fucking things," he muttered. "I knew you shouldn't have come."

He was angry, not in the scornful way he'd been in those early days when Rayan had fucked up on a job but in a way that made him grip the steering wheel with both hands. Rayan stared at those hands. He could see the redness along the knuckles even in the low light. His fault. Mathias was right—he shouldn't have come. He was no longer able to protect himself, let alone Mathias.

"What happened in there?" he asked, if only to distract them from his failure.

"It's done," Mathias said curtly. "Truman and the family are done."

Rayan attempted to read his impossible expression.

"And Allen...?" Mathias returned.

The full weight of what Rayan had done came crashing down on him. He fought to control the panic that constricted his throat. He'd gone behind Mathias's back to make a deal with the inspector. There was no version of reality in which that would go down well, and judging by the grim look on Mathias's face, things were already far from good.

Rayan recalled their conversation back at the man's apartment and how Mathias had been adamant about staying and taking his chances here. Mathias's loyalty to the family was his blind spot, and as the ship began to sink, it would pull him under. This loyalty—the need to prove that he wouldn't buckle under pressure or betray the allegiances to which he'd given his word—had prevented Mathias from using the photos to his own advantage.

But Rayan couldn't stand the thought of what would happen if Allen succeeded in taking Mathias down. Over the past few years, he'd watched parts of Mathias emerge from the darkness, bit by bit. When Mathias had returned from his short stint in jail, for a moment, it had felt like he'd once again disappeared from view. He couldn't let Mathias lose what had been so painstakingly reclaimed. So Rayan had taken his chances, hoping that he could save Mathias without destroying what they had.

"I got her out," Rayan said evenly.

"Bet she was an ungrateful little shrew about it too."

Rayan thought about how the inspector had gripped his arm. He'd felt the clench of terror in her fingers. "That about sums it up," he said, staring straight ahead.

Mathias pulled the car up to the curb a street away from the safe house. "You hesitated," he said into the silence of the cab. "You haven't done that since the beginning."

Beside him in the passenger seat, Rayan pressed his lips hard together.

"Give it to me."

Rayan reached for the gun in his waistband and placed it down on the dashboard. "I could've done it," he said, his voice tight, unconvincing.

"I won't let you put me in that position again. From here on, you stay out of this, understood?"

"Mathias—"

"Don't fucking start with me," he growled. "This isn't your world anymore. You'd do well to remember that."

It was just as much for his own sake as it was Rayan's. When he'd stepped out of the warehouse to find the man on the ground, the explosion of rage had been blinding and immediate. He didn't function well when thoughts of Rayan's safety crowded out all reason.

Mathias felt Rayan's eyes on him, but he refused to meet his gaze. There was a click as Rayan opened the passenger door and then a thud as he closed it behind him and disappeared into the darkened street. Mathias let out a slow breath and attempted to straighten the mess in his head. He wasn't sure exactly what would come of cutting ties with Truman, but he did know that it wouldn't stop the Feds. If the threat of retribution hadn't deterred Truman, who would be next?

His eyes fell to the gun on the dashboard. The look on Rayan's face as he stared up at Truman's lackey—that was the kid from before, brought suddenly back to life. He remembered that look from the early days, when Rayan had yet to prove himself as his second.

It would have been about a month after Mathias had taken him on. There had been one attempt prior to this, and Rayan had failed spectacularly, proving right all of Mathias's assumptions. He'd driven Rayan back to the Collections office and told the man he was done with him. But Rayan had refused to get out of the car, imploring him to give him one more chance, and Mathias, taken aback by the intensity of his reaction—this from a kid who barely spoke—had reluctantly agreed.

"You've been here too long not to have skin in the game," Mathias admonished Rayan as they got out of the Mercedes and headed toward the row of tumbledown houses set back from the road. "What happened last time..." They approached the house at the far end of the row, nestled in a forest of ivy and overgrown shrubs. "Choke like that again, and don't bother showing your face tomorrow. Understood?"

"Understood."

"If you're serious about this, then prove it. Loyalty doesn't mean shit unless it's sealed in blood." Mathias came to a stop and turned to his second. "There will be no more chances."

"Yes, boss."

From where they stood on the street, the building looked abandoned. Heavy wooden boards shuttered the windows, and piles of junk mail were strewn about the unmown lawn. Mathias tilted his chin toward the house. "Barry Olman. He's been dodging his debts for months. It's bigger than Collections now. He's spreading rumors to rival groups, threatening to go to the cops. Word's come from up high. We need him quiet."

Rayan nodded, his face blank.

Mathias tested the handle on the back door and was surprised to find it unlocked. So Olman was slippery but not smart. They entered silently, Rayan ahead of him.

The house was dark and in disrepair. Parts of the walls had been smashed in, and loose panels hung haphazardly from the ceiling, allowing a direct view into the attic.

As they stepped into the front room, Mathias spotted a lone figure stretched out on a tattered brown sofa. He was wrapped in a pile of blankets, and in the dimness, Mathias could just make out the top of his head and the shape of an ear. Rayan removed the gun from beneath his jacket and flicked off the safety. On the sofa, the man let out a rumbling snore, almost rousing himself. Rayan stepped over and gave the sofa leg a sharp kick, startling him awake.

"Hey, what the fuck?" The man tumbled off the sofa in a stupor and quickly got to his feet.

"Olman?" Rayan asked.

The man squinted, his eyes still smeared with sleep. "What's it to you, asshole?"

Then it must have dawned on him. Olman hadn't had dealings with either Rayan or Mathias—he'd been on Franco's list—but it wouldn't be difficult to put two and two together and recognize who they represented.

"End it," Mathias instructed his second from the corner of the room. But Rayan stood, the same conflicted look on his face, the same hesitation.

Mathias felt a twinge of foreboding as he remembered the fear in the kid's eyes when they'd first met. *Too soft.* He'd thought it then, and he thought it now. Death was a fact of life in the family. To falter here would cost Rayan more than he knew.

Mathias sucked his teeth, no longer patient. He'd given Rayan a second chance, and he wasn't in the habit of giving anyone the opportunity to disappoint him twice. There was no way around it—the kid wasn't cut out for this. Mathias reached beneath his jacket and unclipped his holster, forced once again to take matters into his own hands.

His second seemed to interpret this as a sign. Before Mathias could step forward, Rayan's face hardened, and he plugged Olman with two perfectly aimed shots, one to the heart and one to the head. The man crumpled to the floor at his feet.

A silence fell over the room. It was so quiet that Mathias could hear Rayan's ragged breathing. He stood deadly still, his arm remaining outstretched, gun aimed at the space Olman had occupied just moments before.

"We're done here," Mathias said, placing a hand on his shoulder.

Rayan started as if coming out of a trance. He dropped his arm and holstered his gun with a series of jerky movements. As Mathias watched his second put himself back together, he felt an unfamiliar sense of responsibility, as though by crossing paths with Rayan that fateful day by the river, he'd unwittingly cursed him. But

Mathias hadn't seen the conflicted look again. From then on, there was no hesitation.

Back in the car, Mathias stared at the gun on the dashboard, the black barrel illuminated by the soft glow of a nearby streetlamp. Then he reached out and tossed the pistol into the glove compartment. He snapped it shut with a click. As he sat back in his seat, his body flooded with a wave of relief.

Mathias had thought he'd taken something from Rayan—torn it from him—when he'd forced his hand all those years ago. But it had never really gone. Whatever Rayan had done to function as he had during his time working for the family had faded, and Mathias was glad for it. He turned the key in the ignition and pulled the car out onto the street, his mind clearing. There was one more person he needed to see.

23

Frances sat on the sofa in her living room and looked down at the coffee table, where she'd assembled the contents of the envelope Rayan had given her. Across a series of twelve photos was a damning account of evidence against not just Hamilton Police Chief Roger Wainwright but the entire Hamilton Police Department. There was an image of Truman handing money to Wainwright in a swanky restaurant and another of the cop smoking a cigarette while his subordinate slipped a suspicious-looking envelope to the Reapers' head outside one of his strip clubs. Even more perplexing was the photo of Truman holding open a car door for the HPD chief, who was leaving the vehicle with his arms around two scantily clad women. Knowing what she knew about the women in Truman's employ, the legality of both their profession and their presence in the country—not to mention their age—was very much in question.

She sighed and picked up the bottle of beer sweating on the coaster by her elbow. She took a long swig and set it back on the table. She had a professional obligation to raise those allegations of corruption against Wainwright with the deputy commissioner. And the second she did, the full force of the RCMP would descend on the case. As Gill had said, it came down to optics, and a right-leaning government hard on crime would jump at the chance to throw the entire weight of its resources at the first sniff of police corruption. What she had on the table before her was more than a sniff.

But by handing in this evidence, she was bound to her deal with Rayan. That meant putting the Montreal investigation, already mired, on ice. The tip-off had centered on Mathias and his involvement in the Reapers-assisted shipments. With him off-limits, there was nothing left to keep it going.

It was the perfect tactic—to turn the eye of the law back on itself. Meanwhile, Mathias Beauvais and the host of other family players assembled in Montreal would return to being inconsequential, flying under the radar and escaping capture once again. Her hand had been forced. If it was ever discovered that she'd withheld these photos, she would be implicated in the fallout—sixteen years of clawing her way up the chain of command would be down the fucking drain.

Frances reached over to pick up a close-up image of Truman and Wainwright sharing a drink, the Reaper's mouth turned up in a grin. This evening, cornered in the back room of that dingy warehouse, she'd realized there was nothing Truman wouldn't do to protect himself, be it bribing the chief of a municipal police department or quietly dispatching a federal inspector who'd asked one too many questions. Why had Mathias, then—cut from the same cloth—come to bail her out?

And then there was Rayan. Frances pulled her laptop from the bag by her feet, placed it on the table beside the mosaic of photos, and logged into the agency database. She typed in the young man's name and pulled up the case file she'd created then scrolled through her notes—the attempts she'd made to connect him to the Montreal crime family and his father's disjointed testimony, which the old man had recanted several days later over the phone, flustered and speaking in a panicked mumble.

It was an empty case full of dead ends and question marks. She still hadn't been able to determine the true nature of his activities in Toronto or the reason for his sudden reappearance in Montreal. And then, after interfering with Truman's plans, he'd handed her the envelope of photos.

What do I do to make sure it's not him?

It didn't make his or Mathias's actions any clearer. But what did that matter now?

Frances moved the cursor over to the file settings and selected a tag from the drop-down menu. The case updated, a red label appearing over Rayan's photo: Suspended.

On the sofa beside her, Frances's phone rang. It was her sister.

"Brie's final recital was today. You said you would come," Diana said when she picked up, her tone accusatory.

Frances rolled her eyes. As if she'd spent the night lounging around watching television. She could still conjure the smell of the gangster's breath as he'd leaned in, his fingers digging into the flesh of her wrist.

"I'm sorry. Tell her I was sad to miss it."

"Were you, though? I thought you said after Ethan that you wanted to start putting family first. Prioritizing the relationships in your life."

"That's unfair, Diana," Frances said, the heat rising to her cheeks. Her sister was clueless, completely off base. "Of course that's what I want. But I've got things on my plate—people relying on me. I can't just drop everything for a dance recital."

She felt a coldness descend on the other end of the line. "I saw him, by the way," Diana said. "Ethan, at the supermarket the other day. With someone else."

Frances wondered if her sister had been saving up that particular piece of information, waiting for a time to invoke maximum effect. Well, now was as good a time as any. It seemed she was getting the stuffing kicked out of her tonight.

"Oh?" she replied breezily. "And...?"

"She's young, blond. Probably desperate to lock him down. I remember Ethan was keen to have kids. He waited for you long enough."

"Fuck you."

"No, fuck you, Frances. I believed you this time. I thought what happened with Ethan was enough for you to take stock and figure out what really mattered. And I thought me and the kids were part of that. But it's the same as always—you get so caught up, so obsessed, you can't cut yourself loose. You know, at the end of the day, no matter how many cases you solve, you still have to come home to yourself—"

Frances hung up the phone, reached for her beer, and drained it. Then she stood and walked to the window, goose bumps prickling across her skin.

In those horrible weeks of fighting before they finally broke up, Ethan had accused her of choosing work over him. "You're not your job, and until you realize that, there's no room in your life for anything else." She hadn't disputed it. After all, he was right.

And then it hit her—what had almost happened tonight. Frances felt her chest tighten and her breathing go shallow. She placed a hand on her stomach and tried to pull the air into her lungs, long and slow, but it kept catching in her throat. She stared out the window at an unfamiliar city, standing in an empty apartment that wasn't her own, completely alone.

Mathias drove to Laval, navigating the route through the city streets from memory, his thoughts elsewhere. He'd talked a big game to Truman about the family's backing, but the truth was they'd already begun to distance themselves from him. Mathias had become too dangerous, a man with a target etched on his back. It wasn't just Allen and her rabid pursuit of him—he'd now made an enemy of the Red Reapers. And with Giovanni's lofty plan to convert Collections into another faceless corporation, Mathias found himself pushed even further to the periphery. He'd been reduced to what he'd always despised among the bloated ranks of family elite: deadweight.

Disappear with me. Rayan's words circled his mind.

Leaving was not an impossible prospect logistically. The question wasn't whether he could do it but what it would mean if he did. He'd left the city before when he'd been reassigned to Hamilton, and the experience had been seared with humiliation.

Why doesn't this feel the same? What exactly am I fighting to hold on to in Montreal? Mathias reached for the desire that had fueled his ambition from the very beginning, when he had first started out with the family and refused to take no for an answer. But he couldn't find it.

And then there was Rayan. After tonight, it was clear that he was no longer equipped to live in this world, and Mathias was doing him no favors by keeping him here. Rayan was stuck in limbo, torn between Mathias's life and his own.

Mathias pulled the car up outside Château Suzdal and cut the engine. A Russian soldier led him into the front of the restaurant, where the tables were strewn with the remains of a large gathering. Belkov sat at a booth in the corner, drinking.

"Eightieth birthday," he announced when Mathias sat down across from him. Belkov flipped over an empty glass and poured him a drink. "Can you imagine getting to be that old?"

"I'd rather take one to the head," Mathias said, picking up the glass.

"Likewise," the Russian replied. They lifted their glasses in unison and downed their shots.

"Truman's cut off. Thought you should know, in case he decides to start something."

"Let him try."

"Give Gurin a heads-up. The Reapers have more weight to throw around in Hamilton."

Belkov nodded. "While I appreciate the warning, what does this mean for everything else?"

Fuck all. Mathias felt the shift in him then—the slow admission of defeat. "Allen's not backing down."

"And the family?"

"What about the family?"

Belkov gave him an indulgent look. "Come on, Mathias. I know how they get when the cops start sniffing."

Mathias fixed the man with a hard stare.

Belkov returned a knowing smile. "And so do you. Seems you're backed hard into a corner, my friend. Not much left to do except—" He laughed, shaking his head in awe. "No, could it be? I never thought I'd see the day when you'd hightail it out of Montreal."

"I'm not running," Mathias snapped. Yet wasn't that exactly what he was considering? "But perhaps it makes sense to leave for a while, see if the heat dies down."

"What does the big boss have to say about that?"

It's nothing personal, just self-preservation. "I imagine he'd be relieved."

"His loss," Belkov grunted. "So you came here to plead for my cooperation? Make sure as soon as your ass is gone, I don't slam my boot down on Bianchi's throat?"

"No. Though maybe you'd consider that basic courtesy on account of our history."

The Russian snorted.

Mathias was struck by the realization that this wasn't the first time he'd found himself at odds with the family, and both times, the Bratva boss had held firm, refusing to pull away. He remembered how after Junior's attempted hit, Belkov had become enraged at Mathias's insinuation that he'd offer up his own soldiers as cannon fodder. *There is still loyalty among us,* he'd said.

Mathias gave a wry smile. Loyalty could be found in the strangest places. "I will give my thanks, though. For your assistance over the years."

Belkov cocked his head, observing him carefully. Then he reached his hand across the table, and Mathias shook it. "I can't make any promises for Bianchi or that group of yours, but for you, I'll extend a personal guarantee. No matter where you end up, if you find yourself in need of assistance, the Bratva will answer."

Mathias released his hand with a curt nod, and Belkov filled both their glasses to the brim. "*Santé.*" Mathias brought his final drink with the Russian to his lips and downed it.

When Mathias let himself into the safe house, Rayan was sitting on the sofa with a book splayed across his lap. Mathias stepped over to the small table in the corner of the living room and saw Rayan had made his move. He took in the state of the board then lifted his queen and captured the man's rook. "Check."

Rayan was looking at him, his expression guarded.

"But you knew that already."

"I had a feeling," Rayan said, closing the book and placing it down beside him. He stared at the cover, appearing to choose his words carefully. "You were right, earlier. I hesitated."

"Rayan—"

"I thought I was still that person, but I don't think I am anymore."

"I don't want you to be."

Rayan's gaze snapped to his face, and Mathias moved into the room. He stood across from Rayan and slipped his hands into his pockets, his fingers grazing the smooth edge of his lighter, which he traced absently with his thumb. "What do you know about Northern France?"

Rayan blinked, taken off guard. He shook his head. "Nothing."

"There's a property I own in Calais, a small coastal city."

Recognition slowly registered in Rayan's eyes. "There was always a plan B."

Mathias sighed. "I've been doing this a long time. It would've been foolish not to have one. Just never thought I'd have to execute it."

"So you're leaving." The statement filled the room, lodging in the space between them.

Mathias looked at Rayan—the swell of his lips, those unwavering brown eyes. "Will you come?"

"Of course." There was no hesitation.

"You don't know the first thing about the place," Mathias scoffed.

Rayan shrugged and got to his feet. "It doesn't matter."

He thought about the way Rayan waited until he believed Mathias was asleep to burrow against him, how soft his hair was when wound through Mathias's fingers, how his forehead furrowed while he was reading, silently mouthing certain words as if committing them to memory.

"Why?" Mathias asked hollowly.

"When you left me at Guillet's, you told me my time would come," Rayan said. "You looked at me like I had a future. And now I have one because of you."

Mathias frowned. He remembered the exchange only vaguely. He'd been compelled by the need to offer Rayan something—a shred of hope to bookend their grim encounter. At the time, it had felt like tossing scraps to a dog under the table, but it had clearly meant something to the man.

Rayan walked over to stand before Mathias. "You say you're not a good person. You act like there's nothing behind the wall. But I've seen it. *Good* isn't a fixed state—it can be there when you think it's not. And when it's someone important, it's there in everything you do, even while you look the other way—even when no one else can see it."

That first day in Cyprus, when Rayan had believed Mathias had come to clip him, Mathias had thought if his intentions could be so plainly mistaken—if his love, already strange and fledgling, was indistinguishable from the threat of death—then he truly must be a monster. Yet Rayan had seen him, all of him, and wanted him anyway. For two years, he'd stood by the door each time Mathias left, a look in his eyes as though willing him to turn back, and said nothing. Because they both knew that was how it had to be.

Could it be different? Does such a reality exist? Mathias had been convinced it didn't and his very being was molded in the shape of his allegiance to the family. Now he wasn't so sure.

"It's not going to be easy," Mathias said quietly.

"Nothing ever is."

Of course Rayan knew that. "Come here."

Rayan stepped into his arms, and Mathias pulled him close. He brought his mouth to Rayan's and felt the whir in his head cease as he kissed him—soft, slow, impossibly warm. Mathias brushed his fingers against the man's cheek, and Rayan leaned into the touch.

"What made you change your mind about leaving?" Rayan asked.

Mathias stared down at him. That uncurbed softness had the power to bend him. "You can't stay here, Rayan," he said finally, no longer able to deny the truth. "And I can't stay without you."

Something imperceptible flickered in Rayan's eyes, then he dropped his head and pressed his face into Mathias's neck. "You know I love you," he said, his voice a fierce whisper.

The words were hard enough to hear and even more impossible to say. They revealed a missing part of Mathias's programming, a language never used that had long been forgotten.

"I know," Mathias said.

24

When Mathias had returned to the safe house the previous evening, Rayan had been moments from coming clean about his conversation with Allen. It couldn't stay buried between them, despite Rayan's growing dread of how Mathias would react when he found out. But before he could tell him, Mathias had revealed his intention to leave, and Rayan knew if he brought it up then, it would destroy any chance of getting the man out of Montreal. Perhaps if he waited until they were out of the country, he would be able to convince Mathias of his reasoning.

Even as he thought it, Rayan cringed at his own naivety. He was thinking like a philosophy student. Mathias didn't give a shit about a well-reasoned argument. He viewed loyalty in absolutes—you were either friend or foe, with him or against him. Philosophical arguments might be even-tempered. Mathias was not.

The simple fact remained: Rayan had made his decision, and he had to be willing to live with the fallout. While he couldn't bear to lose what they had—and he continued to blindly tell himself it wouldn't come to that—the prospect of losing Mathias entirely to prison—or worse—was unthinkable. If he wanted to keep Mathias safe long enough to get him out, Rayan would have to keep his mouth shut.

In the end, there wasn't much for Rayan to prepare. He was already living out of a duffel bag, having returned once again to a transient life. There were parallels, to be sure. He felt a familiar unsteadiness, the same way his abrupt exit from Toronto had kicked up dust from the past. But this was different. This time, he wasn't going alone.

Nothing in his old apartment was worth going back for. Mathias had assured him everything else could be settled after they'd left, lest they risk setting off any surveillance alarm bells. Despite his initial reluctance, Mathias was curiously prepared when it came to the logistics of disappearing. Then again, it made sense that Mathias—who never left anything to chance—would have a contingency plan.

He was unsentimental that way—things were things, money was money, people were people. Rayan secretly counted himself as the exception to that last rule.

One thing remained unresolved. It had started as a wisp of an idea and was launched fully into being by Mathias's words the night Rayan had seen his life condensed into a bleak stack of paperwork. The man's assertion had rung true— Rayan had always been a passive participant in the events of his past, thrown quickly into their paralyzing grip and allowing the guilt and shame to control him. He couldn't put right past wrongs, but he could decide how to confront them.

Mathias had stayed over, and Rayan lay in bed, listening to him in the shower while the morning sunlight broke through the gaps in the window blinds. Mathias emerged from the bathroom with an air of grim determination that followed him out to the living room, where he plucked his jacket from the back of the sofa and shrugged it on. Rayan met him at the door as he was pulling on his coat. He brought a hand to Mathias's chin and lowered his face to kiss him. Only then did some of the stiffness leave the man's shoulders.

He held Rayan close for a moment, exhaling into his neck, and then released him. "There are things to take care of. I'll be in touch."

After Mathias left, Rayan looked up the hospital he'd seen named in his mother's coroner's report and called the patient records department. He was directed through a series of bureaucratic gatekeepers only to be told that none of the records from the time of her death had been digitalized. Short of submitting an official information request to access a storeroom of archived medical files, there was no way of determining exactly where she'd ended up. As for his brother, Rayan was given a number and told the section of the cemetery in Laval where he'd been buried in a pauper's grave.

Resolute, Rayan decided to take his chances and venture from the safe house despite the risk. When he got to the cemetery, he walked through the rows of small wooden markers until he came upon the one bearing his brother's number. He stood there for a long time, looking down at the grass-covered section of dirt as though it would somehow translate to repentance. It pained him to think his brother had ended up here, nameless and forgotten.

Instead of heading back, Rayan caught a bus and rode it east across the suburb. The Islamic Cemetery of Quebec was a short walk from the bus stop. He found himself rooted outside the gate, his courage deserting him.

Forgive me, Mama.

As though she had conjured him, a short, balding man appeared by the front door of the squat brick building inside the compound and began walking toward

Rayan. He lifted the latch on the gate and beckoned him inside. "*As-salamu alaikum.*"

Rayan repeated the greeting woodenly.

"Are you here to offer *du'ā's* today, young man?"

"No, I don't... I'm nonpracticing."

The man gave him a kind smile. "Son, all are welcome here. I'm Imam Amir. What can I help you with?"

"I'd like to see the plots."

The imam nodded. "Are they coming from a facility? We can help make the arrangements."

"They're already gone. But I wanted something..." He wasn't sure what he wanted—just not a number on a wooden marker.

"To honor their memory?"

Rayan nodded.

"Come with me." Imam Amir ushered him into the building and led Rayan through a series of corridors that smelled of agarwood and sparked a flurry of memories, like a key unlocking a cage.

"Who are you wanting to memorialize?"

"My mother. And my brother."

The imam stopped to look at him. "We'll want two plaques, then. Side by side so they can be together."

Rayan's breath stalled in his lungs. The two of them, lost separately to the world beyond, would finally be reunited. While he could no longer be with their mother, the least he could do was ensure that Tahir didn't share the same fate.

"Together," Rayan murmured, astonished at the peace that thought brought him.

They walked outside to a large area of land behind the building, filled with modest graves. The imam paused to recite a short greeting to the cemetery's inhabitants, wishing them peace. Rayan gazed out across the grassy field, where a line of mature oaks marked the perimeter. In the far corner by the boundary fence was a stone garden dotted with small concrete plaques.

Imam Amir led him down to the garden and gestured toward several available spots. "We know a ritual burial isn't always possible. Family may live overseas or have been put to rest elsewhere, so the plaques allow us to hold a place in their honor."

Rayan stopped when he reached a section of the garden that was shaded by nearby trees, tranquil, quiet. "Here."

"A beautiful place. Inside, we can discuss your chosen verses."

Rayan followed him back through the cemetery and into the reception building. The man opened the door to a small room off the hallway and stepped inside. From the doorway, Rayan could see the prayer rug in the corner, positioned before an alcove in the wall where the Quran lay open. He froze, unable to cross the threshold. To him, it was no longer anything but superstition, yet to his mother, it had been important. He could not bring what he'd become through that door.

"I can't," Rayan said, a tightness in his throat.

The old man turned and gave him a thoughtful look. "Wherever your life has taken you, son, and the ways in which you have strayed from the path, know that Allah's divine mercy has the power to pardon even the gravest sins." Imam Amir pulled out a chair across from the desk and indicated for Rayan to sit.

He made his way into the room, and they both sat down, the imam reaching for his glasses resting on the desk and placing them carefully on the bridge of his nose. "Now, let us talk of your mother and brother. Tell me their names."

Rayan said their names and, like a river bursting its banks, began to speak—about his mother and those Saturday mornings, the books she'd given him, the nights when he'd been sick and she'd kneel by his bed, stroking his hair. He spoke of his brother and the fights they'd had, the rivalry, and those days on the street with nothing but the knowledge that each was all the other had. Before him, Imam Amir sat perfectly still, listening.

Rayan spoke until the words dried up in his mouth and he fell silent. Then the imam picked up his pen and, in scrawling cursive, wrote two separate lines of scripture onto a sheet of paper. He slid it toward Rayan, and it was as though the man had known his mother and Tahir without ever having met them. Rayan nodded, and Imam Amir smiled, gathering everything up into a neat bundle.

"The plaques will be ready in a few weeks and installed shortly after." The imam took Rayan's payment and stood. "It was a pleasure meeting you, young man."

Rayan got to his feet and was struck by a resounding sadness. To think he'd denied them this peace for all those years. "I should've done this a long time ago."

Imam Amir laid a hand on Rayan's shoulder. "But you are here now. And that is all that matters."

Mathias's mother was unusually reserved when he arrived at her apartment that afternoon. Now that the decision had been made, there was a list of things that required his attention, and he wanted to make the most of the lull that had followed their interference in Truman's plan. Allen had gone quiet, but he knew it was only a matter of time before she appeared to lay down the next obstacle for him to vault over.

His mother stood at the front door, her forehead furrowing, before leading Mathias into the kitchen and reaching for the kettle to heat water for coffee. This wasn't one of his regular calls—she was well aware that he wouldn't willingly visit her more than once in the span of a month. Even that had been too frequent for Mathias, the need to leave kicking in as soon as he set foot inside. It felt oddly freeing to be here on his own terms rather than out of some misplaced sense of filial duty.

Marguerite made the coffee in silence, and Mathias took a seat at the kitchen table, watching her. As an adult, he'd grown accustomed to her endless chatter, but this felt more like the mother of his childhood—cold, sullen. They'd shared the same space but had always seemed to occupy different parts of it. When Mathias was young, she would breeze past him without a word, as if he was in her way and it was easier to simply pretend he wasn't there. Unless she needed him, of course, and then there was nowhere in the apartment to hide. Even then, he'd known it wasn't really him she needed—he just happened to be the person closest.

His mother placed two cups of coffee down on the table and sat across from him. She pressed her lined lips together, small wrinkles appearing at the corners of her mouth. Despite the impromptu nature of his visit, her makeup was applied perfectly.

"This is unexpected," she said.

"You're always at me to come by, so here I am."

"No," she said, shaking her head. "Something's different. You're different."

Mathias realized on some level, she already knew he was leaving—she was primed for it. His mother could smell desertion coming from a mile away. His gaze moved to the collection of vitamins and supplements lined up along the kitchen counter, a shrine to his mother's unrelenting effort to maintain herself and delay the inevitable. Staring at the jars and vials, he recalled another bottle—small, amber, with a prescription label affixed to the front.

"When I was eleven," Mathias said, the memory coming back to him in slow motion, "he called to say he wouldn't come anymore, and you emptied a bottle of pills into your hand. Said if I didn't call him back and make him change his mind, you'd swallow them."

His mother bristled. "That's what you want to do—come here and rehash old memories? When did you get so nostalgic?"

"I picked up the phone, but I left off the last number."

His mother stood jerkily, picking up the cups of untouched coffee as though rescinding her offer.

"I stood there, pretending it rang and rang." Mathias looked up at her. "Because I wanted you to do it."

The cups trembled in his mother's hands. "Is this some cruel joke? Why are you talking about this all of a sudden?"

"I was eleven, with a father who didn't want me and a mother I wanted dead."

She stepped away from the table and slammed the cups down on the kitchen counter, the coffee sloshing over the tops and spilling down the sides.

"He changed his mind anyway, didn't he?" Mathias said. "Then ten years later, he changed it back. This time for good."

Her blue eyes burned. "You think I don't know you hate me? You think you haven't made that clear all these years?"

"And you don't hate me?" he spat. "I was raised knowing everything went bad after I came along."

His mother didn't deny it, and he didn't expect her to. If Mathias had been a pawn, an object in their poisonous love affair, she had been too. Except his mother had chosen her fate, and that was too pathetic to hate.

"I don't think that anymore," he said quietly. "Maybe that's what's different."

Marguerite blinked, her face wiped clean. She stared at him, her eyes welling with tears. "I just wanted him to love me more than anyone else."

Mathias felt a tearing in his chest. *How petty.* What a shallow riptide he'd been pulled into. He'd been tossed about in its turbulence for too long.

"I'm going away," he said. "I might not be back."

"Why? What's happened?"

"Nothing." *Everything.* "It felt like time for a change." Mathias stood and pulled out a slip of paper from his jacket. He placed it on the table. "I've made arrangements. Monthly payments into an account under your name. You'll be taken care of."

"And you?"

He thought of the darkened room with the locked door, dinners of cold canned soup alone at the kitchen table, the glare of the television as it taunted him with lives so unlike his own—fathers who doted on their children, mothers who remembered birthdays.

Mathias smirked. "If I learned one thing from you, it was that I can take care of myself."

25

Deputy Commissioner Gill's face shifted rapidly from astonishment to disappointment as he shuffled through the stack of photos Frances had handed him in his office at the RCMP headquarters in Ottawa. On the drive over from Montreal, she'd tried to predict exactly how the man would react to the news. He wasn't nearly as surprised as she'd imagined. Perhaps in his time on the force, he'd become well acquainted with the various ways a case might turn.

"Beauvais gave you these?"

"No, his subordinate."

"Just what we need—more scrutiny." The deputy commissioner tossed the photos down on his desk. "You know, Inspector, sometimes I wonder if we're more susceptible to this sort of thing because we spend our days in the muck. We know exactly how it's done and how to cover it up."

"That doesn't make it any better."

"Of course it doesn't. If anything, it makes it worse," he said, pressing his thumbs against the bridge of his nose. "So, what are we handing over in return?"

"A moratorium on the investigation into Beauvais's involvement with the Hamilton shipments." Frances thrummed her fingers against Gill's desk. "You could say I was somewhat ambushed on this one. Caught between a rock and a hard place."

The deputy commissioner looked up. "If the commissioner asks, I'll back your call. I'd say we got off rather lightly, considering. If I'm being honest, I could barely justify sending you out there, let alone the continued man-hours. Maybe Beauvais has done us a favor."

"How can you say that?" she snapped, forgetting herself. "He was clearly involved, and those shipments were just the tip of the iceberg. If I had more time—"

"Well, you're out of time, Inspector," Gill said, gesturing at the pile of photos. "It's done. I'll go ahead and officially suspend the investigation. I need you to roll back any active alerts and outstanding surveillance measures you have going. We can't be seen to be tracking the man—or anyone else for that matter—without legitimate cause. You know as well as I do that our methods have been subject to a considerable amount of pushback in recent years."

"I shouldn't have agreed to it," she muttered.

"Look, I appreciate the dedication, but we've got to be realistic here," the deputy commissioner said matter-of-factly. "You had a call to make, and it's clear—not just to me, but I imagine, very shortly, to a hell of a lot of big players in the government—that this business with Wainwright was the more pressing of the two. I know it's hard for you to admit when you're beat, Frances, but it's time to pull back."

Not hard—fucking impossible. She'd always pushed through to an outcome that, if not a complete success, was damn near close to it. That was what rattled her about all of this—not just that she hadn't succeeded but that she'd so clearly been made to look like a failure.

"I'd like you to start tying things up in Montreal. Let the local office take the lead," Gill said, sweeping the photos into a folder on his desk. "I've got a few cases coming up that I could use your help with."

She'd traipsed off with such bold intentions, thinking she could accomplish what others had tried and failed, only to return months later empty-handed. But the look on the deputy commissioner's face was enough to make her hold her tongue. The man would not be swayed.

"Yes, sir," Frances said, quashing her humiliation.

Frances left the office immediately after their meeting. She couldn't bear to stand around shooting the shit with her old colleagues. She'd be back here before long anyway.

Her mind ground against the disappointment as she drove aimlessly through town, refusing to head back to her empty house. Frances pulled up outside a popular dive bar she and Ethan used to frequent. It was barely five, and the place looked dead. She headed straight for the bar and ordered a vodka tonic, which she knocked back, and then promptly ordered another.

Frances was on her third drink when a well-dressed man slipped into the seat beside her, not bothering to ask whether it was taken. He turned to her, brimming with confidence, and gave her a brilliant smile, his whitened teeth glistening in the dim room. He must have been at least forty, but his laid-back demeanor made him seem younger. She returned the smile—he seemed friendly enough. She wondered how long it had been since she'd engaged in easy conversation that hadn't been riddled with threats and lies.

Too long, she decided, crossing her legs and giving the man her full attention.

"Drinking alone?" he asked smoothly.

"Not anymore."

The man's beer arrived, and he raised it jovially. "I'll drink to that."

They clinked glasses, and he moved in closer. In the back of her mind, she had a sneaking suspicion that he was the kind of guy with a sixth sense for sniffing out lonely women. "I'm Kyle."

"Frances," she replied before picking up her glass and downing the remainder of her drink.

The next few hours passed in a blur. She remembered getting up to go to the bathroom at some point, and when she got back, Kyle had leaned over and given her a sloppy, open-mouthed kiss, which she returned. The next thing she knew, they were heading out the door together, his arm looped around her waist as she discovered her legs were laughably unsteady. Kyle mentioned that his apartment was nearby, and Frances turned to give him a wide smile.

"I'd love to see it."

They walked down the street to a two-story block of condos, and Kyle led her into the elevator, his hand moving down from her waist to cup her ass. He fumbled with his keys when they reached the door to his apartment and grabbed her as soon as he managed to shut the door behind them, pushing his tongue into her open mouth. She liked the feel of his hands on her, rough and clumsy as he removed her coat. It felt good to be touched, and even through her drunken haze, she liked that he wanted her.

They collapsed on the sofa, and Kyle popped the buttons of her blouse while yanking it open impatiently to fondle her breasts. He stood and wrenched off her pants then thumbed open his jeans and pulled his cock out from the open zipper. He knelt on the sofa, spreading her legs and moving between them.

"Condom," Frances said lazily, pressing her palm against his chest to hold him off.

Kyle gave a low laugh. "I think we're good," he said, pushing her underwear to one side and thrusting into her, unsheathed.

Frances was struck by a vivid memory—how Ethan would run his fingers down the inside of her thigh as his other hand reached into the nightstand drawer to grab that little square of foil, not wanting to break their rhythm, while at the same time honoring the mechanics of the exchange.

A shot of sobriety flooded her system, and she drew her leg back and kicked Kyle hard in the face, knocking him backward onto the carpet. She got to her feet, looking down at him sprawled on the floor, clutching his nose and gasping. "I'm a cop, you asshole," she growled. "Don't you ever fucking try that with anyone else."

Frances yanked on her pants and grabbed her coat then moved to the front door, let herself out, and slammed it behind her. She ignored the look the other woman gave her in the elevator as she stood, buttoning up her blouse. Once back outside, Frances retraced her steps to the bar and reached into her pocket for her phone, thankful it hadn't fallen out during their ill-fated encounter. She punched in the number of a taxi service.

"Frances?"

She looked up to see Ethan and a group of his friends about to step into the bar. Her heart dropped. *How small is this fucking town?*

He motioned for his friends to go on ahead and stepped over. "It's been a while," he said with an easy smile.

He'd grown out his beard, and his hair was shorter, buzzed along the sides, but she saw the familiar streaks of gray at the roots. She'd been with him when he'd found the first one, barely containing her laughter at his horrified expression. The gray hair had grown on him, though—just another thing he'd taken on board with that evenhanded steadiness of his. A steadiness she'd taken for granted. He was still the one she compared all the others to, and none of them ever measured up.

Frances felt her chest tighten. "Has it?" she asked, the phone dangling from her hand.

Ethan tilted his head to one side, studying her. "I think you missed one," he said gently and reached over to fasten the errant button in the middle of her blouse. Frances realized how she must have looked, and her stomach turned.

"Do you need a ride?" he asked.

"No," she said adamantly.

"Let's try that again, this time without the infuriating stubbornness," he said, seeing right through her. "Do you need a ride?"

Frances nodded.

They rode the short distance to her neighborhood and parked on the street.

Ethan let her into her house like he still lived there. He looked around at the empty spots where his furniture had been. "I see you've gone minimalist."

Frances pulled up a stool in the kitchen and sat down. "Keep going," she goaded him. "How else have I proven you right? Cold, single-minded, career-obsessed... Am I forgetting parts of your breakup speech?"

Ethan sighed and shoved his hands into the pockets of his jeans. He wore a faded Wolf Parade T-shirt beneath his unbuttoned winter coat. "Frances, are you all right?"

"I'm fine. Just peachy."

"And the bad guys?" he teased, the way he used to, equating her work with some cheesy superhero comic. "Still kicking their asses?"

"Good, bad—I can't tell the two apart anymore," she said, her voice curling bitterly.

It was true. The clarity that had always been there, propelling her from one investigation to the next, had abandoned her. She recalled the relief she'd felt when Rayan had appeared in the back room of the warehouse in Montreal. To think she'd been safer with him than at Kyle's condo...

Ethan frowned. "What's going on?"

"They're shelving my investigation. Months of work up in smoke. I'm tanking, Ethan. You left. And my sister, she's asking about kids, setting me up on dates. I can't fail at everything. What the fuck do I have left?"

Ethan's eyes softened. "You're so much more than the work, Frances. I know that's hard for you to believe—God knows we fought about it more than I care to remember—but it's the truth. Honestly, the sooner you get that through your head, the happier you'll be." He stepped over, took one of her hands, and gave it a squeeze. "You win some, you lose some. And then you move on."

"Like you did?"

Ethan gave a short laugh and withdrew his hand. "Yeah, I did."

"What does she do?"

"She's a vet."

"Bit more work-life balance, I gather."

He snorted, and they shared a look—one of their old ones. It felt like only yesterday they'd shared everything—secrets whispered in the dark, dreams for the future, a bed, a home.

"I think it took you leaving for me to realize you were the love of my life," she blurted.

A pained look crossed Ethan's face. "Frances—"

"And my job falling to pieces is so hard because it's what I gave you up for." They stood in silence until she managed a soft laugh to disguise her embarrassment. "But I'm happy for you," she lied. "Really, I am."

26

"Surprised to find you here."

Mathias glanced up to see Giovanni coming down the cemetery path with a newspaper tucked under his arm and the air of a grandfather who'd wandered off from his handlers. "Wouldn't have pegged you for the sentimental type."

Beyond Giovanni, Henri stood at the entrance gate, watching. The boss's car idled in the parking lot, his driver waiting behind the wheel.

"He liked the stocks," Giovanni said, holding up the newspaper, which was folded to the financial section. He stepped past Mathias to drop it on top of Tony's grave. "Liked to play the market. He was a dumb old bastard sometimes. Never really knew what he was doing." The boss laughed. "But that's all of us, isn't it? Dabbling in things we don't fully understand."

The remark hit upon something, disturbing a smattering of thoughts that moved too quickly to capture.

"Heard you pulled the pin with Truman."

"As promised," Mathias replied. "I was waiting to tie up a few loose ends, but now's as good a time as any to tell you. I'm leaving."

Giovanni made a small grunt of acknowledgment. "So, you finally came to your senses, then. And what—you're here for the old man's blessing?"

They both looked down at Tony's grave.

"Collections is yours. Do what you want with it," Mathias said. "Far be it for me to fight you on progress with things as they stand. Tony wouldn't have liked it, but we're beyond that now."

"That's the difference between you and Tony—he was happy where he was, but you, Mathias, could never seem to climb high enough. You were never quite satisfied with your lot."

There's more hands on this than you think.

Mathias's blood went cold. The tip-off. If there was one person insidious enough to manipulate the federal police like a puppet on a string… He was a fool not to have seen it. But for some time now, he'd been sorely off his game.

"It was you."

Their eyes met, and Mathias saw in them the cold steel of a giant with the power to move mountains and crush unsuspecting men beneath his feet.

Giovanni sighed. "I can't fault you. It's in your nature and—I'll admit—was a very useful tool to have at my disposal. Until I realized it was only a matter of time before that ambition was used against me."

"Why didn't you—"

"Have you clipped?" The boss gave a low chuckle. "Where's the fun in that? I saw what happened with Piero. I didn't want to make the mistake of unleashing your particular brand of revenge if that failed." He slipped his hands into the pockets of his slacks and rocked back on his heels. "Besides, it's a little uncouth for the boss to whack one of his own council, don't you think? Wouldn't exactly send the right message."

"But enlisting the Feds to take me down—that hits the right note?" Mathias sneered. "And that bullshit with Collections… That was about covering your own ass. With me gone, there's no one even remotely qualified to run the fucking thing, so you figured you'd outsource."

Giovanni cocked his head and smiled. "See, this is why you made this difficult for me, Beauvais. Because I see myself in you. I admire your grit, your competence. You would've made a good boss—would've been my first pick, if we're being honest. But I could never shake the suspicion that you'd take it from me with a knife to the back."

Mathias had trouble recognizing the feeling that seized his chest, unsure why the boss's words pierced him like they did. He was no stranger to treachery, but this was a man he admired and had never thought to deceive.

"I wouldn't have taken it from you," Mathias said, the words stripped down so only the truth remained.

"Who knows what our future selves are capable of?" Giovanni said. "But I've survived this long by anticipating danger before it comes. I couldn't risk having you challenge me for the position. You can thank your second for the inside wire."

Mathias reeled. *Who else is in on this? Enzo, with his well-timed warning? Did I really think, after being blindsided once, it wouldn't happen again?* He remembered how he'd practically begged the boss to give him one last chance. The thought made him sick.

There was a flap of wings as a pigeon launched from the tree above their heads. Giovanni reached into the pocket of his jacket and pulled out his cigarettes. He offered the pack to Mathias, who refused to take it—an honor slighted. They stood before each other, no longer boss and subordinate but two men.

"You and the Quintino hatched this little plan?"

"The Quintino weren't involved." Giovanni placed a cigarette between his lips and lit it. "This was personal, between you and me."

"After everything I've done, you would let me rot in prison?"

"Or rot in the ground. It's up to you. Those are the only options left if you're not gone by tomorrow."

Mathias's mind skipped ahead, the runway he'd given himself immediately contracting. It was as though the walls around him were closing in. "And Truman?" he asked, buying himself time, his thoughts moving at lightning speed. "You put the heat on him to cover your tracks."

"I did you a favor there, Mathias," Giovanni replied, exhaling smoke through his teeth. "Look how quickly he turned on you. Glad you cleaned up that mess before I had to get involved."

Mathias shook his head in disbelief. "I've done many things, Bianchi, but roll over on one of my own?"

"I hardly rolled over on you. I gave them crumbs, a few details to get you noticed. If you move fast, you might even escape a conviction. And don't pretend you haven't used the Feds to your advantage. You've had someone on the inside for years."

"I used them, not the other way around," Mathias spat.

Giovanni squinted out across the maze of headstones. He raised the cigarette to his mouth and took a slow drag. Above them, the wind sent the clouds racing across the sky. "Your father buried here?"

Mathias remained silent.

Unfazed by his impudence, the boss continued. "Of course he is. Every Italian in the city ends up in this place. You know, he and I had something to do with each other back in the early days. Not much—he liked to find a comfortable spot where he could sit back, whereas I was forever chasing forward. Never made a real impression, but Christ, was he stupid. Knocking up his *goomah,* for one." Giovanni gave a short laugh, shaking his head in awe. "I mean, how fucking stupid can a man be?" His words were like salt in an open wound. "And two, overlooking the son with the most potential. The only one who'd go on to accomplish anything." Giovanni stared at him evenly. "Do you know what your brothers do?"

"No." Mathias had never been curious. The less he knew about the men who shared his blood, the better.

"One's the manager at a car rental company, and the other coaches high school hockey." The boss splayed his hands out before him as if that information was some code to be unspooled. "But there's the rub—if you'd been handed everything, Mathias, you'd be as dumb and useless as the other two." The man took another drag, a thin stream of white curling from the corner of his mouth. "You know how this game plays out. You saw it when Piero tried to have you whacked and you took the fall. This isn't the fucking schoolyard. There are no rules. Nothing is fair." Giovanni gave a rueful smile. "And yet here I am, laying it all on the line, attempting to do right by you. I must be getting old."

"Do right by me?" Mathias snarled. "That's rich."

The smile disappeared, and Giovanni's face hardened. Mathias felt the cold unfurling of things unsaid passing between them. He could be indignant, but if the boss wanted him dead, he stood now in the old man's good graces. That could change in an instant, depending on how he proceeded.

"Don't be like your father, Mathias. Don't be stupid. Do us both a favor and leave."

It rose like a beast inside him—the instinctive urge to eviscerate those who stood against him. Yet Mathias had followed that path and seen where it led, and that kind of wrath didn't belong to the life that lay beyond, a life that terrified him, in which he no longer recognized himself, but in which there existed someone who recognized him.

"Why would you let me leave?"

Giovanni gave a shrug. "Maybe I owe you. Without you, I wouldn't be sitting where I am today. I'd like to settle that particular debt."

Mathias took the ring from the finger on his right hand and dropped it onto the paving stones at his feet. "Consider my oath renounced," he said in a low voice. Then he strode past Giovanni and down the path toward the cemetery gate.

"Mathias," the boss called over his shoulder. "If you know what's good for you, you won't come back."

After leaving the cemetery, Mathias got in his car and drove to the Collections office, his mind tunneling into a singular focus. He'd once been convinced that in life, everyone was out to get him and if he didn't remain constantly vigilant, he would be eradicated. He wondered when he'd stopped believing that. It felt as though he was looking down to discover parts of himself missing, unsure exactly when they'd disappeared and who the fuck he was without them.

Mathias found his second seated behind the desk in Tony's office. The sight of him there lodged a dark splinter of fury in his temple. He felt the creep of realization—unwittingly, in his increasing absence, he'd phased Jacques out of a job, refusing to have him sit in on meetings, leaving him to clean up messes at the office while Mathias went off on his own. No wonder Jacques had gone in search of something more—the position and the recognition he thought he deserved.

Jacques stood up quickly when Mathias appeared, rearranging his face a half second too late to hide his surprise. "Didn't know you were coming in," he said, either completely unaware of the situation or entirely confident in his ability to read it.

Mathias was pretty sure it was the former. "I need to be in Sherbrooke for a meeting. Get moving," Mathias said, turning and walking out of the office as his second scrambled to keep up.

In the parking lot, Jacques got into the passenger side of the car, and Mathias pulled out onto the street. They drove in silence as Jacques gazed absently out the window. Mathias couldn't pinpoint exactly what it was about the man that had always seemed so unremarkable. He'd never been curious about what Jacques was thinking or whether he had anything to contribute to an unfolding situation. Mathias had simply registered him as a presence—he was either there, or he wasn't.

When they were far enough out of the city, Mathias turned off the highway and navigated the car along a series of back roads. It began to snow, tiny wisps of white that smeared against the windshield. Mathias waited until the road was empty of other cars before pulling the Bentley into a concealed driveway that led to a small produce farm. He cut the ignition.

"I heard a noise from the engine," he said, flicking the button beside the steering wheel to pop the hood. "Go check the oil."

When Jacques was outside, Mathias reached into the glove compartment, where he'd stashed the gun he'd taken from Rayan. He checked the chamber, got out of the car, and walked around to where his second stood peering under the hood.

"Boss, doesn't look like—" Jacques stopped when he saw Mathias with his pistol raised.

"Back up," Mathias instructed quietly. "Gun on the ground."

Jacques took a few steps backward, slowly extracted his weapon from the holster beneath his jacket, and tossed it onto the ground between them.

"Phone."

The man's phone soon followed.

With the gun still trained on his second, Mathias bent to retrieve them. He slipped the phone into his pocket and tucked Jacques's gun into the waistband of his slacks. Then he lunged forward and smashed the side of his pistol against Jacques's face. Jacques let out a pained grunt but otherwise remained silent, watching Mathias carefully as the blood streamed from his nose.

"Did you go to him, or did he come to you?"

Jacques frowned. "Who?"

"Bianchi."

"The boss?"

"Who the fuck else?" Mathias barked.

"What's this about?"

Mathias aimed his gun and fired a shot at the ground by the man's feet.

Jacques jumped back. "He asked to see me once," he said quickly, the words catching on one another. "He asked about you."

"What about me?"

"Whether I knew anything, whether you'd said anything." Jacques swallowed. "About your ambitions."

Mathias felt a coldness slide down his spine. "And what did you tell him?"

Jacques looked at him, and Mathias could see the fear growing in his eyes, as though it had only now dawned on him. "What you told Piero that day we found him at the safe house. Before..."

Before I blew his brains out. Mathias had little recollection of that day. The memory had grown fractured and hazy. He recalled the anger and the relief when it was finally done, mixed with a gnawing concern for Rayan's condition and the fog of grief at losing Tony.

Take a good look at my face...

Then Mathias remembered the throwaway threat—his pledge to one day head the family, a way to stick the knife in one last time and send Piero off with a bitter taste in his mouth. He'd only half meant it. The words were a lofty brag, to kick Russo's son where it hurt. And now they had come back to bite him.

"Fucking fink."

Jacques recoiled. "It was the boss. I'm supposed to lie to the boss?"

"You're a grunt! The boss asks you a question, you say you don't know," Mathias growled. "You don't talk behind my back."

"I didn't think—"

"What was he offering?" Mathias cut in. "A title, your own team? Or if I know Bianchi, the chance to replace me and run the whole fucking division."

Mathias had handed the office over to his second enough times for him to be well-versed in how things operated. Jacques had even taken charge on several occasions while he was out of town, and Mathias had mistaken his eagerness for obedience while the man plotted against him.

"Well, it'll be a disappointment to hear the old man's handing Collections to a bunch of suits offshore. You never had a fucking chance."

Jacques stared at him blankly. "He didn't offer me anything."

Mathias snorted, but his second's expression didn't change. *Is it possible he gave that information freely, with no consideration for who it would be used against and no thought for what he might extract in return?*

"Bullshit," Mathias snapped. "And when you met again, what did you tell him?"

Jacques shook his head. "He never asked to meet again."

Mathias almost laughed. Somehow, he believed him. Jacques Laberge, ambitious but lacking the brains to get ahead. Easy prey for Giovanni, who'd gotten what he wanted from the man without having to lift a finger. A master at playing people for his own gain—look how well he'd played Mathias.

He saw how toxic Giovanni's paranoia had become. He'd risen to the head of the family only to be choked by constant suspicion, a life lived looking over his shoulder. That fear must have come with the territory and would explain Giorgio Russo's sudden purges and his reluctance to widen his inner circle. Mathias had experienced something similar in the months following Junior's attempted hit, when staying alive had meant preempting disaster. Maybe there had been a time when Mathias had wanted his shot at the top, when advancement was all he had.

"Take off your shoes."

Jacques flinched and then, as though resigning himself to his fate, kicked off his shoes and tossed them at Mathias's feet. Mathias threw them into the open car and moved to slam the hood closed, his gun remaining fixed on Jacques.

"You're leaving me here?" Jacques cried. His teeth began to chatter, and his socks were sodden with icy sludge.

"Why not?" Mathias said coldly. "You running your mouth almost put me six feet under."

Once, he would have simply knocked him off. Quick, easy, a single shot between the eyes. But the window was narrowing fast, the opportunity to escape diminishing by the second. Mathias could not afford to make a mistake. It was always the last hurdle that tripped you. When you were tired and losing focus, errors were made. And the discovery of his second's bullet-ridden body in the Quebec countryside would be a surefire way to send the full weight of federal law enforcement down on him.

Mathias got in the car and gunned the engine, leaving Jacques in the snow on the side of the road. By the time the man made it back to Montreal—if he made it back—Mathias would be long gone.

27

Frances had just turned off the highway into Montreal and was heading to the Quebec divisional office when she got the call from the security dispatch office at Montréal-Trudeau International Airport. She'd returned from her brief visit to Ottawa to meet with the deputy commissioner and had received instructions to stay on in the city until the end of the week. After that, she would head back to HQ and be reassigned to another case.

Part of her dreaded returning to her life in Ottawa. She'd replayed the interaction with Ethan in her mind, unable to shake the lingering humiliation. He'd been gracious—as expected—even offering to meet up for coffee when she was back in the city. Fortunately, she'd had the sense to refuse. After showing him the depths of her painful desperation, she thought it best for both of them that he keep his distance.

It wouldn't take her long to pack up the Montreal apartment. She figured she'd dump everything she needed in the trunk of her car and let work figure out the rest. The divisional office would be happy to see the back of her. Frances certainly wasn't expecting a going-away party.

"Inspector," the airport security officer said over the phone as she slowed for a changing light. "We've received an electronic alert from the Air France counter that Mathias Beauvais has checked into a flight departing for Paris at twenty hundred hours."

There had been a list of things Frances was still working through in her wrap-up of the investigation. Following the deputy commissioner's instruction after Mathias's botched arrest, she'd already removed his plates from the automated recognition watchlist with Transport Canada. But she'd neglected to cancel the airport travel alerts she'd set up after securing his arrest warrant. Half convinced he'd run before they could take him in, Frances had figured it didn't hurt to be proactive.

So, Mathias thinks he can just walk away from everything and leave the country, scot-free? The thought set off a wave of fury. Her hand might have been forced, but she still had some power.

Before she could think about what she was doing, Frances spoke. "Detain him. I'll be there momentarily."

It was blatant insubordination. She'd received clear instructions from Gill to suspend all activities associated with the investigation. There was no longer any reason—or legal precedent—for her to detain Mathias.

"Roger that, Inspector," the security officer said and hung up.

Frances sat staring at the screen of her phone as though she'd imagined the call. *I know it's hard for you to admit when you're beat.* Behind her came a loud honk, then another, and she glanced up, startled, to see the light was green.

"Fuck it," she muttered, making a hard turn through the intersection and heading back in the opposite direction, toward the airport, not entirely sure what she would do when she got there.

Mathias had said he'd be in touch, but knowing what was involved with a maneuver of this kind, Rayan had expected it to be some time before he heard from the man, so when he received a call from him the following afternoon, he was more than a little surprised. Mathias spoke quickly, and his tone was clipped. Rayan was to get his things, only what he could carry, and be at the airport in an hour. Mathias would meet him there. It was as though the entire plan had been condensed, launched forward at speed. But Rayan knew not to ask questions.

He was already half-packed, so it didn't take him long to collect his things. He moved around the safe house, unplugging switches and turning off lights, not sure exactly what would happen to the apartment once he stepped out the door. Rayan walked several streets before hailing a taxi and paid in cash once the driver dropped him at the airport.

It was busy, and he took advantage of the crowds to blend in as he made his way through the terminal. Following Mathias's instructions, he located the Air France counter and purchased a one-way ticket to Charles de Gaulle. They would travel separately, Rayan's flight departing first, with Mathias following later in the evening.

Stepping back from the counter with his ticket, he caught a glimpse of Mathias standing by the book rack in a nearby convenience store. Their eyes met for an instant before Rayan looked away as though he hadn't seen him. He walked casually toward the store, navigating around a couple wearing matching khaki shorts, and busied himself by examining a display of sunglasses.

"You're on the flight at six?" Mathias asked quietly from across the aisle, his eyes lowered to the paperback he was idly flipping through.

"That's right."

"I'll follow at eight," Mathias said. "Everything else remains the same: wait forty-eight hours at the meeting point. Otherwise, continue on alone."

The thought made Rayan's throat constrict, but he'd agreed to the plan the evening Mathias had laid everything out at the safe house. At the time, they were accounting for contingencies so hypothetical Rayan hadn't given them much weight. But here they were, only two days later, summoned by an urgency Mathias didn't have time to explain, and suddenly the prospect that one of them might not make it out seemed very real.

He glanced over to see Mathias looking up, his gaze following a group of uniformed airport security personnel as they advanced across the terminal in their direction. Rayan felt his stomach drop. *Fucking Allen.* She had given him her word. That was what he got for trusting a cop.

Mathias snapped the book in his hand shut, tossed it back on the shelf, and strode past Rayan. "Go. I want you on that plane."

"No." Rayan's hand shot out and grabbed his elbow.

"Of all the times to be difficult—" Mathias wrenched his arm free, and his face darkened in anger.

That look used to frighten Rayan, but not anymore. Nothing about the man frightened him anymore. "I've run before, and I don't want that life if you're not in it," Rayan said, staring him down.

Mathias dug his fingers into Rayan's shoulder, his face inches from his own. "And I don't want this one if they take you too." His expression briefly softened. "Do it for me."

Rayan felt the hand drop from his shoulder, and then Mathias was walking out of the store, staring straight ahead, cutting an imposing figure in his designer suit.

"Mathias Beauvais!" one of the officers called out, breaking into a stride. "Airport security—you're coming with us."

Rayan thought of all the times it had been him standing between Mathias and trouble, putting himself in harm's way. He wasn't accustomed to the sight of Mathias's back, placed as it was in front of him, shielding him from impending danger. Two security officers flanked Mathias and restrained his arms while a third slapped a set of cuffs on his wrists. The image was so confronting that Rayan found himself moving forward on instinct, compelled by years of conditioning—Mathias's protection his sole objective.

He froze mid-step when he saw Mathias's face, turned slightly to look at him as airport security led him through the small crowd of onlookers that had gathered. His eyes bored into Rayan's for the briefest of seconds but long enough to ensure that the message was clear. Rayan had spent years intuiting the man's expressions, and this one needed no elaboration. This one he couldn't ignore.

Frances arrived at the airport in time to find security officers cuffing Mathias by the Air France counter. As she approached, she saw Mathias glance behind him, his expression changing before her eyes. Gone was the hardened scowl, that threatening stare—instead, his features shifted to reveal a flash of tenderness that made her stop dead in her tracks. Following his gaze, she was stunned to spot Rayan Nadeau standing stock-still by the entrance to a nearby store, watching the unfolding scene. Mathias gave a curt shake of his head and looked away, his face slipping back into a blank mask.

And then she knew. The apartment in Toronto, Mathias's assistance in extracting Rayan from the family, Rayan's desperate bid to intervene on the man's behalf. Mathias Beauvais, one of Quebec's most notorious criminal figures, had almost succeeded in concealing his biggest vulnerability. But she had seen it now—the missing piece of the puzzle.

Frances made her way separately to the terminal's security office, where she was informed that Mathias had been detained in one of the interrogation rooms. She told the officers waiting outside to leave and closed the door behind her. Mathias sat with his cuffed wrists resting on the table in the center of the room, his eyes darkening when he saw her. She reached for the recording console mounted to the table, disabled the camera, and flicked off the audio.

Mathias raised an eyebrow, his mouth curling into an amused smirk. "Is this the part where you take to me with your fists?"

Frances dropped her bag and took a seat across from him. "Tell me, do you think people are capable of change, or are we cursed to repeat the same mistakes for the rest of our lives?"

"Do the Feds hawk their inspectors out for free therapy now?" Mathias sneered. "This is all inherently fascinating, Allen, but I'll save my answers for when my lawyer's present."

She reached into her bag and pulled out a folder. She'd left the original photos Rayan had given her with the deputy commissioner, but she'd made copies to bring back with her and file with the rest of the investigation paperwork at the Montreal office. She opened the folder, took out the photos, and splayed them across the table between them.

"Appreciate the help, by the way," she said.

Mathias could not hide the shock that transformed his face. Frances suppressed her own surprise. She'd never before succeeded in unseating his herculean self-control.

Mathias stared at the photos for a long time before looking up at her with that familiar piercing gaze. "Where did you get these?"

"Nadeau didn't tell you? He seemed willing to do anything to get us to step back."

"Idiot," Mathias hissed.

"I'm not so sure about that," she said, recalling how expertly Rayan had negotiated his terms. "This was enough to get you off the hook—for now."

Mathias's forehead furrowed, his eyes narrowing.

"He made a deal—the photos in exchange for turning a blind eye to your involvement with the shipments. A municipal police chief in bed with the Red Reapers? You couldn't buy that kind of negative publicity. No doubt, the prime minister will order a full investigation."

Mathias tutted. "Police corruption. How disheartening."

Frances scowled. "Meanwhile, without you, I've got nothing to justify the funding to keep the investigation open."

"Then why the fuck are you here?"

"Because I know you were behind it," she snapped. "The shipments—God knows what else—and if I'd just had more time, I would've nailed you for it."

"Seems we've both run out of time," Mathias said cryptically.

"Optics be damned," Frances continued, bringing her hand down on the table. "My superiors might be happy doling out resources based on what appeals to the government's yardstick of success, but I'm more concerned with the concept of justice. So now I'm put in the unfortunate position of deciding whether to follow my principles and stop you from getting on that plane."

"You've gone rogue?" Mathias mocked. "On some moral crusade—or worse—a personal vendetta? You wouldn't be the first." He gave a bitter laugh. "You ground me, and you're going to need something that sticks. Then try to scrabble together the funds to take me to trial—and I can assure you, Inspector, you will need them. Even if you make it that far, do you think the prosecution is immune to bribes, threats? What about the judge or members of the jury? And if you still believe I'll accept a plea in exchange for names, you haven't learned a fucking thing." Mathias sat forward in his chair, utterly fearless. "The way I see it, you let me leave, and you still get something." He tilted his chin toward the photos on the table. "You try to keep me here, and I'll make life very difficult for you. You'll find your ass at some reception desk back in Ottawa, taking messages."

He wasn't wrong. As she'd walked into the room, seeing Mathias cuffed yet entirely composed—drawing from a deep well of resilience neither Frances nor the RCMP could possibly hope to run dry—it had dawned on her that he would never bend to her will or repent or plead remorse for his crimes. He would pay his expensive lawyer, and they would distort the truth to match their story. Or they would find someone else to pin it on, paid handsomely for their troubles. And Mathias Beauvais would continue his challenge to the law, unencumbered.

Unless... There was one thing that would change the entire state of play, one thing that clearly meant something to the man, that could be twisted and wielded against him like a knife.

"Are you wondering if he got out?" Frances asked quietly. "Or if he's being held in the room next door?"

Mathias's shoulders stiffened, but this time, his face gave nothing away. He glared at her, silent and unmoving.

"The reason he was wiped from the records—that was you, wasn't it? You were protecting Nadeau, obscuring his involvement."

"If you took him in—"

The threat hung empty in the air, and she knew he felt it. They both did. The unspoken shift. His one exploitable weakness coming into view.

If they were both here at the airport, then they were leaving together. And to leave with Rayan meant Mathias was willing to give up everything. Frances felt a hard spike in her chest. He was doing what she'd been unable to.

She dug her nails into the flesh of her palm under the table. She couldn't fucking do it. She couldn't use Rayan against him.

"I didn't."

Mathias set his jaw, his lips pressed shut.

"I closed his case. There was nothing there. Not enough worth pursuing, anyhow. But you, on the other hand..." Frances fixed him with a hard look. "Why did you intervene that night with Truman?"

"I didn't do shit."

192

"You sent Nadeau to get me out. If you hadn't, I take it I wouldn't be here right now."

Mathias said nothing.

"It would've solved all your problems—sit back and let the cop investigating you get killed." She let out an ironic laugh. "Maybe you're not entirely devoid of decency."

She thought of Ethan's words: *You win some, you lose some. And then you move on.*

If Mathias left, he would be out of Canada and out of her jurisdiction—cut off from the family that had funneled him to power. Perhaps that was enough of a victory. She would still have succeeded in getting him off the streets.

"And I'm not entirely incapable of leniency," she said. "There's a list. Your name gets on it, and you're never let into the country again."

"What do you think I'm doing?" Mathias said in a low voice. "Going on vacation?"

Frances shook her head ruefully. "I thought I had you figured out, Beauvais. Now I'm not so sure. What I do know is I don't want you here. Which is something I think we both agree on. You leave today, and you're not ever coming back."

Mathias leaned back in his chair, returned to his former state of impenetrability, those cold gray eyes meeting hers. "Don't worry, Allen. You'll get the next one."

28

Once the inspector had released him, Mathias cleared security and walked to the gate, where he waited to board his flight. On the outside, he remained perfectly composed, but Mathias could barely see straight for the blinding rage that curdled his insides.

They had scheduled separate flights hours apart and arranged a place to meet once they got to the city. Paris he knew well—where to stay, how to navigate the streets discreetly. But it wasn't safe in the long term. The city was too conspicuous, too well-trodden. He and Rayan would continue north, toward the smattering of small villages along the coast.

Mathias was still reeling after seeing the collection of photos—like an apparition, spirited from his safe and into the glaring light of the interrogation room—and knowing who had facilitated that particular transaction. Yet it was also the reason he stood here now—why Allen had pulled back and allowed him to leave the country. Thwarted by a government focused more on looking good than serving justice, she'd propped the window open long enough for him to escape.

While the end might have justified Rayan's means, Mathias couldn't get past the jagged stab of betrayal. Different from Giovanni and Jacques, this one cut deep. He wasn't sure when Rayan had done it. The thought of him taking advantage of what Mathias had believed to be an immutable trust—one he'd never extended to anyone else—sucked the air from his lungs.

Mathias hadn't even noticed the photos missing. He'd taken only the essentials from the safe, not registering the disappearance of the envelope, since their plan to leave the city had been fast-tracked by Giovanni's ultimatum. It came as a rolling series of blows, each betrayal further evidence of how spectacularly he'd failed. After a life lived in eagle-eyed pursuit of his ambition, Mathias had foolishly allowed himself to take his foot off the gas, and everything had collapsed around him like a house of cards.

He was barely aware of getting on the plane or the journey across the Atlantic. At the airport, he hailed a taxi to a large commercial hotel on the outskirts of the city. There, a key awaited him at the reception desk under another name, allowing him access to a room on the fifth floor, where Rayan was waiting.

When he opened the door to the room, Rayan appeared before him, still in his traveling clothes, relief washing over his face. "I thought they'd got you," he said, letting out a shaky breath as Mathias walked past him and dropped his bag to the floor.

Mathias turned, his voice blistering. "You fucking snake."

Rayan stepped back, his mouth drawn.

"You took the photos," Mathias growled, his hands clenching into fists. "And used them to cut a deal with Allen."

"Mathias—"

Mathias lunged forward, grabbed the front of Rayan's shirt, and slammed him against the wall. "It's not enough for the boss to turn on me and for my own second to be in on it, but to have you sneaking around with that fucking cop?"

Rayan looked at him, confusion lining his face. "The boss?"

Mathias's head throbbed, further fueling his fury. "He tipped off the Feds, convinced I was after his job. A cleaner way to get me out, less potential for bloodshed—after seeing how well I managed the last takeover."

Rayan shook his head. "You wouldn't have ousted Giovanni. You respect him too much."

Something about the conviction of his words eased the pounding at Mathias's temples and momentarily calmed the doubt that had seized him since Allen slid those photos across the table. Despite the man being privy to Mathias's laundry list of deeds over the years, Rayan hadn't fallen prey to the same conclusion as the boss, somehow aware of the invisible line that existed—proof that Rayan knew him better than anyone else.

Mathias released him. "Apparently, he wasn't convinced."

They stood, mistrust crackling between them, the fallout of weeks of brutal pressure that had concluded with both of their lives upended.

"I know you came to the same conclusion," Rayan said in a low voice. "You knew those photos had a chance to change the course of the investigation."

Mathias had known. As soon as he'd held the glossy images in his hand, he'd realized what they could do.

"But you wouldn't have used them."

"No."

"Because you'd never make a deal with the Feds. They can accuse you of everything else, but you're not a rat. And that's important. That means something to you." Rayan glared at him, resolute. "You're the only thing that means something to me. Rat, lie, kill—for you, I'll fucking do it. Two years on the outside couldn't change that, and I wasn't going to let you stop me. So I did it. I did it so you didn't have to."

As much as Mathias hated to admit it, there was an underlying truth to Rayan's assertion. Even when the situation had begun to look increasingly dire, that was one thing he couldn't bring himself to do. "What happened to playing model citizen?" Mathias taunted. "Come down from your high horse?"

"I told you, I know how to survive."

After he'd made Rayan hand over the gun, Mathias had believed that the man had succeeded in shedding his ill-gotten gains—the sullied skills he'd taken on to serve the family and to serve him. But he realized Rayan hadn't completely rid himself of his scrappiness and innate survival instincts. Those were baked in.

"That day with Junior, I don't remember thinking," Rayan said, refusing to back down. "I just knew I couldn't let anything happen to you. I found those photos, and I had to try. If there was a chance to get Allen off your back, I was going to take it."

"That wasn't your call to make," Mathias snarled.

"Yes, it was," Rayan replied, his voice rising. "The same way it was my call to pull my gun on the kid. I wasn't going to wait around for permission. You would've gone down rather than give the Feds the satisfaction. But it wasn't just prison you were looking at. You told me yourself the family won't hesitate to protect their larger interests—even if it meant making you disappear."

"You went behind my back," Mathias admonished him.

"Like you cutting me off so I would leave?" Rayan countered. "You knew I wouldn't have otherwise."

Mathias was struck by the parallel. He recalled his paralyzing fear for Rayan's safety following the shooting and how it had overshadowed everything else. "That was different," he said, sounding unconvincing even to himself.

"Was it? Did you think I'd just wait around for the family to finish you off—until it was your photo Allen showed me next?" Rayan's voice caught, and he swallowed hard. "If that's betrayal, fine, call it. I'd lose this—us—if it meant keeping you alive."

He fell silent as they reached an impasse, neither of them able to cross it. In the past twenty-four hours, Mathias had been turned on his head and shaken so that his bones rattled. He was stripped raw, confronted by his own failings, his convictions thrown back in his face.

"I hurt you," Rayan said finally. "I'm sorry."

"You're sorry?" Mathias sneered. "What do I fucking look like, a child?" He felt like one, alone again in the dark.

"So, what's left?" Rayan asked tightly. "You get even, make me pay?"

Mathias struggled with the emptiness his words evoked. Those were the only acceptable solutions. He didn't know anything else.

"If I broke something, let me fix it," Rayan implored.

I'm tired of losing everything.

Mathias stared at the man fighting for him. Rayan had nothing to gain and everything to lose. And they'd lost so much already.

Mathias clenched his jaw, and the anger that had clouded his vision began to thin. He moved forward and raised a hand to grip Rayan's chin, his fingers digging into the flesh of his cheeks.

Mathias yanked Rayan's face upward and leaned in, barely able to keep his voice even. "Don't cross me."

But even as he spoke the words, they felt less like a threat and more like a plea. *I couldn't fucking bear it...*

Rayan reached for him, and his hand trembled as it gripped the back of Mathias's jacket. Mathias knew then how worried he'd been, waiting here for him to show. He stepped back and shoved Rayan roughly onto the bed, the lingering fury morphing into something else, heady but no less volatile. Mathias wanted the heat of Rayan's skin beneath his fingers. He wanted to make Rayan feel the turmoil surging through his blood—a different way of getting even.

He threw off his jacket and pulled Rayan's shirt over his head then moved to free him from his pants. Rayan's hands worked the buckle of his belt as Mathias tugged at the buttons on his shirt and let it slip from his shoulders to the floor. Soon there was nothing between them. Mathias crushed Rayan beneath him on the bed and felt Rayan's arms encircle his waist. With their faces almost touching, a sudden stillness fell over them as though one final barrier existed, a soreness still fresh. Then Mathias leaned down to graze Rayan's lips, and the man let out a soft gasp—a last gulp of air before diving underwater. Rayan opened his mouth and pressed against him with a fierceness that reminded Mathias of that first time in the rain, when something had passed through them like lightning. He kissed him back, letting in the hot wetness of Rayan's tongue and letting go of the fear.

They broke away, breathing hard. Rayan reached up to place his hands on Mathias's shoulders and pushed him onto his back. Rayan straddled his legs and lowered his head to bring Mathias's cock to his lips, refusing to look away as he took him into his mouth. Mathias masked a groan as Rayan stared him down, his brown eyes dull with lust.

There was something devotional about the way Rayan sucked cock—like a fucking religious experience, his tongue worshipping every inch. Mathias grabbed a fistful of Rayan's black hair and let him set the pace, yielding to the heat of his mouth as he moved languidly along his shaft. He struggled to stay vigilant. It was too easy to give in to the sensation of Rayan's hand as it circled the base of his cock. Mathias's eyes were drawn to his face—every line of it memorized—anticipating each flutter of desire that crossed Rayan's features. He tempered the flight of his pulse as the pressure built at the base of his spine.

Not yet ready to be undone, Mathias slipped a hand beneath Rayan's jaw to still him. He rolled Rayan onto his stomach and spread his thighs. Rayan reached an arm behind him, and Mathias gripped his wrist and pulled him taut. He brought his other hand to Rayan's mouth and guided two fingers past the willing confines of his lips. Mathias removed them, wet and slick, and reached back to ease one finger then another inside as Rayan buried his face into the mattress to hide the moan. If Mathias were a patient man, he would deal to Rayan like this, far more in control with his fingers than his cock. Capable of unending endurance, he would sit back while he reduced Rayan to a keening mess. But every shudder of Rayan's body only served to fuel the growing thrum between Mathias's legs, leaving him achingly hard and incapable of patience.

He removed his fingers, and Rayan tensed, glancing over his shoulder to reveal the hunger in his eyes. Rayan flipped onto his back and gazed up at him.

"Say it," Mathias demanded.

Rayan's chest rose and fell, his lips parting. "Fuck me," he said, his voice thick.

The request made Mathias pause—its directness, the need that permeated each word, and the way Rayan expected him to fulfill it. This was still new—not the wanting but the realization that what Rayan wanted, only Mathias could give. He spat into his hand and ran it along the length of his cock then lifted Rayan's legs and moved between his thighs. Mathias looked down, taking him in—the swollen lips, the delicate curve of his dark eyelashes. He eased forward, and Rayan's eyebrows knitted together as he let out a sharp breath. Wrapping his arms around him, Mathias buried his face into Rayan's neck and inhaled him into his lungs.

There had been a moment, as security had led him away, when he thought he'd never again know that smell.

Mathias entered him slowly, inch by inch. He was in no rush, his movements controlled, wanting to draw this out and make it last. Mathias lowered his head so their foreheads touched, watching the pleasure flicker across Rayan's face as he cored him.

"All of you," Rayan demanded, threading his fingers through Mathias's hair.

Mathias pulled out then pushed back in to the hilt, stemming the shiver of desire as a strangled growl tore from Rayan's throat. The sound spurred something inside him, his arousal flaring, taking over the rational brain, his blood pulsing hot in his veins. He raised himself onto his hands and began to thrust. Rayan let out a grunt of surprise. Mathias fucked him hard, needing the man to know he was bested. Because standing alone at the airport, he'd been sure Rayan had bested him.

Mathias reached down to run his hand along Rayan's straining cock, and Rayan gripped his wrist to stop him. "Don't... I'm going to—"

Mathias smirked, his breath quickening at the sight of Rayan's obvious undoing. "That's the point."

"Not yet..." Rayan groaned. "I want you to—"

Capturing Rayan's lips with his own, Mathias pushed his mouth open, and the man's arms tightened around his back, nails digging into Mathias's shoulders. He withdrew completely then plunged deep, Rayan letting out a guttural cry as he clenched around him, and Mathias felt the rapid unfurling of his own release. It stole his breath, and he pulled Rayan to him as they came together. Mathias held him there until the tension left their bodies.

After, Rayan lay on his side against him, his head resting on Mathias's shoulder and one arm curved across his stomach. "You can blame me," he said softly. "For leaving."

"Where's the sense in that?" Mathias retorted. He'd naively assumed leaving was his choice to make, only to discover the truth was far more complicated. Mathias kneaded the bridge of his nose in frustration. "I should have seen it coming—Jacques, Giovanni. All the signs were there. I was too distracted to notice." He reached over and ran his fingers along the side of Rayan's face and down the smooth flank of his chest. "That life was easier when you weren't a factor."

Rayan's expression turned reflective, and Mathias let out a slow breath.

"This... you... It's meant to feel like this?" Mathias had no frame of reference for these feelings. He knew what it was not to be loved, but loving was still an alien experience. It left him exposed to everything he'd worked so hard to barricade himself against.

"Like what?" Rayan asked.

Mathias grimaced, his thoughts returning to the interrogation room and the moment Allen had blindsided him with Rayan's involvement. He'd felt like he'd been sliced open and his guts scooped out onto the floor. "Painful."

Rayan took a moment before answering. "Sometimes." He shifted against Mathias, his skin slick with the remnants of their shared pleasure. "But would you trade in the rest not to feel it?"

Mathias stilled. He had done so before—traded in a lifetime of good not to feel the pain.

29

The students were restless that afternoon. Rayan pushed the desks aside and laid out large squares of paper on the floor and small jars of black paint. He asked them to write one word in their native language about what being here meant to them.

"Not in French, monsieur?"

"Not today."

They'd been excited then, released from the stuffy confines of an imposed language and allowed free expression. The words bloomed on the paper like flowers, many of which he recognized: family, money, peace.

Rayan picked up his own brush, trailed it in the paint, and pulled it inexpertly across a blank piece of paper. He remembered how his mother had guided his hand as she taught him the Arabic alphabet—the stroke of a pen unlocking each letter like a code.

The word looked strange written down. For him, not tethered to any real cultural history, it had never been a place or a country. It had always meant a person. Someone who tied him to the world, helped him determine his place in it. His mother, his brother, and now...

After the lesson, the students rolled up their papers and took them home. They were part of a cultural immersion class for youth, which Rayan taught at the newly opened Calais Center for New Migrants. In recent years, the coastal town had found itself inundated with people fleeing conflict across the Mediterranean, arriving in Europe on makeshift boats and inflatable rafts after battling treacherous conditions. From Calais, many attempted another perilous journey across the English Channel, a journey some never completed. In Rayan's classes were children who'd lost parents, siblings, grandparents, aunts, and uncles.

Northern France was dotted with towns like this, reeling with an influx of migrants who knew little of the language, the culture, or what the future would look like. Eventually, many of the refugees would be distributed around the rest of the country or across the border to Germany, Belgium, or the UK.

The center taught acclimation courses and provided resources and amenities to those in limbo. Rayan had started as a volunteer in the kitchens before the center manager had pushed him to take on one of the classes. He'd discovered Rayan spoke Arabic and declared his Quebec dialect quaint, viewing him as the perfect cross-cultural ambassador, despite Rayan having arrived in France only several months prior. Rayan's first instinct was to decline, compelled by a deep-rooted need to remain hidden. But then he'd remembered Professor Hofstein and his mitzvahs. *The greatest good for the greatest number of people.*

Rayan finished packing up the classroom, rolled up the piece of paper with his painted scrawl, and made his way to the exit, where he saw one of his students waiting on the steps outside.

"Do we get to do that again next week, monsieur?" the boy asked as Rayan passed him. Omar was his name, and he'd come here with his family from Syria. He was short and reedy, his jet-black hair sticking straight up.

"We'll see."

"My mama says they don't like seeing the letters. She tells me not to write them down."

Rayan stopped on the bottom step. "Some people don't like things that are different. Doesn't mean they're not important." He looked at Omar pointedly. "Do you think they're important?"

The kid nodded.

"There we go."

"Anyway, thanks, *akhi.*" Omar shot him a cheeky smile and sprinted off across the courtyard.

Rayan stood, his hand gripping the handrail. Then he let out a breath. "*Akhi,*" he said quietly, tasting the word again.

The walk from the center to the house took Rayan along the harbor. He slowed as he approached the row of buildings by the entrance to the dock. The sign above the warehouse at the end of the row read Importations Fleurdelisé. Rayan grinned at the thought of making an unexpected stop—he could already picture the scowl of irritation on the man's face. Instead, he crossed the road and rounded the corner past a brightly painted souvenir kiosk.

The house sat on a quiet street a few blocks from the ocean. Narrow but tall, it was made of solid white brick and had withstood war and Nazi invasion. After turning the key in the lock, Rayan stepped inside to find it warm. Mathias usually left after

Rayan in the morning and always kept the heat on. They'd left Montreal at the tail end of winter and had spent the spring and summer in the mild climes of coastal France. It would soon be their first winter here, and while it wasn't balmy Cyprus, it wouldn't get nearly as frigid as Canada.

Rayan took off his shoes and placed them on the rack in the hallway beside a pair of black leather Oxfords. Sometimes Rayan opened the wardrobe just to see their clothes hanging together. He remembered once thinking it an utter fantasy to wake every morning in Mathias's bed. Now Rayan awoke each day to the man's face or the curve of his neck, with Mathias's back pressed against him or his arm wrapped around him, and it took a second to convince himself it was real.

Rayan had wondered what it would be like to be together after spending so much time rationing contact. In some ways, it resembled those early years, when he'd wait each morning for the moment Mathias arrived at the Collections office, and the man was almost always tired, sometimes hungover, and usually preoccupied with a situation that needed righting. Rayan's most important job would be to get Mathias's coffee. It still felt like the most important task of the day.

But getting to this point hadn't been easy. After their arrival in France, Mathias had moved through the initial days with purposeful efficiency—making arrangements and tying up loose ends they'd left back in Montreal. Then he'd ground to a sudden halt as though his inner mechanism had broken down. For two weeks, he didn't leave the house. He would sit smoking on the balcony, looking out at the sea or staring at the same page of the newspaper. Some days, he simply remained in bed, refusing to eat. Rayan had never seen him like this. Unsure what to do, Rayan had continued through the rituals of the day—making food, walking to the store for groceries, and bringing back books, which he'd leave around the house, hoping Mathias might take an interest. Mathias's mood had scared him, reminding him of another time, when his mother had grown so listless it was like she was no longer there.

At night, Rayan had lain beside Mathias with his hands clenched at his sides, desperate to reach out and hold him, but the man would not be touched. He knew that the structure Mathias had built to make sense of the world and his place in it had disappeared. He'd gone from having everything—status, power, respect—to nothing. He also knew Mathias hadn't told him everything about their hurried exit from the country, only that they could no longer return. Mathias's departure from Montreal had come on the back of a string of betrayals, and Rayan's actions had further compounded the ordeal. While Rayan had steeled himself to face the full force of Mathias's wrath, he'd been unprepared for the pain in the man's eyes when he'd confronted him.

And then one morning, as though a switch had flipped, Mathias got out of bed and went to the bathroom to shower and shave. He'd dressed carefully in one of his suits, placed a series of documents in a small case, and left the house. When he returned later that afternoon, he was more himself than Rayan had seen him in weeks. He'd taken Rayan against the wall in the hallway, quick and furious, and later, as they lay intertwined in bed, had told him he'd purchased a local art-and-antiques-import business.

"I didn't know you were interested in art," Rayan remarked.

"I'm not," Mathias said with a shrug. "The owner was desperate to sell, and I got it for a bargain. Hasn't run a profit in years, but the client list is solid, and I like a challenge."

It wasn't so much that he liked a challenge—more that he needed one. Mathias measured himself by what he pushed up against—the harder, the better. That was what had been missing after he cut ties with the family, rendering him aimless and lost.

The business was good for him. While not quite like skimming a percentage off multimillion-dollar construction contracts, the enterprise came with its own set of difficulties. Calais was a microcosm of Montreal. There were wheels to be greased and favors to be negotiated. In a short time, Mathias had managed to integrate himself with the inner workings of the town. Clients began to come to him from around the country and farther afield, with bespoke requests and often astounding amounts of money.

In contrast, Rayan had found himself drawn to the plight of the people who continued to flock to the small seaside village, set adrift in a new land—buoyed by hope but dogged by tragedy. He felt a pull to the work that he couldn't explain. Before leaving Montreal, he'd sent Professor Hofstein his completed thesis in the mail, with no return address. He hadn't expected anything to come of it and merely wanted to close out the chapter. Rayan had been surprised, months later, to get the email from the university with his confirmation, asking for an address to send his degree certificate. Either the RCMP's inquiry had led to nothing, or the university was simply happy to take his money without question. Rayan hadn't replied—he had no need for a certificate—but he'd felt a quiet pride at seeing his name beside the title of his degree. He'd wanted to see if he could do it, and now that it was done, Rayan had no interest in taking it any further.

Teaching at the center had started as a temporary preoccupation but become something bigger, more important. The pay was next to nothing—as Mathias took pains to point out. He would observe Rayan as he gathered his materials each morning. "They keep coming, and they'll just keep shipping them out. How will a few months of learning French change any of that?"

"It's something though, isn't it?"

And Mathias would sigh, shaking his head. Rayan knew what it was like to have nothing, and he knew what it was like to feel that knowledge gave him something.

Rayan walked into the kitchen, dropped his bag, and placed the rolled-up piece of paper on the counter. He took out a stockpot from the cabinet, filled it with water, and put it on the stove to boil. From down the hall came a click and then a soft thud as the front door opened and closed. Rayan hadn't expected him back for another few hours.

Mathias strode into the kitchen, and his eyes fell on the paper from Rayan's class. He plucked it from the counter and unrolled it, one eyebrow raised. "I thought you were supposed to be teaching them French," he said, dropping it back down.

Rayan shrugged. "Sometimes you need to make peace with the old to learn something new."

"Two years of philosophy, and now you're a fucking oracle?"

Rayan snickered. "A little early, isn't it? Not like you to slack off."

"Who's slacking?" Mathias said with a smirk. "I got my hands on an original Monet."

The skills that had served Mathias so well in the family had proven effectively transferrable. Rayan knew he didn't tell him everything about the business, no doubt to avoid implicating him. There were bound to be aspects of it that brushed up against the law—or at least stretched the interpretation of it. Mathias was well-versed in the ways the world worked and how best to place himself in it. Nothing had changed there.

Mathias stepped over to the fridge, and as he passed, his hand grazed the small of Rayan's back. Rayan remembered a time when he would have given anything for that casual brush of contact. Now it came easily, built into the groove of the day without him realizing. Rayan caught Mathias's arm, moving to kiss him—seamless, like a song paused and then restarted.

"Don't start something you can't finish," Mathias murmured, pushing him up against the counter.

"Who said anything about not finishing?" Rayan asked, his arms encircling the man's neck, and he tilted his chin to capture Mathias's mouth once again.

Behind him, the piece of paper curled on the counter, the curves of black paint forming a neat word that contained multitudes: *home*.

A Life Imagined

Having cut ties with the family, former mafioso Mathias Beauvais adjusts to the challenges of staying on the right side of the law—for the most part, at least. When his business draws the attention of a prominent criminal group intent on using it to disguise their smuggling operation, he may have to fall back on a few well-worn tactics to keep them at bay.

Spurred on by a deep-seated need for redemption, Rayan Ayari finds himself drawn into the escalating conflict between the residents of Calais and the city's growing refugee population and is forced to confront the possibility that he may never absolve himself from the deeds of the past.

Meanwhile, Mathias and Rayan navigate a future together in which hiding is no longer a necessity and begin to realize just how much they've come to rely on one another. But when chaos strikes the Montreal underground, Mathias receives a surprise visitor from his old life who challenges his resolve to leave the family and brings his newly built world into question.

A Life Chosen

A recent promotion leads Mathias Beauvais—an ambitious captain in the Montreal mafia—and his subordinate, Rayan Nadeau, to uncover a deeper plot to betray the very organization they work for. With their loyalty in question and their lives on the line, the two find themselves drawn to each other, fighting a pull that has been present since their first meeting.

Mathias has spent years having to prove himself, combating the stigma of his birth to establish his place within the family's ranks. But when succession threatens to overturn the group, he finds his priorities have shifted from his own advancement to the man at his side.

Rayan had nothing before he met Mathias. In an effort to hide the true nature of his devotion to his boss, he's dedicated himself entirely to Mathias's success. However, as the situation becomes increasingly dire, his feelings for Mathias threaten to hinder his ability to protect him.

About the Author

Sydney Rutherford is fond of travel, a morally ambiguous protagonist, and the fragility of the human condition. She writes contemporary m/m romance with a penchant for noir, and currently resides in Aotearoa New Zealand.

Find out more about her books at sydneyrutherford.com or sign up to the mailing list for bonus content and upcoming releases.

Thank you for reading. If you enjoyed this book, please leave a review.

www.ingramcontent.com/pod-product-compliance
Lightning Source LLC
Chambersburg PA
CBHW051249250626
47155CB00009B/3220